THE SMALL BLACK KNIFE

A Selection of Recent Titles by Pamela Hill

CHARMED DESCENT
CURTMANTLE
INADVISABLE MARRIAGES
MAN FROM THE NORTH
MURDER IN STORE

THE SMALL BLACK KNIFE

Pamela Hill

This first world edition published in Great Britain 1999 by
SEVERN HOUSE PUBLISHERS LTD of
9–15 High Street, Sutton, Surrey SM1 1DF.
This first world edition published in the U.S.A. 1999 by
SEVERN HOUSE PUBLISHERS INC of
595 Madison Avenue, New York, N.Y. 10022.

British Library Cataloguing in Publication Data

Hill, Pamela, 1920-
The small black knife
1. Detective and mystery stories
I. Title
823.9'14 [F]

ISBN 0-7278-2234-9

Typeset by Hewer Text Ltd
Edinburgh, Scotland.
Printed and bound in Great Britain by
MPG Books Ltd, Bodmin, Cornwall.

Part One

One

"Last bike on the road, you are, and don't forget it. When you pack in, so will I. They won't see me pushin' one of them bleedin' trolleys up through Bellenden woods."

Jeremiah Beale, long-term postman from Brennan, pumped up a doubtful tyre and then pressed on. He always did the last part on foot anyway, but the lack of logic in his late pronouncement was not apparent to him. In any case all the houses on the Bellenden estate were near each other. Everyone in them knew everyone else, that was if you didn't count the Hawk, whom nobody knew if they could help it. Jerry pitied her husband, who was known hereabouts as the Dove for his sufferings, which he endured with patience. Any other man would have left her.

The name in question was in fact Partridge, so birds came into it. Jerry Beale took out the mail for what Mrs P. had started to call Lesser Bellenden since they'd arrived two years ago. Before that it had been 4 The Cottages, not that they were in a row. Mr Hedley lived by himself in one, with a visiting housekeeper, and had enough room in front to have erected that ruddy great glasshouse where they kept the washing and the car and them orchids he was so fond of growing and took to shows. Like the Crystal Palace, all of that was, and that's what everyone called it. He'd even delivered letters addressed to W. Hedley, Esquire, Crystal Palace, Brennan, but the postcode was all right so it got there. Lady Bellenden hadn't minded the putting up of the glasshouse because it wasn't attached to anything and could be taken down as easily as it had gone up, at least you supposed so.

Then there was the Dower House, which by now was the

rectory by permission of her ladyship, the other having been sold off for church funds. A bit further off was the odd-job man's cottage, not that there was ever mail for *him*. Beyond that was Miss Reston's studio where she made her pottery, and last of all the big house itself, where her ladyship lived alone since the death of my lord. Eighty, she'd be, if not more. She kept a couple to see to things.

Beale sorted out the rest of the bag's contents attached to his bicycle carrier. Lesser Bellenden was almost the last of the morning round, and once he'd got past that he'd look forward to a nice cup of tea with Mrs Houston, Mr Hedley's housekeeper at the Palace; she'd have arrived by now, and they both liked a bit of gossip, though Dora, his own wife, said it wasn't Christian. Dora would be working by now cleaning up at Lesser B., and would have made him a cup herself, except that the Hawk got difficult about such things, depending on how she was feeling. It was better not to risk it, Dora said. He'd told her not to worry, there were plenty of jobs for good cleaning women, and Dora was one of the best, kept their own little house like a new pin. However Dora said she liked to please Mrs Partridge. "She's only a poor soul," she kept saying. In his opinion, from what he'd heard, Mrs P. was a bitch. However, Dora kept telling him to mind his own business and stop paying attention to what everyone said.

As if he was not very good at this, Jerry turned over the mail and had a good look at it. There was a small square white envelope in thick paper for Lady Bellenden. That would be an invitation to something or other. Her ladyship didn't get many now, and liked to go to what she could. She still drove her car. That dog – well, he, Jerry, didn't want to get bitten, but if it happened he wouldn't report it like some did. McGinty was the old lady's only comfort now my lord was dead. A devoted couple, they'd been; no heirs, a pity.

Beale stared down at Mr Hedley's bundle, two magazines from horticultural societies, it said so on the outside. The Rector had a missionary magazine and an electricity bill. That left the parcel for Mr Partridge at Lesser B. It was heavy, and he was glad to get rid of it. It was probably a script. The Dove had once been a lecturer, that was known, and some of his letters had used to have more after the name and Dr before it. However, in a place like this people were liable to ask for free advice about their veins and the like, not knowing there were other kinds of doctor. By now, the Dove read scripts for a living, or perhaps had something put away. He'd need money to support the Hawk. She—

"Here I am, Jerry. I caught up with you and the bike after all."

Beale turned with swift pleasure at the sound of his own wife's voice. He, Jerry, could never get over the wonder in his mind that Dora had married him rather than all the others that might have been after her. He was old enough, when all was said, to be her father, and neither rich nor handsome; a postman. They had been married now twelve years, happy as could be, except there were no children. Now, though, perhaps . . .

Dora was smiling. Joy flooded him. There she was, trim and neat in her working clothes, blue eyes like speedwells, not that you saw any nowadays; colour like a rose. Had the doctor—?

"What're you gawpin' at, Beale? Get on with the mail."

"Dora, I wanted to know."

"Well, I was going to tell you at home, when I could say it proper. It's on, this time. October."

She leaned over and kissed him. He felt as if he was walking on air. Married all these years, with that one accident at the beginning, and now – and now here they were again. He hoped it would be a boy. He'd take him fishing, teach him to handle a gun. That wouldn't be all; they'd see to it, he and Dora, that their son became something better than a postman. College, perhaps; maybe even Oxford or Cambridge, you could get there these days on them grants. Visions of the future soared in glory in Beale's mind, like the potter's in the Arabian Nights. However, being a shy man all he said aloud was, "You'll have to tell Mrs P. to get someone else to clean for her. You don't want to go draggin' furniture about. Look after yourself."

Dora smiled on, her rosy face dimpling. "Get along with you. It isn't for seven months. Anyway she won't find it easy to get anyone else to come, what with her being like she is, and that Peters."

"Don't you let Peters near you."

"I don't. Go away, now, or she'll say I'm late." She kissed him again, speaking gently. "Don't worry, love. D'you suppose I don't want the baby as much as you do?"

They walked along together in silence for a time, as he wouldn't let her take the heavy parcel for him to Lesser Bellenden. It was against regulations, he told her, to spare her feelings.

On the way, in the companionable quietness, they passed a steep flat face of grey rock. The path wound upwards among the still-bare spring trees to where the ground levelled, and a large sprawling grey house could be seen in the distance. They passed that, and came to a smaller one. This was so isolated that for a long time it had been difficult to let after the death of Lord Bellenden some years ago. His widow had had to shoulder the burden of death duties; the five-year arrangement customary with heirs had not been possible, as there was none. Behind the smaller house again was a dilapidated cottage, in which the odd-job man Peters lived. He wasn't liked, any more than Mrs P. The small, closed society of Brennan, which knew everything, knew why.

Jerry Beale entered the latticed front porch of Lesser Bellenden, knocked on the door and waited till it was opened by a tall man with a thin tired face who peered over half-glasses. The postman touched his cap – Mr Partridge was a gentleman, you could tell – and handed the package over. It hadn't been sent by recorded delivery; a risk, that. Dora meantime had tactfully gone round to the back entrance. Inside, she hung up her coat, got on an apron, then busied herself with the tasks she knew now up here by heart; cleaning the wood ash out of the grate in the sitting-room Mrs P. called a lounge when she wasn't thinking; laying the fire ready for lighting later on; filling the kettle and leaving it ready for when Mrs Partridge should come down. She'd be still in bed, and presently Dora would take her up a cup of tea. Mr P., poor man, would have got his own breakfast as usual. She'd do his dishes for him presently. There was nobody else about, and Peters wouldn't come in today, thank goodness, for his money, it not being a Friday. He'd left piled logs ready in the basket beside the grate.

Dora's husband had meantime continued his round, again in the saddle, towards Mary Reston's studio with a pottery catalogue to deliver. He would call last of all at the Crystal Palace, then go home. Dora had left the stew ready to put on; she'd be back later in time for them to have it together, nice and hot. He was lucky. She was a good wife. Today's glorious news was only one thing more. His cup overflowed. *Goodness and mercy all my life shall surely follow me.* He freewheeled down the rough hill again with abandon, feeling twenty-five.

Two

Julius Partridge, BSc, PhD Econ. – he never stressed his doctorate up here, but not for the reasons Jerry Beale had worked out – had taken the newly delivered script into his study, where he could read undisturbed and alone. Elaine knew that she must not come in or she wouldn't get her evening drink; it was one way in which he could control her. As for little Mrs Beale, she had instructions not to clean in here unless specifically asked to do so by himself.

The script was one he had been expecting; Henschel, in London, had said it showed exceptional promise in its field, but needed a few cuts. It was by a new writer. An almost boyish excitement stirred in Partridge as he undid the string. It was one of the few pleasures still left him to help promote talent, as he had done at Cambridge. After all, it didn't matter if it was done at third hand; or shouldn't.

Partridge's scholar's gaze rested briefly on the pear tree beyond the window, at this season void of anything much but buds. Shrewdness and acumen had availed him little in marrying at forty-two. He would have been better by far in bachelor solitude in his room at Caius, or engaged in good talk with his fellows over dinner and the college burgundy. Elaine . . .

His mind shied away. He'd been a fool, of course; deceived by a certain childlike quality she could lay on at will. It had seemed out of place in a secretary, down in the office; the appealing heart-shaped face, the great dark eyes containing only innocence. 'I'm afraid I'm awfully slow at this, Dr Partridge. It takes me ages to get the correctable ribbon on. It turns round and looks at me. Could you . . . ?"

That had been the beginning, before computers. It had ended in bed, on their wedding night. Even he could tell she'd been with other men, but it was too late; she made a tearful confession, probably lies; she told them easily. He still tried to retain some affection for her, despite everything: some responsibility he couldn't shed. She would be lying upstairs in bed now, drinking tea taken up by Mrs Beale. The sound of Dora's vacuum cleaner came, a faint constant whine, from the sitting-room. There was enough for them to live here quietly, pay the rent, pay the cleaning woman. He had once threatened to leave Elaine, but she'd turned into a sobbing dependent child again, clinging to him. By now, he was used to the state of affairs. It was no longer a marriage, but they kept up appearances as far as that went. It was easier here than at close quarters in various universities, with the other wives at get-togethers drawing away in their own close group. The grapevine never failed. Well, he must get to work. He sat down at his desk, and pulled the script towards him.

He began to read, oblivious of the things that lay in the secondary stratum of his mind; the locked cupboard in the wall behind him, the keys in his pocket, reassuringly. Once a day he would pour Elaine a small glass of whisky or brandy; otherwise life became impossible. However, it was still too early for that. He could forget everything, for the time, except the intriguing handwritten facts spread out in front of him.

Sloping writing stared up at him from the page, clear facts and figures. They were large and easy to read. Here and there Henschel had already made an editor's mark. Nevertheless he himself must judge the whole thing objectively, as if it hadn't been read or commented on by anyone. Already he was sure he would agree with Henschel's verdict, but it was too soon to persuade oneself; read on, read on.

Dora Beale knocked on the Hawk's door, opened it, set the teacup and saucer carefully down on the bedside table, and opened the curtains on either side the window. The bright day flooded in.

Elaine Partridge stirred on her pillow, turning her swathed

head towards the expected tea. She wore a turban, underneath which were curlers. Julius Partridge slept elsewhere. Elaine reached out a hand with stubby, degenerate thumbs, took hold of the cup and drank.

"It's a fine day, Mrs Partridge," ventured Dora. She liked, without seeming familiar, to speak to the poor thing and cheer her up; no one else did, except her ladyship when she looked in. Besides, she, Dora, was so greatly filled with joy about the coming baby that it overflowed onto everyone and everything she met; she'd even given the sitting-room carpet an extra going over.

"Well, it's spring, so it ought to be fine. You sound very cheerful today, Beale." Elaine set down the cup, and yawned; there was nothing to get up for, this woman was paid to do the work. She fixed treacle-brown eyes on Dora's face.

Dora suddenly told her the glorious truth. She couldn't keep it to herself. "Twelve years Beale and me's been married," she reminded the other. Elaine's expression grew bored:

"How tiresome," she said. "Now I suppose you'll leave, like they all do." The human race bred like rabbits. It was almost impossible to find any reasonable woman to come, because of Peters in the cottage, who made passes at them. He didn't have enough to do chopping wood; the grass wasn't ready yet for mowing.

Dora had flushed. "It isn't tiresome to me, Mrs Partridge," she said firmly. The Hawk gave her short hard laugh.

"You wait till you're busy yelling, having it, and changing nappies, then keeping the brat quiet, not that anyone does now. I shall need you presently; I want you to help me shift the freezer across to the other plug. I shall be down in about half an hour." She didn't eat breakfast.

"Mrs Partridge, I don't think perhaps I ought. It's heavy. Maybe Peters would do it." What was it Jerry had said only this morning about looking after herself? She saw the Hawk's thin eyebrows raise themselves incredulously.

"No need to start pampering yourself yet; I don't want Peters inside. When I come down, leave what you're doing and come and lend me a hand, as they say in the navy." She was suddenly pleasant and charming, in the way she had.

It was almost, Dora thought later on, as though she'd had the notion about shifting the freezer as soon as she heard about the baby. She tried once more, timidly; the Hawk could make ugly scenes.

"Peters could lift it with one hand. I'd see him out. He does as I say." It was true; Peters didn't try any nonsense with her again after the first time, when she'd slapped his face. Elaine began to shout, still lying in bed.

"Then you do as *I* say; I pay you, don't I? In any case Peters will be up in the wood by now, and I can't wait all day. Stop arguing and do as you're told."

Dora walked out of the bedroom and went downstairs to put away her cleaning things, wringing out the cloths valiantly to rid herself of her anger. There was no doubt that she was a fool to go on here; Jerry had told her so often enough, hearing the things the Hawk said now and again. However the habit of compassion – Dora had been brought up chapel – was strong, and as usual she gave in, or knew she would when Mrs P. came downstairs. Meantime, she began to polish the spoons. She didn't like sitting about doing nothing. She'd set them in a gleaming row before Elaine appeared, in trousers and a loose tunic, her grey-black hair combed out. She hadn't washed her face.

The sitting-room fire lit easily, and Elaine started throwing odd bundles of papers and emptied boxes in, having taken them out of the opened freezer. She put aside a brace of pheasants, stiff with ice, by themselves, and said brightly "There, now I've lightened it. You take that end. I want it against the far wall, opposite where it is now. No, not that way, the other."

They were in the kitchen, which adjoined. The freezer was very heavy, more so than Dora had foreseen. By the time they had pulled and pushed it halfway she was panting. "I'll have to stop, Mrs Partridge," she said. "I can't go on, it isn't safe."

"Nonsense, you're stronger than I am. You can't leave it like that, in the middle of the floor." In Elaine Partridge's eyes a diamond-bright devil gleamed for instants, then was gone.

Half an hour later, with the freezer in place, Dora Beale began to have cramps. Presently she felt blood. "Please," she called. "Please get the doctor."

Elaine raced along to her husband's study door, and hammered on it; she welcomed theatrical roles. His face looked out at her, a stranger's.

"You'll have to take Mrs Beale home in the car," she told him; that would stop his reading. "She's had a stroke, or something."

After they had driven off, Beale behaving as though her legs were made of asparagus, Elaine stood watching the car lurch down the drive. *That* wouldn't do the pregnancy any good; girls who got into trouble in the old days had always used to be sent for a carriage-drive. Where had she read that? She'd tried to acquire bits and pieces of culture at first, when she'd married Julius, to keep up with the bitches at staff parties, whoever they thought they were. It hadn't made any difference.

Julius hadn't been her husband for years now. He'd told her he was impotent. There wasn't any reason why he should be, still under fifty. There hadn't been any other women, and there were none here, certainly, in this God-forsaken place he'd brought her to. Elaine wandered into the forbidden study, staring down at whatever he'd been reading. It didn't mean a thing, all those figures. She tried not to remember Dora Beale lying with her feet up on the sofa, face white as a sheet. Julius had offered to fetch the doctor. "No, sir, I'd rather go home," Dora had replied gently; and he'd taken her there. Home.

He'd gone out in his old working jacket, picking Dora Beale up in his arms to carry her out to the car. It had given one an unpleasant sensation to see a young woman in Julius's arms. His other jacket, the one he liked people to see him in, hung still on the hook behind the door. Perhaps—

Elaine moved quickly. The stubby fingers rummaged through the pockets, and emerged in triumph, holding a bunch of keys. He'd been in such a hurry to attend to Dora Beale he'd forgotten to take them out of her way. Elaine's eyes gleamed. She went to the cupboard in the wall, grasping the keys close as if a hand might reach out, even now, and take them away. It wasn't difficult to find the key that unlocked the booze door.

The lock turned; the forbidden door opened. Inside were rows of bottles, carefully stacked. Julius ordered them from some club to save money. He knew about wine. He knew about most things, or thought he did; but not this. Elaine smiled, went down on her knees and found the bottle of brandy which was newly opened. He'd doled out her daily allowance to her yesterday evening. Elaine set the neck to her lips and drank and drank. When that bottle was empty she found another. There was an opener, and she used it. She was beginning to feel a sensation coming over her of wellbeing, of aggressive power. Anyone could do anything. She, Elaine Partridge, was as good as anybody. When she had drunk enough for the time being, she stood up, balancing with her hands against the wall. Beyond the cupboard was the room, Julius's sacred study, and on his desk whatever it was that had been taking up his attention, leaving none for herself; she hadn't forgotten the look he gave her when she knocked on the door about wretched Dora Beale. She'd see to that. She'd make Julius notice her, the way he had at the beginning. She was the same person, wasn't she? And he . . . he was the same fair, thin man she'd seen standing at the counter of the Caius outer office, that first day, asking about something or other, and he'd helped her fix the ribbon. It hadn't stopped there. Why should it stop now? Nothing else was in the way but . . . this.

She moved to the bulky typescript, lifted it bodily from the desk, and carried it down to the sitting-room fire, which Beale had lit. Elaine stoked the flames with papers until the typed figures turned grey, the paper itself to ash. It didn't all burn; some merely scorched. More logs were needed, and Beale's miscarriage, if that was what it was, had prevented her from carrying enough in before being carried out. Elaine grinned at her own pun.

There would be other logs in the shed. Elaine lifted the round basket which was used for carrying them into the house, and made for the door. The sunlight outside struck her eyes like a knife. Halfway between the entrance and the shed she suddenly collapsed on the ground and lay there without moving, while the basket rolled a little way, then, sent back by its handle, changed direction and rolled back again, then once more, back and forth repeatedly, till it lay likewise still.

The man Peters lived by himself in the cottage behind the house. Nobody else would have lived there; it was derelict, but he didn't want council housing, neighbours wouldn't mind their own business. This place suited him very well, and the job of hewing wood; he was a big, powerful fellow, and there were few things he couldn't turn his hand to. There was, accordingly, no wife to interfere; though he liked a woman now and then. He did his own cooking and at times, his washing; and on Friday nights, when the Dove paid him his wages, he'd walk down to the Lamb and Flag for a pint or two, then go upstairs after hours by long-standing arrangement with Betty the barmaid. He'd been aggrieved, last week, to find that Betty was not available. A client was courting her. That was all women wanted, a wedding ring and to be able to call themselves Mrs. No doubt it had been a hint that he himself ought to marry her, but he was doing nicely for himself, liked to be free, and that was that. To listen to the Hawk's tongue up at the house was enough to put you off the notion of one, about and wagging. He knew all about *her*, the Hawk, the bitch; forbidden him the house, she had, after he'd tickled up little Dora Beale. Not much of a life, the Dove hadn't; a wonder he didn't take to his own locked cupboard. Peters knew all about that. He knew most things. He belonged to a race of tinkers who could send messages across the hills from the north in less time than it took to telegraph in the old days, or whatever they did in this; when one of them died, everyone came to his funeral from all parts.

Anyway his business now was hewing logs, up in the pinewood behind Bellenden House. He made himself a pot of tea and drank it, good and strong; then damped the fire, got on his coat and a knitted cap to keep him warm, and got ready to go out to the shed to see what needed doing. As well there was no shortage of trees up in the forest, with all them do-gooders talking about the fate of the planet. It'd see him out, that was the main point.

He heaved his axe into his handcart, and wheeled it round towards the entrance. On the way he had to pass Lesser Bellenden, and saw a crumpled figure lying motionless on the ground. The Hawk, that was. Nothing surprised Peters. He laid down the handles of the barrow, walked over, and stirred her with his foot. Out cold, she was. Must have got at the cupboard. The Dove's car had driven off some time ago; he'd heard it from where he sat drinking his tea. Mrs P. had had her licence taken away. As for Dora Beale, there was no sign of her, or of anyone.

The house door was open, creaking a bit on its hinge. Peters bent, picked up Elaine's unresisting weight in his arms, and carried her inside. Forbidden him the house, had she? He knew it well enough from old days, when it had stood empty. He knew where she slept.

He mounted the stairs, still carrying her. There was scarcely anything of her, he thought. Drunks were often like that, nothing of them but skin and bone, in spite of all the papers said about calories. Betty was a great reader of the papers.

He reached the room, laid Elaine Partridge down on her bed and stood surveying her. Whatever they said, she was a woman; and he hadn't had one for a week. Peters began to feel a certain sensation in his parts. Partridge couldn't be back for some time yet, in the nature of things; nobody could drive fast over them stones. There was time for a quick one; she was still out cold. Peters unfastened his fly, then lifted a powerful leg over Elaine.

She came to before he'd finished, and began to cry and claw at his face. "You be quiet," he told her. "No need to say anything about it, see?" She wouldn't want, after all, to lose her standing with the county. He silenced her, in the way he could silence Betty.

Suddenly Elaine began to writhe with pleasure and cling to him with her legs. "Go on," she breathed. "Do it again. God, for a man. Go on, go on."

Peters withdrew, shocked. This was a nympho. It was a

different matter when a man wanted a woman; a woman wanting a man was, in some way, taboo. He rose from her, deaf to her pleadings, went downstairs and out. He'd get on with the logging; no reason why not. The only trouble was that she might follow him up there. Panic claimed him; but otherwise, he could always deny that anything at all had happened. Knowing women, he didn't think she'd say a word to anyone, certainly not to Mr P.

Julius himself had been delayed, fetching the doctor and then Beale. It appeared that the baby was not lost, but Dora must rest for a day or two. There would be no question of her coming back here, the husband had said grimly. Well, that would mean a neglected house; but that was the least of it. He was filled with cold anger against Elaine. He put the car in the garage – it had once held a pony and trap – locked it, and turned to meet the man Peters, returning from the wood with a cartload of logs.

"Mornin', sir." The man sounded pert. Julius grunted in reply, and Peters was quiet thereafter. Usually the Dove had a pleasant word about the weather, but not today. Peters heard him go into the house and shut the door.

"Julius! Darling! Julius! Come quickly, something's happened."

Partridge heard the demanding voice with weariness. He was still afflicted, had been so all the way back in the car, with the remembrance of poor little Dora Beale, lying ill on her bed, and the haggard husband, called home from sorting. "Dragged a freezer, you say?" Partridge recalled the outrage in the words. It made him unwilling to face Elaine. He knew her well enough; she would have some lie ready to account for it, half convincing him.

"Come quickly. I'm in my room. Come in."

He went up, feeling his own deliberation in the way he trod the stairs. They were carpeted in lilac cording; it was cheap and wore well. One noticed details always. He turned the handle of Elaine's room and went in. She was lying on the bed. Wasn't she well? The thing that had happened left him incapable of compassion. He stared down, aware that her cheeks were wet with tears. She could produce them at will.

"He raped me. Peters came and raped me, here on the bed. If only you'd been in, it wouldn't have happened."

Words kept pouring from her; he listened, uncertain which to believe and which to discard. Peters had been with them ever since they came; why should he suddenly have done this? Partridge made himself put a hand on Elaine's forehead, to see, he supposed, if she was feverish. She seized his hand, kissed it and held it fast.

"Oh, Ju. If only things were as they used to be, this wouldn't have happened. People know you're not with me much. You sleep alone. You're cooped up in that study all day, by yourself, except to eat: even then you hardly speak to me. I'm not part of your life any more." The tear-filled eyes gazed up at him. "If only things were as they used to be," she repeated. "I'm your wife; does that mean nothing?"

"Are you?" His face was suddenly bitter; his glance turned.

"Oh, that – that old priest in the bank – don't believe it, he was lying." She sat up, her mouth suddenly firm.

He patted her absently, as one might pat a dog; then went out and downstairs. The first thing was to speak to Peters. The latter, having stacked the logs in the shed, was back in his cottage. Smoke rose from the chimney; there was a smell of cooking onions. Julius knocked on the door. The great broad figure emerged, in shirt-sleeves. Peters' face reminded Partridge, for the first time, of an archaic mask of a sated god, with an Etruscan smile.

He spoke directly, aware of a great weariness. "My wife says you mishandled her. Is that the case?"

"Mishandled?" The voice was jaunty. "Don't know what you can mean by that, sir. I found Mrs Partridge lyin' in the entry, not herself by any means, and carried her up to her room. When I left she still hadn't come round. I came downstairs and went about my business with the logs. That's all, sir."

It sounded plausible; God knew it could have happened either way; the man was as much a liar as Elaine. "I am afraid you will have to find another situation," said Partridge firmly. "I will give you a reference; you've been a good worker. For my wife's sake, however, I cannot have you staying on here."

"What's that you say? What's that?" The great fists were doubled, the sly gaze bright with anger. "I been hereabouts more years than you remember," said Peters slowly. "Born and brought up in these parts, I was. There's nothin' goes on in this place I don't hear of, and there's a deal I could say about you and your missus, come to that."

"That is not the point," said Partridge coldly. "I will give you a week's wages, and you will go." There had been no agreement about the cottage; it was officially unfit for habitation. He could hear Peters shouting on, adding abuse to what he had already implied. It did not occur to Julius that the man could have felled him. He turned and walked away, saying clearly, "You will be out of here before the end of the week. Call on me before then for your money and reference. You are fortunate that I do not have you charged, but the less said about all this the better."

"You can say that again," sneered Peters.

His glance burned into Partridge's back as the latter returned to his house. He shut the door and locked it with the key which stood behind it, then recalled the others in his study; he should have taken them with him in the car. He'd forgotten about it in the anxiety over Dora. He went straight to his study. There was no need to look in his jacket pocket; the cupboard door gaped open, there was chaos among the bottles inside, several lying on their sides, empty; how much had she drunk? He kept calm; the bunch of keys was still in the outer lock, and he retrieved them, locked the cupboard and bestowed the keys safely. It was not till then, shutting the desk drawer, that he noticed that the typescript from Henschel was missing. He did not trouble to search the room. He went up again to Elaine. She was lying down again on the bed.

"You know," he told her coldly, "that Mrs Beale narrowly escaped a miscarriage because you made her move a heavy freezer. You will have to do the housework yourself in future until we find someone." No cleaning woman, no odd-job man. Never mind all that. Her eyes had opened wide.

"A miscarriage? She never told me there was anything like that, or of course I wouldn't have asked her. It isn't my fault. You always blame me."

"I saw Peters just now, and have given him notice. He will leave at once. Whether it will be easy to replace him I do not know."

"Of course it'll be easy. Anyone can chop wood. You could, instead of reading all day. Did you fetch the police about what he did to me?"

"Do you want the police to know about what you say has happened? It is better to leave things as they are. The man is going. Keep your door locked in future."

"You don't care about me. You don't care what happens to me. You bring me up here to this God-forsaken place, then lock yourself away all day. I never see you. You never speak to me."

His face was grim. "What," he asked her, "have you done with the typescript I was reading on my desk?"

An expression, half cunning, half like a mischievous child, spread over her face. "It took you away from me all the time," she said. "Like the others."

"What have you done with it? It was the only copy of a work by a new writer, who might have made himself famous and the firm as well." There might, in fact, be another copy; he hoped so, for everyone's sake.

"The firm! The firm! If you think so much of Henschel's bloody firm, why not have stayed in town? Why come here to this, where I—"

"You know very well why. I dared not let you be within reach of a wine merchant's. My life is only tolerable even here if I lock away all strong drink so that you cannot lay your hands on it. For the last time, Elaine, where is the typescript?"

"In the fire!" screamed Elaine. "In the bloody fire. You think you can make a prisoner of me. Can you blame me if I want a drink? You're no comfort to me. You won't sleep with me. I don't believe you can't, there's nothing wrong with you. I'm going to tell the doctor about you. He'll give you pills. You're not a man at all. You don't even care about what that one did to me today. You don't care about anything that happens to me. The world's full of givers and takers, and you're one of the takers, always were."

She was sitting up again, shouting, but he had gone. He found the fire in the sitting-room almost out, close-packed pages stuffed against the dying heat. He tried to save them, but it was too late; many were destroyed. Unless there really was a copy, or the author had rough notes of his work, the loss was irreparable.

He decided to go for a walk; it was one way to keep sane, and he used it often. He took a stout stick, put on his deerstalker and coat, and went out. By now it was the afternoon; with luck he could walk round Bigod, returning by evening. He didn't feel hungry. Nor could he stay in the house.

Three

Lady Bellenden was in the habit of taking her bull terrier, McGinty, for a walk in the woods each morning at six sharp, rain or shine. As she had been a widow now some years and could please herself, there was no real need to undertake the task so early, at this time of year scarcely broad daylight. However, it was probable that McGinty, himself a dog of habit, would remind her by shoving his nose, then himself, under the blankets where she lay in bed if she failed in her duty. Because the childless old lady doted on him, therefore, six o'clock it was.

They skirted her immaculate garden; gardening was one thing she kept up. Although like all his breed McGinty was an individualist and went where he chose, he had gathered, in course of a long and indulged life, that going among the plants to relieve nature was not popular. It was impossible to punish him, because, as every owner knows, hitting a bull terrier is like hitting concrete. However, McGinty was good-natured himself and appreciated the like quality in other people, particularly his mistress and his only just recalled, but still unforgotten, master. He bustled alongside Lady Bellenden now, occasionally going off on his own for brief forays, as the wide woods and his eccentricities permitted him to do.

Lady Bellenden avoided, as she nearly always did, the path that led up to Lesser B. One reason was that Elaine had complained that the early walk disturbed her, and although this was nonsense – McGinty seldom if ever barked, believing in deeds rather than words – the old lady preferred to avoid unpleasantness. There were after all plenty of other paths. She reached up a hand to settle her battered and ancient felt hat more securely on her head, and set out, with a stride astonishing in one of her years and small stature, for the rockface which met one coming up from the village, just as the postman did each day. Beale was back on his rounds again despite the unfortunate mishap, of which one had of course heard, the other day to his wife. It was still several hours before he would bring any letters.

Lady Bellenden's faded eyes glowed wistfully. She looked forward to mail; there wasn't always much these days, except at Christmas; everyone had died. There were of course bills, which Winifred Bellenden paid by return, thereby avoiding polite reminders; and specialist plant catalogues, which she would exchange and compare with Bill Hedley's over at the Crystal Palace. She'd been criticised for allowing him to put that up, but one had to encourage somebody like him in a hobby such as indoor orchid-growing. He—

"What have you found, sir? Rabbits?" There were sometimes poachers still though the game now was sparse, and anyway Beale was allowed to come up at nights in the season and shoot. He didn't use a dog, and had perhaps not found the quarry. "Fetch," said Lady Bellenden uselessly; McGinty had no talents as a gundog. They'd once had pointers. She peered over to where the dog was scratching and worrying, his white body active, his tail whipping furiously sideways. Winifred strode over.

"McGinty. Heel."

It was something large. It was wrapped in a tweed caped coat and deerstalker. It was a man, neck broken, head turned into last year's leaves. The foxes had nibbled at the exposed cheek in the night.

It was Julius Partridge. His torch was still lit, lying some way off.

Lady Bellenden stood quite still for instants, feeling slightly sick, making no sound. She had taken the dog by his collar. Somebody would have to tell Elaine. She had resisted the temptation to switch off the torch.

* * *

Peters had not yet evicted himself from the dilapidated cottage; he had till the end of the week. He had turned over, and was just in the process of looking forward to another hour in bed – no need to work, he'd been paid off – when he heard urgent knocking at the door. He hoped it wasn't that damned woman.

It was a woman's voice. "Peters! Peters! Come quickly."

Not to her, he wouldn't. However he decided it wasn't the Hawk. The voice was deeper, harsher. He decided it must be old Lady Bellenden. What did she want? She wasn't a bad old girl.

He threw off the blankets, struggled into his trousers, and pulling his shirt over his head went to the door. Lady Bellenden was standing outside, in her old togs as usual, with the dog on its lead, he was glad to see. McGinty and Peters understood one another rather too well.

"Mr Partridge is dead," Lady Bellenden said calmly. "I found him a few moments ago. He must have fallen over the rockface last night in the dark. I want you to go for the doctor and the police."

"Use your telephone," he said sullenly. He didn't want to be mixed up in anything. The faded eyes raised themselves, their gaze direct and unafraid.

"I shall do so, when I have informed Mrs Partridge," she replied evenly. "Meantime I must be certain the doctor is on his way. Be as quick as you can."

As soon as she was out of sight he grabbed a few belongings, a couple of cleanish shirts and a spare pair of shoes. He wasn't going near any doctor nor no police, not he, after what had happened a couple of days ago. The narks would pick on him at once. Fallen down the rockface, indeed! The Dove knew the woods well enough, walked in them often. He wouldn't have fallen by himself even in the dark. It was best to be out of the way. Peters had kin in the hills, horse-copers, tinkers, their families. They'd hide him for as long as it was needed. The law couldn't find everybody, say what you liked. He could vanish among them like a half-pint, and no questions asked.

He made his way swiftly down the path and then aside, staring on the way at the tweed-clad body with its head turned at so odd an angle. Poor bugger, he was better off dead. Within moments the trees, even so early in the year, had swallowed the man Peters up. In fact, they never found him for questioning.

Lady Bellenden strode manfully up the path to the Partridge house with McGinty, thankfully again freed from his leash, ploughing resolutely behind her. No doubt she should have gone straight to her own telephone, as the man Peters had rather impertinently suggested; but it was in her blood first to tell the widow of the death. The doctor should, however, be here very shortly. It was a pity to have to waken such as Elaine so early in the morning, but Winifred Bellenden quailed at nothing. It would not, however, be a pleasant or easy task to break the news.

She grasped the bell and pulled. A rusty jangle echoed through the house, ending, as Lady Bellenden knew of old, in a row of capering metal bells attached overhead to a wooden board in the kitchen. It was a period piece and poor Julius Partridge had appreciated it; his wife hadn't.

"Who the hell is it? Is that you, Ju?"

A scurry of footsteps had sounded inside. The door was flung open by Elaine in her dressing gown, hair loose for once and not too clean. Its hanging grey-black masses gave her the air of a witch. The eyes peered through it.

"Oh, God, it's Win. Why're you here at this hour? I thought it was Julius. He went out last night and I didn't hear him come in. I left cold ham for him in the fridge, but I don't suppose he's touched it. What do you want? Don't bring that dog in here."

"I am afraid he has to come in," said the old lady firmly. She knew well enough that if she were to leave McGinty outside again tied up, he would strangle himself with the indignity; and left free, he would go straight as an arrow down to the dead man lying below the rock and gnaw at the already savaged face. She supposed it was true to have to say animals hadn't reason in such instances. She laid her hand on her dog's back, a gesture he understood.

"There's bad news," she said gently.

"Julius? Oh God. I knew something must be wrong. Oh God. Tell me. Don't stand there."

Her face had blanched, her mouth hung open; a witch contemplating the malefic vision. "I found him," said Winifred. "He must have fallen over the rock." There was no means of saying it otherwise than plainly; the poor creature had to be told.

"Is he . . . dead?" She then answered her own question. "He can't be dead, he can't be, not Julius. There was nothing wrong with him. It's a mistake. Let me go to him. Wait till I get a coat on. Is he—"

Suddenly, tears were running down her face. "Take me to him," she whimpered. "I must see him. Tell me where he is, and I'll get dressed and come." She made no offer to ask the old woman inside to sit on a chair.

"You must remember him as he was," said Lady Bellenden firmly. "You will be asked to identify him. He has lain out all night." She disliked the possibility of further description; Elaine would see the havoc soon enough.

"As he was? Of course I remember him as he was. I'll never forget him. I'm his wife, aren't I?" She had madc no effort to go and dress; already the glance had wavered, fixing itself malevolently on the dog. McGinty growled. Lady Bellenden made herself speak up.

"Dress yourself, before the doctor and the police come." She thought of a crumb of comfort. "He must have died at once," she said, "with the fall."

"I'm going to lie down," said Elaine. "Take that dog away."

"Best thing to do, but be ready for the doctor; he should be on his way. I sent Peters. I will take McGinty home and then return. I will then make you a cup of strong tea and bring it up to you if Mrs Beale is not yet here."

"She won't be back," said Elaine spitefully. She appeared to have forgotten about the death. It might be shock. She put out a hand to the older woman suddenly.

"If you go away, I'll be alone," she said. "Don't leave me. Promise you won't go away till someone comes?"

"Well, I will put my dog in the house and come straight back. The doctor may be here before then." She reassured herself; he might be out on a case, otherwise one would have expected his car by now. Meantime, there was no one but herself to help this poor creature. One did one's duty by anyone in distress.

Time passed, she had returned without McGinty, had made and delivered the tea and had a cup herself. Elaine was giving orders about whom to telephone; it would probably be better if she did so for herself. Winifred tried the doctor's number; it was engaged. By now it was surgery time; Peters couldn't have got to him at once. Lady Bellenden began to feel trapped. She could not leave the house to get hold of any of the other neighbours; every few moments, Elaine would call to her from where she still lay in bed, asking her to come upstairs. When she did, on rheumatic joints, it was to listen to a flow of hoarse unrelated talk, of the past, of the important people they'd known at Cambridge. That that might have been true on the surface the old lady was aware; there would have been courtesy for Julius, tacit acceptance for his wife till she became outrageous. It was the same here. Winifred had recognised unhappiness when she saw it; the man's. He had said nothing, but that kind of thing came out by one means or the other.

"Come upstairs," called the voice again. She'd only just got down; and McGinty would be hungry, he hadn't had his food. He expected a bite and a biscuit just after his walk, and there hadn't been time to get them. Winifred imagined his narrow, shrewd eyes watching for her, face inscrutable as always; but he had his feelings. Where was the doctor? Where were the police? Nobody here had eaten any breakfast. Sooner or later, her own man Stevens was bound to know there was something up, and would come round in the end, perhaps; but in the meantime the dead body was still lying below the rock. Beale the postman mustn't find him. Winifred used the telephone again. It was out of order.

She kept calm, went to the fridge, found the cold ham Julius Partridge would never now eat, nibbled a bite for herself and took some up to Elaine, who shuddered.

"I couldn't touch food. What do you take me for?" Her manner was at once pert and majestic, an actress queen with her servant. "You ought to eat," said Lady Bellenden. She tried to smile. "If you won't, McGinty and I will share it, if you don't mind. I won't go down to the shops."

"Help yourselves, do," said Elaine ungraciously. She began sobbing and crying again. "I can't believe it about my husband, I won't believe he's dead. He walked out of the door last night for a turn in the woods, the way he often does – did. I went to bed. I can't think what happened. Why don't you telephone? Someone ought to come." She was petulant. "I'll have to write to everyone," she said. However she made no movement to get out of bed, and Lady Bellenden refrained from saying that if she was able to think of it, she might as well do it. Once she was occupied, one could go down in the car to the police station.

"The post's late," said Elaine. "That bloody Beale takes his time."

"Perhaps there are no letters for anybody." She didn't mention the possibility that his wife might be worse; Elaine had enough on her plate, if one could so put it.

She hoped Stevens would come soon. Apart from her own isolation, finding the body would not be pleasant for anyone. A child might find it on the way to school.

Just then the bell jangled; someone was at the door at last. Lady Bellenden went to open it, full of thankfulness.

Outside stood a tall broad man with close-cropped white hair and a square jaw: Bill Hedley, the orchid-grower from the Crystal Palace. She had never been as glad to see anyone; but his face was grim.

"I've just found Partridge," he said, as though he knew she must already know.

She nodded. "I found him myself earlier this morning. The telephone is out of order. I sent Peters down at the time to the village to fetch the doctor, but he hasn't come here." She turned her head cautiously, inviting him in. "Elaine's upstairs," she murmured. "It has been a great shock." The words sounded trite.

"As it's a matter for the police, she will have to identify the body, poor woman." He stepped over the threshold, blotting out the daylight beyond the door. "How long have you been with her?" he asked. "You look tired; don't overdo it."

"Several hours. It's only that I cannot get away to do the things that ought to be done, and she – she can't be left. She's lying on her bed."

"I'll send Mrs Houston to relieve you at once, and ring from there," he promised. That Peters was a rascal. He knew the type from his army days, sly as boots, never admittedly near trouble. "I'll deal with the police when they come; I'll wait down there," he promised. "After that, anything else I can do—"

"See if you can find out what has happened to the post. Mrs Beale may be ill again."

Hedley promised again to do what he might, and went striding away in almost too manly a fashion. Lady Bellenden waited in relief till his housekeeper came round, then went home and fed McGinty. Her conscience made her, after that, come round to Lesser Bellenden yet again; by now, it wouldn't be a lone siege, and she ought to be helpful.

Mrs Houston was seeing to things downstairs, saying Mr Hedley would report the fault to the telephone people. "I have already done so," said Winifred. She ascended the staircase again.

"I heard a man's voice," Elaine called. "Was it the police?"

She knew, evidently, that the police must come. "It might have been Mr Hedley," Winifred Bellenden replied. For some reason, although the residents here mostly used one another's Christian names with ease, she couldn't speak of him as Bill to Elaine Partridge.

Elaine was lying where she had lain all morning, a refilled teacup by her side. "I can't bear abnormal people," she said. "It's true, I suppose, that the Japanese did something to him in the war? I heard that." Her eyes gleamed, not with tears: with a kind of triumph.

"I would not dream of asking him," replied Lady Bellenden. It was true, she knew. Bill Hedley had been growing green peppers in the jungle as a very young sergeant, to give some vitamin C to the rest when they were all working as half-starved prisoners on the Burma railway. His punishment on discovery had been unspeakable. She passed quickly on to the presence of Mrs Houston downstairs. "If you like to tell me what to give her to do, she'll get on with it. Then she'll bring you some lunch."

"I tell you I don't want any bloody lunch. I'd rather you stayed; you've been so kind. I don't want her nosing round here. Servants always gossip. I'd rather you were here when, when – oh, Julius—"

"I will try to stay for a little while," said Lady Bellenden gently. It was certainly better for her to be here when they came, as in the end they must. "There are one or two things, however, that I must go and do," she admitted.

"What things?"

"The ordinary things about the house; you know them as well as I do." That wasn't true; Elaine did no housekeeping, nothing in the garden; it was merely shaved grass, seen to by Peters last autumn and beginning to straggle. "Also, I must let my dog out," Winifred added. "He's been shut in now several hours."

Elaine uttered a vulgar, never before heard epithet about McGinty. "But you will come back?" she went on, incredibly. "You promise? Promise me."

"I will certainly do so as soon as possible." There was nothing for it but to remain courteous and to remember that the woman was both shocked and ill. Lady Bellenden picked up the teacup to take it downstairs.

"What time?"

Lady Bellenden began to realise something of what the late Julius Partridge had had to endure. "When I can," she said with firmness, and at that moment there was a knock on the bedroom door which revealed Mrs Houston, standing outside with something on a tray. One ought perhaps to stay to persuade Elaine to eat it, but Winifred Bellenden escaped while she might.

She came back, valiant as ever, in an hour and a half, having seen to the house and watered her germinating meconopsis seeds, which had been in danger of drying. She arranged for Stevens to come and call for her if she did not return within a stated time. By now, news of the death might have spread as far as Brennan, and it would surely not be long before other neighbours came round to help out. They hadn't liked Elaine, but they had liked Julius, and would do their best for his widow.

Mrs Houston opened the door. "The police is here," she said in a whisper. "The doctor's been down at the body. They're upstairs with her now." She passed her tongue over her middle-aged lips. "Standing with a glass of brandy, she was, in the study; wouldn't eat anything, not that there was much in the house except eggs. I made her an omelette, but she wouldn't touch it. The farm boy called with their milk, I should say with hers." She gazed in conspiratorial fashion at Lady Bellenden.

"I think," said the latter, not commenting on the variously related disasters, "that this is the day Mr and Mrs Partridge used to go down to the village and fill up the car boot with stores for the week. I can relieve you now, if you like, or else go down."

"Mr Hedley says he'll have a bite at the Lamb and Flag today, to leave me free here for as long as I'm needed. Shocking thing about poor Dora Beale, wasn't it? They say the husband's more upset than the wife. The baby might be saved, it seems, after all, though you never know with them sorts of accidents. I remember—"

Lady Bellenden, having long given up wondering how the grapevine operated as it did in Brennan, nodded her head briskly to stop the flow.

"Kept the place nice and clean, she has, poor Dora," remarked the housekeeper, a stream diverted slightly. "There wasn't much for me to do except dust."

"I had better perhaps go up to Mrs Partridge now, to see if she needs assistance," said Lady Bellenden. At that point there came a belligerent shout from upstairs.

"Naturally my husband left me the keys. This isn't the Middle Ages. He had no reason to keep anything in his pockets. I can't help what you found."

"Madam, it's a case of what we didn't find," replied the sergeant audibly as Lady Bellenden mounted the by now dreadfully familiar stairs. He greeted her respectfully as she looked in, at the same time saying "Not a single article, not a tobacco pouch. That's not like most men." He winked at the old lady, but respectfully; she was liked hereabouts, was old Lady B. No side about her.

"My husband didn't smoke a pipe. He liked the occasional cigarette."

"As you say, Mrs Partridge. That'll be all meantime, but we'll need you later."

"I shall be here, of course. I have no means of leaving since you took my driving licence away."

The sergeant took refuge in silence, and left. The young constable had taken all of it down in his notebook; the second constable had been left guarding the body. They had asked now, politely, if the latter might be brought back up here till the van came from Llanaff. There was no mortuary in Brennan.

Elaine was still in her dressing gown, her hair stuffed by now into a soiled headband. She sipped at the brandy. "Of course bring him here," she said. "It's his home, isn't it?" She began to cry. "Oh, Julius, oh, Julius, I still can't believe it, I can't." The tears ran down her face. Lady Bellenden came and put an arm round her.

"Leave me alone," said Elaine angrily. "Why is the house full of people?"

"Is it necessary for her to have to identify the body?" asked Winifred later. "I can do so; I have already seen it. It was I who found it, and I knew the dead man well."

"I'm sorry, my lady, but it must be done by the next of kin. That's the law."

She had persuaded Elaine, at last, to go and dress. "What time did you discover the body?" the sergeant asked.

"Shortly after six o'clock this morning. I was taking my dog, as I always do, for his walk then. He observed something and went over. I recognised the late Mr Partridge by his tweed coat and deerstalker."

"Did you look at the facc?" put in the constable ruthlessly. The sergeant frowned; young Parkes spoke out of place now and again, he'd often told him so.

"At what was left of it," replied Lady Ballenden drily. Both men looked at her in admiration; most women, let alone an old one like that, would have been in screaming hysterics, even now. In fact she was a lot more help than the widow. Winifred went on to tell them something else.

"I went at once to the cottages to instruct the man Peters to come and inform you and the doctor," she said. "He promised to go at once."

"He's gone at once, all right," said the sergeant grimly. "We went there first of all, knowing his like. He's scarpered."

"Perhaps they will find him by means of television?" suggested Lady Bellenden. She didn't like it, wouldn't have it in the house; it saved a licence and watching a lot of rubbish. However, they traced people by such means, one understood; it might be considered. "Peters was a tinker," she said charitably, meaning he wouldn't take orders easily.

"You can add an 's' to the beginning of that, my lady. He's wanted for a good deal, but we haven't been able to pin anything on him till now, and now you can put a fiver on it he's turned into some of his relations as looks just like him, and was somewhere else at the time, with witnesses."

Elaine emerged at that point in a dark woollen dress, with her hair combed and her face washed: a discreet and sorrowing widow.

They brought Partridge's body home, the ruined face covered by a sheet. The doctor, obtained at last, remained in attendance; he offered to give Elaine a sedative, which she took. The body was laid meantime on the table downstairs. Contrary to expectations, Elaine made no scene when she was compelled to look on the terrible face. She merely nodded, said the body was that of her husband, and turned away.

By that time the antique bell had jangled to admit yet another neighbour with an offer of help; this time a stocky young woman of about thirty-five, with dark cropped hair, a linen smock and sandals with a serape thrown over everything for warmth, and gloveless hands showing a rim of white dried clay below the square, competent fingernails. Her manner was brisk and abrupt.

"I've heard. Can I do anything?" Mary Reston asked Mrs Houston, who opened the door.

"Maybe you'd like to go up and see her," replied Bill Hedley's housekeeper. Elaine by then was lying down again, but nobody could blame her.

Mary went up. The door opened and the two women looked at each other. They began to address one another stiffly, neither sounding at ease. "Do you need any letters written?" Mary asked.

Elaine suddenly came out with a list of business acquaintances, professors, newspapers, a step-aunt in Canada. Like Winifred Bellenden earlier, Mary thought that if she had all that worked out in her head, she might as well get on with it herself; such things eased a death. She did not say as much aloud, however, but wrote down a list and took it back to her studio, where there was a typewriter somewhere.

The next person to be given a list was Lady Bellenden herself, who, unwearied in well-doing, had called to ask if there was anything she could bring from the shops. "Next time, you can come with me in my car," she said. It was not normally her own day for going in. Elaine was quite ready with orders for this and that: grocer, baker, butcher and – a large order, this – the wine merchant. Lady Bellenden made it clear that she would say the order was for Elaine and not for herself.

She drove down to the village in her elderly, mostly reliable Morris, almost all of whose parts had at one time or another been replaced. She'd often wondered whether it wouldn't be cheaper to get another car, but was fond of this one. It would probably see her out. McGinty sat as usual in his royal place in front. She never had any trouble about parcels left inside with the door unlocked; one sight of McGinty was enough for thieves. Having made the purchases and arranged them separately for Elaine and for herself, the old lady began to feel a little tired; but there was one errand she must still perform, if only for the sake of her unsleeping conscience. She had been troubled over the matter of the keys said to be missing from Julius's pocket; she knew well enough he had kept them there, not by being told but no doubt by natural intuition. It wasn't, as the police had said, like a man to have empty pockets. Men were like schoolboys who hadn't grown up; if you cleared a pocket out, all kinds of things emerged; string, knives, bait for fishing, lumps of sugar for a pony. Tears rose briefly in the faded eyes; she could remember clearing out her husband's things when *he*'d died. She was certain Elaine was lying; after all she did so constantly. It wasn't, granted, her own affair, but perhaps she ought to make certain. One person who might be able to enlighten her was Dora Beale, and anyway it would be charitable to call on the poor young woman. Coming to clean twice weekly she would have observed the Partridges as well as anyone. One didn't, of course, pry.

She knocked at last at the green-painted door of the council house where the postman lived. It was opened by Dora herself, a little pale, but otherwise tidy and cheerful as usual. She greeted Lady Bellenden with pleased shyness.

"It's good of your ladyship to call. Yes, I'm better. I was finding the day slow to pass, though, with Beale back at his work and me not supposed to do much yet, the doctor says. I've got the kettle ready; might I make you a cup of tea, my lady?" Perhaps, she thought, she was being forward, but Lady Bellenden didn't seem to mind. She was never on her high horse, not like some.

"I would be very glad of one. Are not you supposed to be in bed?" She had followed the younger woman into a scrupulously clean parlour, with a hand-crocheted mat set on the table and a geranium in a plastic pot on top of that, in its saucer. Everything shone with care and attention.

"There wasn't any need, not after the first day when it still wasn't certain whether I'd lose it or not," said Dora. "It seems to be all right, nothing's come." She recalled that she was perhaps speaking in too earthy a fashion to be respectful, and hastily said, "Beale's like a fussy old hen, to be sure. It might have been a lot worse. How is poor Mrs Partridge? It was a terrible thing to happen. A nice man, he was. I'll get the tea."

She was preparing, Winifred knew, to set out an elaborate

tray, no doubt with more lace mats, perhaps even a display of the best china. "Let me come and have it with you in the kitchen," she said practically. "It saves carrying things through."

"Well, if your ladyship doesn't mind the kitchen—"

"Of course I don't mind kitchens, I've got one of my own." She was shown by Dora into an equally clean and shining apartment, small, with a table and chairs, a framed wall-sampler which had been a wedding present from Jerry's mother, now deceased, and more geraniums on the sill beyond the gleaming metal sink. Dora set about making tea in a brown pot. Winifred switched to other matters before returning to the Partridge death, by then drinking her welcome tea. "Did he leave his keys with her, or keep them in his pocket?" she asked at last, roundly. Dora choked a little on her scalding tea, and shook her head.

"He always kept them himself, that I know, so's she couldn't get into the cupboard," she said. The speedwell eyes – Lady Bellenden, like Beale, remembered speedwells in the hedgerows – raised themselves to the old lady's face. "I don't like saying it, but there was drink kept in there, and he wouldn't let her get at it," she continued. "I was only in the study now and again. He didn't like that room disturbed, because he did his reading in it." She set down the teacup suddenly. "Poor man, it's sad to think he'll never read anything any more. It's hard to believe it, really."

"So the keys would be kept in his pocket?"

"Like as not. I don't recall ever setting eyes on them." Dora stirred the sugar in her cup, feeling sure she'd said too much. Why would her ladyship want to be so certain about the keys? She'd ask Jerry when he came in. He'd know.

Lady Bellenden rose to leave shortly. "Thank you, my dear," she said on the doorstep. "You have refreshed me. I feel much less tired now. Look after yourself, and the baby."

She left Dora standing on the scrubbed doorstep, the pale sun shining on her neat black hair. Thinking over the whole matter as she drove home, Winifred decided that she would not give the information to the police. Julius Partridge was dead, and nothing would bring him back to life. That he had not fallen over the rock by accident was almost certain if his pockets had been searched and emptied, but it might have happened subsequently. One didn't like to think of that part any more than the other.

She made herself concentrate on nursing the old car up the rough, familiar drive home. To have got the estate roads tarred would have been possible, no doubt, with a council grant, but she liked them as they were. The people who came up to live at Bellenden liked solitude for its own sake, every one for different reasons; Hedley with what might have been a wrecked life, but for his passion for orchid-growing; Mary with her pottery and her visits from the blind man Oldham; and the likes of Peters, by now, as the police put it, having scarpered.

Winifred slowed to negotiate twin stone gateposts between which tall iron gates had used to open and close. They marked the entry to Bellenden House, and Lord Bellenden had removed the gates with his own hands twenty years ago; there wasn't a lodge, he said, and no point in keeping them, it merely meant you had to get out and back in again twice over to shut them at last. She smiled fondly, remembering him. They hadn't had any children, she didn't know why. "There's you, at any rate," she said to McGinty, who accepted the tribute with his customary aplomb. She put in the car to its port and reached home thankfully, sending Stevens round with Elaine's parcels. At present, she herself really could not face Elaine again.

* * *

Julius Partridge's funeral was well attended, it having been decided that the death was due to an accident. That was a relief, as the insurance wouldn't have paid up for suicide, but everyone present – except Winifred, who alone knew about the keys – was wondering if that after all had been it. The publisher Henschel, grey-faced with shock – he and Partridge had been students together at Trinity long ago – had come from London; and most of the county were present, all the Bellenden inhabitants and others, including blind Basil Oldham, from further afield. Elaine was in her element, having somehow acquired a full-length widow's veil and draped its transparent black folds over her head and face. They weren't worn any more, everyone muttered: she was play-acting. They muttered also that no sane man would fall over a ledge whose location he knew as well as anyone. Also, it wasn't as if Julius had an enemy in the world, except possibly the man Peters, who'd been sacked a few days before. That grudge, on silent agreement, was thought to be the most likely answer. Elaine was unlikely to have done away with her husband; more likely, someone from the back murmured, to have been the other way round. It was Henschel, who was already concerned about the missing typescript. He had had the hardihood to tackle Elaine before the funeral, a fact much resented.

Elaine said she knew nothing about it. "But he was reading it," insisted the publisher. "He wrote to me that he'd received it safely, and would shortly return it with any comments, as he always did promptly. It must be about the house somewhere."

"Look by all means. It's hardly a time to ask me. I knew nothing about Julius's work. He kept it to himself."

Henschel hunted in the study and elsewhere, but without result. He was white with anger, even during the funeral service and the long bumpy drive down to Penarch Crematorium and back. It was unlike Julius to have mislaid a script; and that was the only adequate copy, with alterations. That bitch – he was under no illusions about Elaine – had either hidden or destroyed it. There was nothing to be done except to contact the author again in the hope that he had a rough copy of some kind. "If he hasn't, I'll kill her," Henschel murmured. It would be a loss to the firm, being already paid for in advance, and times weren't easy.

After everyone had gone and the ashes were scattered, Elaine was left standing alone in the room where the service had taken place. She flung back her veil, staring down at a few loose petals from the removed wreaths; no flowers now, no coffin on its trestle. They'd decided the death was accidental, so thank goodness the insurance would pay. She could afford to do more or less as she liked. Perhaps she wouldn't even stay on here. Visions floated through her mind; London, Paris. It didn't matter about that bloody publisher. He'd never paid Julius much.

A knock sounded at the door. Perhaps Henschel had come back to go on with his search, God knew why; or perhaps it was old Win again. She was useful, would take one down to the village shops as required. Otherwise it was like a desert island, and she, Elaine, was marooned here with no chance of a passing sail. She reflected on her own fate for moments, then went to the door. "You needn't waste your bloody time," she shouted, in case it was Henschel.

The knocking continued, impersonally and politely. Elaine flung open the door. It was Stevens, Win Bellenden's man, standing there with a note in his hand.

"Her ladyship said to give you this, madam." His face was wooden. It could not be seen from his expression whether or not he had heard anything, but late that evening, in the privacy of their cottage, he told his wife he'd never heard anything like the way that Mrs P. went on. "Better for her ladyship if she has nothing more to do with that one, she'll only be taken advantage of," he remarked over his supper of toad-in-the-hole, which Mrs Stevens made remarkably well.

"She's too kind-hearted," agreed his spouse, adding that her ladyship had asked if she'd go and help out at Lesser Bellenden on the half-days Dora Beale used to go there and clean. Mrs Stevens had agreed, not without reservations, because the place would get like a pigsty if she didn't; but she had made it clear she wouldn't put up with any of Mrs Partridge's bad language, and to say so. It had not, in fact, yet been said.

Meantime Elaine opened the note. It was written in Lady Bellenden's sprawling hand, easy to read even in the dim light of the porch. *The wine merchant won't supply further goods until you pay his outstanding account*, it read. Elaine crumpled the paper into a ball and flung it into the furthest corner of the room.

She raged about, walking up and down like a madwoman. Win's man had gone; he must have known there would be no reply. Damn all these superior people and their know-all servants! She could show them she was as good as anyone. She'd get out the car and to hell with the police, go down and face the wine merchant this minute, and tell him if that was the way he treated his regular customers she'd take hers elsewhere. She'd—

She'd have a glass of brandy, to steady her. There was some left. It was a relief to be able to get at it again. Julius hadn't understood that she needed a drink fairly often, she was sensitive; people didn't realise how raw her nerves were with one thing and another, and today had been her husband's funeral.

She drank the brandy, seized a coat from the row of hooks in the hall, marched out to the former loose-box where Julius had left the car, found she'd forgotten the keys, went back, located them and came out again, got in at last and switched on the ignition. It was some time since she'd driven. She backed the car out safely, then swivelled it round to get out to the rough path leading past Bellenden. On the way she encountered the latter's bare stone gateposts. For some reason the car cannoned into one and knocked it sideways. Elaine was brought up with a jerk. She got out. The car was a write-off and so was the post. Old Win would no doubt send her a bill for having it put straight. She wouldn't pay. Nobody had any right to leave obstructions of that kind in the way of drivers.

Anyway, now she would have to rely on Win to be driven. It was a nuisance. She left the ruined car where it was, and walked back to the house. They could find it and do what they liked with it. She would go away soon, and live in town, where shops were round the corner.

That episode would have added to Elaine's isolation but for the fact that, for Julius's sake, people began to ply his widow with invitations. Perhaps, it was thought, these would take her out of herself. It was of course mostly necessary to ask Winifred Bellenden as well, but nobody minded that; she continued as Elaine's chauffeuse without complaint. McGinty however made matters complicated, because Elaine objected to his presence in the car and Lady Bellenden could hardly bear to leave him behind. On the whole, however, she considered it her duty to give in: after all she was enjoying a renewal of social life herself as a result of driving Elaine. McGinty took to a certain amount of indignant and solitary barking.

So matters continued, except that Elaine, displaying the kind of shrewd cunning of which she was always capable, looked after number one, as Mrs Stevens put it. For instance, she paid the wine merchant by letter instead of abusing him. He continued, therefore, to supply her; and Beale had returned to his rounds. In their way, things went on for a time as they had done before, though with the absence of Julius and Dora.

Four

Tom Brackenbury had booked in at the Lamb and Flag, Brennan, and had just turned the key in his room door when the telephone rang. He put down his painting gear, the canvas satchel, the portable easel, the ordnance map, and picked up the receiver.

He was surprised that anyone knew where he was. he had stayed here as a boy thirty-odd years ago for climbing and fishing, before disaster had struck the farms; but by now Brennan itself and the houses and fields round about had become a comfortable, sociable refuge for retired people who had made enough money. Tom himself had no relatives here now; old Aunt Kate Millington had died long ago.

The voice was a man's, high-pitched. "That you, Brack? Haven here."

Tom raised an eyebrow. Henry Haven was a fairly well-known writer of suspense novels, whom in the nature of things Brackenbury had run into often in London and who, he knew, had separated from his wife some time ago. No doubt he had retreated to this spot.

"How did you get on to me, Henry?"

"The grapevine. You were spotted as you drove through Penarch. Nothing here remains a secret; you're often the last to know about yourself and what everybody's saying. I say, are you tied up? What about lunch? I can do you an omelette, cheese and a goodish Chianti."

Tom said he would like to come, and the voice at the other end of the line underwent a subtle change and deepened.

"Look, Tom, I'm damned sorry about . . . what happened.

Got to make the best of it now with your friends. I know you have plenty."

Tom murmured something meaningless, as he always did by this time, rather than let his mind dwell on what it had been trying to reject, put into proper focus perhaps, for almost a year now. It seemed longer; it seemed a lifetime without Sheila.

"Glad you can come," said Haven's normal voice. "It'll be just ourselves. I'd better tell you how to get to this place. From where you are in Brennan, drive four miles back on to the Penarch road and take the left-hand fork. About two miles ahead you'll see a jumble of cottages and an old mill, and a square Victorian church tower."

"I know. Leafkillen."

"That's right. I live behind the church in a hovel of my own I bought last year. The lane stops there and reversing is difficult; you may want to leave your car in the village street. It's only a few yards to walk."

"I'll find it. This is very good of you." In fact, he admitted to himself, the pleasure was not entirely genuine. He had wanted to set off right away, with sandwiches, to paint an unfamiliar aspect of Bigod Peak he remembered from a boy, with the one-inch map he had bought on purpose to get him there if he lost himself among a rash of new council houses and altered roads. But the painting could be done at any time if the autumn weather remained good. Autumn, and the Harrods bombing almost a year ago.

He jerked his thoughts away. "Look forward to meeting you again. It's a long way from El Vino's." Tom remembered Haven last in the thick smoky atmosphere of the famous journalists' pub. He had been pinned to the wall by a reviewer who had had to shout his questions against the din of talk.

"About twelve-thirty," Haven said. "Time for a drink first."

"I'll look forward to it," said Tom again, and rang off. He stared at the painting gear, recognising it for what it was; a screen to put up in front of himself, behind which to remain uncommitted. He had once had some talent; had done nothing with it in his involvement with his chosen way of making a living, which was reporting for increasingly influential newspapers. Painting was only a hobby now, no more; a substitute, if one could call it that, for losing himself in work and more work, which had itself then suffered, losing its crisp vitality, its driving force. Now, he was on holiday, another name for sick leave.

The Editor had been understanding. For an unsatisfactory member of the permanent staff of the paper, Brackenbury had been treated well. The kindly grey eyes behind the rimless glasses had contained no hint of what was after all the truth, that readership must rise and not fall. "Take six months off," A.B. said. "Come back when you can. I'll take over the column myself meantime; make me feel young again. You need to get right away, absorb some other interest, do your own thing, as they call it now, for a time, and forget about work, London and the rest of it. It happens, don't forget, to all of us that we have something in our lives we can't bear to look back on. Giving up is not good enough for someone like yourself; you see I value you; you're a fine reporter." And on these words he, Brackenbury, had stumbled out of the office in a kind of incredulity. He must, it followed, do the best he could to repair his life, his thinking. It should be possible. He was forty-four.

He had gone home to the empty house and had tried to consider foreign holidays, a trip to Spain or North Africa. But the prospect of sun-soaked beaches and warm blue sea didn't interest him now there was no Sheila to share them. In fact, there was nowhere he could think of that he wanted to go, nowhere that wouldn't remind him of her, her slim eager body, her fair hair shining in the sun. Then he recalled his boyhood in the shadow of Bigod Peak and the familiar places, the land of lost content. A country holiday in Brennan's only hotel would do, for the time being. The good old Lamb and Flag had been unchanged and he had left his car in its capacious garage. And there he was, getting ready to have lunch with Henry Haven. He would keep on the old green pullover and corduroys in which he had driven up. He gave himself a bath and shave, dressed again, ordered coffee, drank it and went out. It was still before ten o'clock – he had driven up overnight – but he had no time in any case to start painting before lunch. He decided to pass the time checking out on the way to Bigod he remembered. It would take perhaps an hour there and back, and he could take a look at conditions and colours, preferably with a limited palette.

He got the car out and, turning off before the bridge, continued on the inland road, where nothing seemed to have changed much except for a proliferation of council houses at the town end. He supposed practically everyone in them would be unemployed and living on social security: once they would have been agricultural workers, before the EEC. He drove on, found the turning he knew, left the car and followed the woodland path. It was a crisp day that made walking pleasant, but as always in idleness his mind shied back to last Christmas.

He had known something was wrong as soon as he got to the house and found there were no lights on. Sheila had always left the welcome light shining when he was out on a late assignment; her job in an architect's office let her out earlier. If she knew certainly when he would be coming home she would unlatch the garage doors. They hadn't been open. With a mounting premonition of something wrong, Tom had found the latch and turned the key in it and had gone into the dark little hall they'd tried to brighten with white paint and cheerful wallpaper. As soon as he had shut the front door behind him the telephone had started to ring.

It was the police. They had tried to reach him earlier. "It's your wife, Mr Brackenbury. I'm afraid it's bad news." Sheila had gone to Harrods to buy his Christmas present. Among the many wounded by the IRA bomb she was one of the dead, the package for him still clutched in her fingers. It was a boldly striped shirt. He had kept it in a drawer and had never worn it. He had gone to the mortuary and had identified Sheila's pale peaceful face above the turned-down sheet. She hadn't looked as if she had died a violent death. Perhaps she didn't even know what had happened.

He must stop thinking about it, and about his own solitude.

The woods were turning their colours with autumn. To paint them would be trite. Heart red, dun yellow, golden brown. *Driven like ghosts from an enchanter fleeing, yellow, and black, and pale, and hectic red.* He hadn't read Shelley since his schooldays. Some leaves had already fallen on the path. It was a pleasant, secret place. Why hadn't he ever brought Sheila up here? They had both had their jobs, their careers: it had sometimes been difficult to arrange holidays together. There had simply not been enough time.

He climbed on and upward, glad of the physical challenge to muscles softened by town, by constantly driving a car. The path had become stony, perhaps treacherous, and on either side were thick woods, with an occasional break for a narrow track. The tracks led, he remembered, to cottages.

It was quiet; not even a scurrying rabbit or bird disturbed him. This was the way acknowledged climbers sometimes took to Bigod Peak, the difficult north face. He passed a cottage with empty windows presently, and wondered who owned it now. It had once, he supposed, been part of the old Bellenden estate; in Regency days the then Lord Bellenden had used to have hellfire parties here. Now the great house was a ruin, half-seen at last through the wood. Beyond, there had once been gamekeepers' cottages, with stable quarters behind: the kind of places that were being modernised now and sold for tidy sums, or let in summer.

Suddenly he came on the clear view of Bigod Peak, glimpsed beyond the branches, hyacinth colour in the morning sun. Its humped twist was like a human shoulder, its sharp summit clear above, a trail of cloud across. He was alone with the cloud, the woods and the mountain. This was the place where he had hoped to come and paint. He would do it this afternoon, or if not, tomorrow.

He turned to reconnoitre the ground; there might be a better view yet. A little way off there rose a sudden rock-face he remembered, eighty feet or so high, its surface like grey slate. Would he be better to climb to the top and extend his planned view? There would be plenty of time before joining Haven for lunch.

He scuffed the leaves a little, for here they were thick underfoot, undisturbed from last year, the year before that. It made footing uncertain; he trod carefully. Then his senses received a jolt. It was like looking at a picture by Salvador Dali, giraffes on fire, dressing-tables on a beach, a ring with a pattern of corsets. Before him, settled squarely at the base of the steep bare rock, was a vase filled with mixed dahlias.

"Get out of here. What the bloody hell are you doing here? Go on, get out."

The voice was strident, neither a man's nor a woman's. He looked up and saw its owner standing at the top of the rise. It was a woman after all. She was a scarecrow figure, tall and sallow, or perhaps it was dirt; her grey-black hair stuck out in wisps from beneath a soiled knitted cap. She wore a man's Burberry, stained with use and age; ragged trousers, also a man's, and gumboots. Brackenbury thought at first she might be a tinker, but the sounds she made denied this: she continued shouting in good enough English, and when he did not move began to stoop to lift stones to throw. He took it by now that she was mad, or at least eccentric. However, it would be a nuisance if she came back later to disturb him when he was painting. For that reason, if no other, he answered her as pleasantly as he could.

"I believe this is a public way. I do not know you, madam."

"I'm the bloody owner, I tell you. Get out."

He resolved to ask Haven about this creature, but had his thoughts scattered when the stones began to come rattling down. One hit him sharply on the elbow. He raised a hand to protect his face, and called out that he would inform the police. He was beginning to be angry, an emotion he seldom felt. In the end he turned and went; it was time to go to Haven's in any case. She did not shout after him and although he did not turn his head he knew she was still standing there, staring down at the place where he had stood beside the undisturbed and stiffly thrusting dahlias, their garish colours shouting down the autumn woods, their presence an outrage. The odd thing was, as he realised afterwards, that the ugly words and rough voice had been, as Aunt Kate Millington would have put it, a lady's.

"Know her?" said Henry Haven. "Know Elaine Partridge? I should jolly well think I do. She tried to rape me about a month ago." The squeaky voice was as indignant as a woman's. Tom conveyed a mouthful of omelette, excellently cooked, from his fork to his mouth and used the movement to disguise his expression. The vision of Haven being assaulted by any woman amused him; his host was, somehow, asexual. Perhaps that was why the marriage had gone wrong. Tom reflected that Haven was, in a way, like a balding portrait done in pastels instead of oil; there was no deep colour about him. Yet his books were sensitively written, with real people acting as people do. Perhaps writers were always by their nature on the outside, looking in. The little house Haven had bought here was tidy and not too ugly, tucked away where nobody would notice it. Outside the window the grass waved high. Haven did not care for gardening and did not worry about who knew it.

Brackenbury waited for the story about Elaine Partridge, and duly it came out. "Don't know if you have heard about Basil Oldham – tragic, the chap was a brilliant flyer and was blinded about ten years ago in an air crash. His other faculties have taken over, as often happens, and he keeps a sharp ear to the ground and ends up trying to interfere with the lives of other people – not all, but the chosen few. I'd never have dreamed of taking Widow Partridge out to dinner myself—"

"Out to dinner? In rags?"

"Well, they were glad rags; she's a good-looking woman when she takes the trouble to wash herself. It was after Julius died – that was her husband."

"How did he die?"

"He fell over that rock face in the dark. Extraordinary, as he knew his way about quite well and had enough sense to carry a torch at night. His hand was still holding it, switched on, when they found him lying with his neck broken."

"A terrible thing to happen. No wonder it drove her to extremes."

"Not the extremes she goes to. And in my personal opinion," said Haven spitefully, "she pushed him. She played the bereaved widow, of course, and everybody was sorry for her and some still are. Anyway, Basil was one who was so sorry he figured out that she ought to be taken out of herself and invited out to dinner. He wouldn't ask her himself, but he fixed up with good old Maggie and Chips Everbury to ask her, then rang me up and told me I was to have the job of escorting her. That's Basil; nobody else would get away with a thing like that. He does it on purpose."

"So you took her." In its way the story was fantastically funny; the demure Haven and the wild Widow arm-in-arm, dressed up to kill. But perhaps it hadn't happened like that.

"He timed it so that I couldn't very well wriggle out of it," said Haven. "It was a disastrous evening. When I called for her she wanted me to come into the house and drink, and I refused because I knew we wouldn't have got away that night. That made her rude, of course. When we got there, it was pretty bad. Chips and Maggie are the kindest and most tactful people in the world, but that woman's manners are so aggressive nobody could help but notice, and she'd drink taken even before I'd arrived. Later she laid on the charm, and one can still see that that's what must have hooked poor Julius, who wouldn't have been looking for trouble at the time. He came across her in the office, I suppose; she was some kind of secretary when he was lecturing at Cambridge. He couldn't have known what he was taking on when he married her; alcoholics can be very deceptive. In the end – you know what college circles are like – she alienated everyone and Julius had to move elsewhere. It was the same tale at the next place, a redbrick, and the next, which was abroad. Julius was a reserved person and I didn't get all this out of him. Ollie Rowbotham, who'd been in the same college on research, spilt the beans up here, then dropped dead, poor dear chap, on the golf course shortly after they arrived."

"As good a way to go as any other."

"Well, Julius wasn't as lucky. In the end he retired on some kind of reduced pension and bought this cottage at the back of nowhere, put Elaine in it and devoted every hour of every day, and probably every night as well, to keeping her off the bottle. Have some more wine yourself."

Brackenbury reached across his glass. "It sounds to me," he ventured, "as though Partridge might well have flung himself over that rock. No doubt he realised he'd be happier dead."

"No, he had principles about all that. I got to know him quite well – but the police didn't enquire as much as they might. Lady Bellenden – you may not know the old lady lives alone nowadays – said she'd gone out for a walk and found him. She called the doctor and the police, but it was too late. They never did get to the bottom of it, and of course Elaine put on an act to get them to believe it had happened for other reasons, money troubles for instance. He wasn't that sort, poor Julius, but it didn't matter to the law." Haven sounded bitter. "Somehow, the insurance paid."

"So now she lives up there alone?"

"Yes, and drinking her head off with parcels sent up from the grocer's. Fortunately she can't drive – she lost her licence years ago – so most of us are free of her except poor Mary Reston, who lives in one of the near cottages, and Lady Bellenden, of course. Old Lady B. has been very good to Elaine and takes her food to make her eat. She – the Widow – strides into their houses without any by-your-leave, and she may be aggressive or she may be like treacle, which in my opinion is the more disgusting of the two. Anyhow, that night at Chips and Maggie's she tried treacle, then when it didn't work in the car going home she literally grabbed me by the balls. I kicked out and there was nearly a flat spin, but I got her home somehow, dumped her at her door and fled. Not Satan and all his minions would get me near that woman again. She's evil, evil. She may be at – oh, I haven't told you yet. Let's finish with the Widow and then have our cheese."

"Has she tried the rape thing with anyone else?" Tom was not quite prepared to leave the subject, which diverted him.

"Your guess is as good as mine. There was a slight variation on the theme with the postman, Jerry Beale, who's the salt of the earth. He must have had some idea of what things were like, because his wife used to go twice a week to clean for Elaine. Elaine sits about all day, won't lift a finger and won't trouble to cook, hence Lady B.'s charity in case she starves. Well, one fine morning Beale was delivering the mail as usual, and found the Widow lying flat out cold against her own doorstep. He did what any decent person would have done and carried her inside to her own bed. Do you know what that bitch did? Wrote to the Head Post Office complaining that Jerry had tried to rape her and that she was instituting proceedings. Beale got a telling-off, officially that is, but as everybody knew our Widow nothing more was done about it. I question if her lawyer would have taken it on in any case; he's a moderately sane character called George Brown. But it shows you what Elaine's like, treacherous as an alligator, if they are. The Stilton's not bad, or do you prefer Camembert?" He rose. "I'll make coffee. It isn't instant, it's the proper thing."

"You're doing me proud," said Tom. The high-pitched voice replied from the small kitchen, accompanied by the pleasant sound and aroma of freshly grinding coffee beans.

"Glad to see someone different," Haven said. "Did you ever have children, Brack?"

"No. Sheila was an architect and liked her job. I wasn't going to turn her into a nappy-washer and child minder. Did you and your wife have any?" Tit for tat, he thought; he rather doubted if Haven could have sired children.

"One girl, not very bright. She lives with my wife at Stoke Mandeville. We exchange Christmas presents and sometimes Nicky writes."

"But you don't see her?"

"No. I don't want to and neither does she by now. I like it here by myself, in peace."

He brought in the coffee, poured it steaming into small pottery cups, and looked across the birchwood table. "By the way – this is what I didn't say earlier. I'm going tonight to a drinks party at Bill Hedley's. I hope this won't bore you, but I rang him when I heard you were here and said I didn't know if you were free, but if so might I bring you along? Of course he's delighted, but it depends on what your own plans are." Haven put his head on one side, rather like a considering bald eagle. Brackenbury said he would be pleased to come, which was true. Night would have fallen and there would be no light for painting. "I haven't met Hedley, have I?" he asked; it was sometimes difficult to remember among so many.

"You won't have done; he only arrived here a few years ago. He's a retired rubber planter, and must have made a lot of money somehow. He was in prison camp with the Japs during the war in Burma as a very young man, but after that perhaps shook the pagoda tree in some way. He loves gardening and has a special house for rare orchids. He isn't married; maybe something to do with the way the Japs treated certain prisoners in their time. You'll like old Bill; he's a good sort, rather withdrawn at times, but the perfect host."

He set down the empty coffee-cup. "If you like," he said, "I'll call for you at the Lamb and Flag; it's on the way and I can run you there and back."

"Will the Widow be there?"

"God knows. If so there are plenty of corners to hide in."

"Half-past six, then?"

"Fine. Make it five minutes earlier in case we have a puncture on the way. I have a neurosis about them."

"Very well." They finished their coffee and presently Tom took his leave.

On the drive back he saw a tall blind man walking along the road near the hedge, carrying a white stick and accompanied by a black Labrador. The man's face was tilted to the unseen sun. Was it Basil Oldham, who liked interfering with other people's lives and who had arranged Haven's disastrous dinner party? One would find out, doubtless, in time.

Henry Haven called at the Lamb and Flag as arranged, but he was nervous about some expensive noise of recent occurrence in the engine of his car, so they went in Tom's. The way led past the running river, shallow over stones, and then to a winding road among trees, not unlike the path to the rock Tom had followed that morning, but less narrow. "It's quite a way," said Brackenbury.

"Yes, I do apologise for using your petrol after all instead of mine." It was a nervy, fumbling excuse of a kind only a neurotic would make. Tom began to understand even more fully why

Haven's marriage had failed. The man was probably happiest when alone with himself, without the need for constant apology.

They came to a dip in the ground and then climbed once more. An extraordinary sight met Tom's eyes: on the horizon, in the direction of the river, but on high ground, stood something that at first sight might have landed out of space. It proved to be an enormous circular greenhouse, far bigger than the house it served. The evening light caught its myriad surfaces and reflected the dying sun. About it lay a well-kept lawn with shrubs planted gracefully and with knowledge.

"That is the famous orchid house," said Haven. "The funny thing is that you can erect one without planning permission as long as it isn't joined on to the house. In the winter Bill keeps his car in it, and when nobody's about his housekeeper probably hangs out the smalls in it; they'd dry quickly, more so than outside. But it will be on show tonight."

He waved to a man's figure that had appeared in the doorway at the sound of the car. "Bill has the most extraordinarily green fingers," he said. "When he was a prisoner of war working on the Burma Railway he used to find time to grow green peppers and hand them out to the others for Vitamin C. Nobody else would have thought of doing it, there."

They parked the car favourably in the small tarmacadam plot. They were first to arrive, as Tom had known they would be; it was just half-past six. Bill Hedley came out to meet them, shutting the door of the orchid house carefully behind him. He held a tray of glasses. He was a big man, urbane and courteous, with thick snow-white hair closely cut. He shook hands with Tom warmly.

"Very glad you could come. I'm an avid reader of your column. What happens to it when you're somewhere else?"

"My editor kindly took it over and told me to relax for six months. This is the best possible way to begin to do so; it was good of you to invite me."

"Come and see my orchids," Hedley said, and showed them into the great dome. Inside, it was astonishing because of the many blooms so late in the year, and Hedley's informed voice talking on about the crossing of pollen. Orchids of every imaginable species, brown and pink, spotted green and cream and white, blossomed in raised beds. Their scent was fresh and not overpowering. Best of all was a beautiful spray of pure white blossoms, each one with a tiny marking of brown.

"That's my Star of Hanover," said Hedley with pride. He had shut the door behind them all, and whenever other guests appeared went through the process of greeting them and opening and closing the door. "Let me do that," said Brackenbury. "You're holding the drinks tray, and you've only got two hands."

"Thanks very much indeed. Draughts don't do them any good. I'm showing the Star at Stockport next week, hopefully."

Various people were beginning to arrive in small groups from the car park: the glasshouse would hold fifty guests with ease. Brackenbury was introduced to everyone who came in and in his self-appointed task of minding the door, had the first view of all who did, including the ubiquitous Maggie and Chips, erstwhile commandeered hosts of Haven and Elaine. At about seven o'clock he glimpsed the Widow herself, getting out of a battered car driven by a small and very old woman in a formidable and ancient hat. Tom guessed without being told that the latter was Lady Bellenden. She advanced with valiant obstinacy, like the last survivor of some historic onslaught.

"So you're the doorkeeper," she said cheerfully. She had a thin face overlaid with wrinkles and a pair of shrewd diamond-bright eyes; she must be in her late eighties, and two patches of rouge sat squarely, one on either cheek. He was introduced to Elaine Partridge and bowed as if they had never met. The pair passed on and Tom found Haven once more at his elbow.

"I wanted to see the *rencontre*," he said. "The old girl drives her everywhere. As I think I may have told you, she even cooks food for her and takes it along, otherwise the Widow wouldn't eat. They get to that stage, unable to bother about themselves except to pour yet another surreptitious brandy, but if you asked Elaine straight out, she'd swear she never touches anything but a small occasional glass of sherry, only one. Look, she's having it now, with her little finger lifted, looking as if it was poison and she was Sophonisba, drinking it to oblige."

To Tom's relief nobody overheard all this; Haven's obsession was beginning to bore him. He was more interested in the next piece of gossip, about Lady Bellenden herself. "You know the old house is a ruin, and would be impossibly expensive to run by now," Haven said. "It was going to pieces even before Lord B. died, they tell me, and that must be nine or ten years ago. *He* was a character if you like; considered mad, although his views have been taken up nowadays. Spent all his money on defending wildlife in the days when they still shot tigers and brought home the skins. Lady B. took up breeding and showing bull terriers after they came back from India. They're all gone now except for one dog she dotes on, called McGinty. He won't be here tonight because the Widow likes to sit in the front of the car, and so does he."

A matron with blue-rinsed hair paused at that point for a few words. "Henry, I never see you. What are you writing just now? Do tell me about it." Tom left them in unequal combat at the door, as everyone had by this time arrived and he needed another drink. As he turned he ran straight into Elaine Partridge, in a surprisingly becoming red and blue patterned jumper suit, perhaps the glad rags Haven had described. Her grey-black hair had been washed and curled and she looked presentable. Brackenbury decided to treat her like anybody else.

"Good evening, Mrs Partridge."

She was all gush. "Oh, please call me Elaine. Do forgive me for having been so unwelcoming earlier today. So many trippers come up earlier in summer and I thought you were one. The place where you were is where my husband fell to his death." Her eyes remained dry, but in any case had what Tom would have described as a blackcurrant-jelly look about them. Her nose was faintly pink at the tip, but there was no smell of alcohol on her breath. No doubt she was a vodka addict. "I found him, you see," she went on, and Tom began to be embarrassed.

"Dreadful for you," he murmured, and the Widow clasped predatory fingers about his arm. Tom looked about for help, but Haven was firmly elsewhere.

"Yes, too dreadful," Elaine Partridge said. "I keep fresh flowers where he fell. I grow flowers. I take them down, always fresh, every few days."

For some reason he knew that she was lying. Had he met her casually, without knowing anything about her, he would simply have put her down as a slightly forward woman; but the fingers clasped about his sleeve, though not thick, were stubby, with short degenerate thumbs. He did not like her, and wanted to move away. He tried to catch the eye of their host, but Hedley was pouring drinks with his back turned at a small table set up in the glasshouse for the purpose. Tom had a wild vision of the car and the drying smalls, occupying this space when nobody was here. He tried to make civil talk with Elaine, but had the impression that she listened to nothing he said.

"I came because I'm interested in painting a certain view of Bigod Peak from your woods," he told her. "Would it be inconvenient if I came back tomorrow morning? I didn't know they were private."

"They aren't," she said intensely. She was pursing her mouth in a manner peculiar to her, which made it look like the opening orifice of a sea anemone before the fronds emerge. "You must come for a drink," she said. "Promise you'll come." The fingers gave Tom's arm a squeeze.

"I'd really rather, if the light is good, paint while I can—"

"Come at twelve," she said. "We'll have a drink then. You will be in time, won't you? I don't wait about. Come then. Promise."

Hedley rescued Tom at last and said "Go and get yourself a drink, you've been busy with that door all evening," and Tom thankfully left their host with Elaine, who appeared not to see him and turned abruptly towards the flowers, running her hands lasciviously through their immaculate leaves. Hedley was meantime accosted by some other guest, and Elaine continued her sacrilege.

Tom did not risk getting near her again, and neither did anybody else. Suddenly she pounced on the Star of Hanover and picked the whole unique spray, thrusting it into the bodice of her suit.

"I love flowers," she drawled. Nobody answered; a silence had fallen, soon to be replaced by an embarrassed whispering. Hedley was still occupied with giving out drinks. Elaine had begun almost to run round and show herself off, as it were, to different groups into which she was unable to penetrate. In the hiatus, Lady Bellenden, to whom Tom had not yet spoken, came up to him, determinedly making talk.

"I do so enjoy your column," she said. "What—"

He managed to get her away from the subject. "I hear you keep bull terriers," he said. "I've always liked them."

"I only have one left, old McGinty, and he's nine years old next week," she said, the diamond eyes twinkling; he knew that she had noticed the orchid disaster, but was resolutely keeping on playing the game. "They always talk about old ladies being hit on the head," she said. "He's a good watchdog out here in the country. He was born just at the time my husband died: he consoled me then and now."

Tom saw the crowd, the well-bred cultivated crowd no member of which would ever be so brash as even to stub out a cigarette in the famous orchid-beds, mingle and sway. Elaine was somewhere in the place but he had ceased to worry where. "I must introduce you to Mary Reston," Lady Bellenden murmured. She guided Tom to where a stocky woman, perhaps in her forties, was standing chatting with a few acquaintances. Her dark hair was done in a no-nonsense cut with a fringe straight across her forehead. She had pleasant features and her eyes were hazel.

"Where is Basil tonight?" Tom heard someone ask her, and she replied:

"He won't come to parties nowadays, says they confuse him."

"It's understandable, I suppose, when you think of it."

"Mary, this is Mr Brackenbury," said the old lady. "He paints. Mary here is a potter and sculptor, very famous."

In the intervals of wondering how in the world Lady Bellenden could know already that he painted in his spare time, Tom talked to Mary Reston, occasionally witnessing the attractive smile which lightened her rather heavy face.

"You must come and see my work and show me yours," she said. "Are you staying long? Could you come for drinks tomorrow? It's Basil's day and I'd like you to meet him. He always wants to know what has happened and who has been there after a party, although he won't come."

He was aware of a strange lack of possessiveness in her talk, rather like that of an understanding wife referring to her husband. He accepted, then passed her one of the plates which still held a few small squares of smoked salmon on tiny pieces of brown bread and butter, and Mary Reston took one in her square, workmanlike fingers.

It was at that point that there came a sudden crash from further over in the great glasshouse; a second's silence, then a bull's roar which Tom was only mildly surprised to perceive came from Bill Hedley, surveying Elaine, still flaunting the Star of Hanover on her red-and-blue bosom.

"You damned bloody bitch! You blasted drunken tart! You've ruined it!"

Into the appalled silence the Widow spoke icily, a duchess. She fingered the orchid at her breast, then bridled somewhat.

"You damned eunuch," she said clearly, "flowers are about all you're able to handle. Come on, Win, we're going home."

Chiefly in Tom's memory there had come and remained the sad old countenance of Lady Bellenden, wrinkled jaw suddenly loose and trembling, bright eyes wistful. Poor old girl, she likes parties, he thought: she won't want to leave yet to drive that bitch home.

He took a step forward. "I will take Mrs Partridge home, Lady Bellenden," he said firmly. "There is no need for you to leave until you are ready."

"I want to get out of here," shouted Elaine. "These people are bloody nits."

He steered her with a certain iron determination to the car. He would return for Haven later. "Hang on to your chastity, old boy," he heard the high voice mutter as they went.

"You'll have to direct me, Mrs Partridge," Tom said formally when he had got Elaine into the car. "I'm not entirely certain how to find your house." He did not, he thought, on any account, want to get lost with her in the woods.

"Oh, I'll show you," said Elaine suddenly amiable. "You must come in and have a brandy. Don't go back to those buggers. You will come in, won't you?" She harped on it all through the journey until they drew up in front of a small cottage with twin gables. It had been a rough drive. When Tom stopped the engine, a dog barked not far away.

"That's that bloody bull terrier of Win's," Elaine said. "One day I'll murder it."

She got out quite steadily, and switched on a light at the door, then returned and gave her hand to him. She did not let go.

"Do come in, even only for a minute. There's plenty of time before the damned party ends. God knows they probably stay drinking and gossiping all night. It's lonely here and I'm glad to see a visitor."

She raved on. He was sorry for her and weakly allowed himself to be led into the room, which was surprisingly large and cold. A fireplace at one end held unlit logs. Elaine struck matches and set the crumpled paper and twigs alight, then the dry logs. As the flames leapt she turned in triumph. "Now you've got to stay," she said. "I've lit the fire for you."

He was aware of panic. "I have to fetch Haven," he said again. She replied with vituperations resembling those she had flung at Hedley. Brackenbury said nothing: there was no point. He had noticed as soon as he entered the room a thing of significance; while the room had been cleaned and the furniture dusted, the light switches were surrounded with grubby finger-marks. In other words a cleaning woman came, did what she was told, and went away.

Elaine had disappeared into the kitchen. She returned with two filled balloon glasses. Tom could drink with any man, but he was determined not to touch a drop here. "Well, cheers," said the Widow, and took a gulp. She might have been drinking milk. No doubt after the genteel sherry consumed at Hedley's she needed something stronger, and fast.

"Sit down, for God's sake," she told him, and again, "There's plenty of time."

He glanced at his watch. "That's rude," said Elaine. "Everyone's damned rude to me."

"You're damned rude to them." The white orchid, still in her bodice, was beginning to wilt. "Hadn't you better put that in water?" he asked her. He could never bear to see living things spoiled and wasted, and he had been profoundly shocked by the whole episode at Hedley's.

"I'll put it in a better place," said the Widow coarsely. She plumped herself down on the sofa and tried to drag him with her. "God," she said, "aren't you a man? Aren't any of that lot down there men? I'll tell you something. Julius was impotent. What sort of hell of a life d'you suppose I've had?"

The brandy glass was empty. "Get me another," she said aggressively. "You haven't touched yours."

"I'm going," said Tom firmly. He handed her his untouched glass. He then walked out, hearing behind him a babble of words of the same variety as earlier. He shut the door quickly and got into his car, reversing it skilfully in the narrow driveway. On the way down, going with care and almost trembling wih devout thanks for his release, his headlights picked out a man among the brambles, probably a poacher. He carried a rifle, was thick-set and not young. The lights picked out the electric blue of his woollen scarf. He blinked into the dazzle and turned away. Tom did not want to stop. He drove on and, at last and with thankfulness, found himself on the highway, heading once more for the party at Bill Hedley's.

On return there the crowd had thinned, although several people had stayed late out of sympathy for Hedley. The conversation had resumed as usual; somebody had taken away the empty pot in which the Star of Hanover had been grown. Hedley came over when he caught sight of Tom. He appeared to have recovered his natural ease; his face was no longer suffused.

"I must apologise for what happened then, "he said.

"It wasn't your fault."

"I asked for it. I shouldn't have invited that damned woman.

Everyone else has dropped her, and I felt sorry for her. It won't happen here again, I can swear to that. Only, poor old Win Bellenden – ah, here she is."

Lady Bellenden, her hat a trifle askew, came up to press Tom's hand. "That was most exceedingly kind of you," she said. "I don't go out much, and when I do I like to make a night of it. Will you come and visit me and McGinty tomorrow? Come to tea."

He smiled; there was not going to be much time after all for painting. "I'll be glad to come," he said, "and tell you both about Fleet Street."

"That will be very interesting. I shall look forward to it. My late husband had some connections with newspapers, through his photography, you know. You will see some of the photographs when you come."

She raised her glass and passed on. Tom had noted that her hands, unlike the fabled lily fingers of Edwardian aristocrats such as Winifred Bellenden almost was, were gnarled with rheumatism, large, rough and strong, a gardener's hands, a dog-handler's. Presently everyone began to leave and Haven joined Tom; they said goodbye to their host and left, picturing Hedley standing alone at last among the soiled glasses and empty plates, staring at the place where his prized orchid had stood in its glory.

On their way home Brackenbury lured Haven away from much comment about the orchid incident by mentioning the man he had seen, asking if he might be a poacher. For some obscure reason he felt guilty about leaving the Widow unprotected in her lonely cottage. Haven was unimpressed. "Oh, they get the odd rabbit and bird up there still," he said. "The coverts haven't been kept up. The man would be looking after his own business – although, my word, if he did fill the old Widow with shot it would be good news and everyone would cheer him on. Did you ever meet such a woman? Loathsome isn't the word – and the filthy name she called Bill, after what he'd come through in the war in Burma. That was unspeakable."

They had reached the little house with its long waving grass outside. "Will you come in for coffee or another drink?" Haven enquired, but Tom felt he had had enough hospitality for one evening.

He was in the middle of breakfast next day early, so that he could go and put in a morning's painting, when the waitress came to say there was a telephone call. "Will you take it in your room, Mr Brackenbury?" He left the congealing bacon and eggs unwillingly: who the devil wanted him now?

But a voice sobbing with outrage and grief met him at the other end of the line. "This is Winifred Bellenden here. I have to ask you, if you please, not to come to tea today after all; I'm very sorry. A dreadful thing has happened. McGinty's dead, poisoned. I found him this morning. It must have happened last night. There is so much evil here. Do forgive me," and the voice began to tremble again. Brackenbury asked, uselessly, if there was anything he could do.

"How could it have happened? Was he in the house?" he said, knowing that despite her distress talking was good for her, an old woman alone. It must be like losing a child, for a woman who had no children.

"No. You are most kind to ask. The vet is coming, of course, and there will be a post-mortem. But it can only be poison. He was in such good form – he loved his walks, just snuffling round the woods – last night when I got in from the party somewhat late, I did not disturb him, only calling goodnight to him when I went to my room. He has – had – his own little way in and out of the house with swing doors I had specially built for him, out into the run. I was not surprised that he did not bark; he only did that at strangers or for some distinct reason. All that time he must have been lying there, and I went to bed and slept. Perhaps if I had gone in—"

"You wouldn't have been in time," he said, to comfort her.

"Possibly not. But this morning – he must have died in great agony. I am so sorry, Mr Brackenbury. I knew I must get hold of you early, because it is a fine day and you will want to go out and begin painting soon. I do apologise, but I can't see anyone today or quite yet. I hope you will understand."

"Believe me, I do," he said. "If you think of anything at all I can do to help, or even just want to talk, I shall be back by lunchtime." But she rang off, and he was left alone in the room staring at the silent telephone. He found himself filled with slow rage. Who in all the world would do a thing like that? And why?

The waitress was standing ready in the breakfast-room. "I've kept your food and your tea hot," she said, and he thanked her sincerely and drank down the hot tea. They were friendly and helpful here at the Lamb and Flag. "That was Lady Bellenden," he said. "Her dog's dead."

"McGinty? Oh, sir, everybody knew him. He was the world to her. Poor old dear, she'll be in a state. He was all she had left, in that way, you know what I mean. Always sat in the front of the car, he did, sitting up straight like he owned it, that was when Mrs Partridge wasn't in it instead. Oh, what went wrong, sir? McGinty was quite old. Was it his heart?"

"No. He was poisoned. She found him this morning." He rose and crushed the paper napkin in his fingers and left it on the empty plate, and went to his room.

That bloody bull terrier. One day I'll murder it. Had she gone out last night, after he had left her, filled with useless resentment against everything and everybody? If he had stayed, would Lady Bellenden's dog have lived?

The thought of the old lady and her dead dog occupied Brackenbury all through the drive. He had almost forgotten that he was going to paint. If he caught sight of Elaine Partridge he knew he would ask her if, as seemed almost certain, it had happened as he thought. He was sure it hadn't been the man with the gun. The last thing the latter would have wanted to do would have been to draw attention to himself in such a way. And in any case the dog had been in his own run. Someone had come to the end of it, someone McGinty knew.

He parked the car in the same place as yesterday. As he got out he saw a shooting-brake come down the other wooded path. It slowed and a young man's head appeared at the open window.

"If you're looking for Mrs Partridge, she's not at home," he said civilly. "She's down at Lady Bellenden's."

"What?"

Tom was horrified at the news. He stared into the back of the car, where there lay the contorted dead body of a large white bull terrier, its pink tongue protruding stiffly from slavered agonised jaws.

"The late McGinty," he said more as a statement than a question. The young veterinary surgeon met his gaze candidly.

"Poor old girl," he said quietly. "She's nearly out of her mind. Mrs Partridge is therc, trying to cheer her up."

To gloat, thought Tom. What an unspeakable bitch. He was so angry by now that he felt like his old self had used to feel, after rustling a controversy at acid length in the column.

"What would you say killed the dog?" he asked as the brake moved off. "Rat poison, most likely, the old phosphoric kind, smeared on a bit of meat," the vet said. "We'll know more precisely after I've seen his stomach contents."

He drove away, and Tom took out his painting gear from the boot almost unwillingly. It was only a kind of obstinacy which made him persist in his original intention to paint this particular view of the Peak. He found the place, set up his easel, and out of the corner of his eye saw the vase of dahlias, beginning to wilt. *I grow flowers. I keep fresh flowers where he fell.* He recalled her words more or less. She was of course a compulsive liar, thc way alcoholics often got to be. How had all that started? Had it been long before she met and married the decent Julius Partridge, whom everyone seemed to have liked and respected? Had Elaine in fact pushed Julius over the rockface for no more reason than to get the keys to the booze cupboard and perhaps remove a constant watch kept on her movements? Doubtless by now no one would ever know, but Brackenbury was pleased to watch his own mind, as one might do a stopped clock after putting in a fresh battery, starting to function again regularly, steadily.

He began to cover the canvas with brisk, remembered strokes. He found himself thinking still of Lady Bellenden. She was shrewd, and once the first shock had worn off would she guess it was probably none other than the comforting Mrs Partridge who had poisoned her dog? And what would Lady Bellenden do then?

He wondered if it was a piece of Lady Bellenden's own cooked meat that Elaine had smeared with poison; the daily meal brought to her out of kindness. As the old lady and Haven had both expressed it, there was indeed evil here.

For some mysterious and long-buried reason, the shops in Brennan, in addition to their half-day which was Thursday, shut for the whole day every third Wednesday of the month. Accordingly, shoppers were busy all the previous morning and afternoon purchasing food, drink, envelopes, knitting wool or anything else they might need over the two-day period. The little town was crowded when Tom took a walk through it with the purpose of buying a picture postcard to send to his cleaning woman in London.

He struggled through the crowd at the stationer's, chose and paid for the postcard, which was a view of the nearby mountains. Why do I bother to paint? the thought occurred to him; coloured photographs were just as good if not better. But he would take tomorrow morning again at Bigod Peak; that should finish it.

A strident voice accosted his ears from the other side of the street as he made his way towards the Post Office. It could belong to no one but the Widow, who was shouting orders to a small grocer's boy who had carried out large packages for her into, presumably, someone else's car; he saw that it was Mary Reston's. Mary sat quietly at the wheel, with an air of wanting nothing to do with the scene going on at the back. "Put that there. No, in there, and that one down there, and that – no that's Lady Bellenden's, you'll have to keep them separate in front." She ranted on, so that the whole town could probably hear, but the boy might have been a deaf mute; he was probably used to it. He put the things in quietly and went back to the shop. Mary came out to see that the hatchback was closed properly. She must have been rung up and asked to take the Widow into town, as the old lady herself wouldn't be in shape to drive. What an embarrassing nuisance to make of oneself! When Tom passed inescapably by Elaine was treacly, as Haven would have put it, and made as if to paw all over him.

"I say, I was so dreadfully sorry to hear what had happened about your wife. It must be ghastly for you. Don't forget you're coming for drinks when you're up soon; make it early. I don't like to wait." She was not wearing the Burberry, but the old knitted cap was there, this time completely covering her hair.

Mary said tactfully, "We will have to get back now, Elaine."

Elaine said, "Yes, boss," in a spiteful way, and bundled herself presently into the car.

Mary followed. "See you later," she muttered to Tom, who closed the door for both women.

"What does that mean?" he heard the Widow ask as they drove off. "Let me come along."

God forbid, he thought, and made pretence not to hear, walking on to the Post Office which was close by. Owing to the traffic Mary's car drove slowly, and it was just passing as one of the postmen came out of the door with a tray of letters ready to go round the back for sorting. Tom had a slight shock of recognition; here in the grey Post Office uniform was the thickset fellow he had seen in the woods yesterday. Seen in daylight now he had red eyes, as though he had been weeping. He looked ahead and caught sight of Elaine Partridge in the near side of the car, and stood still, then said aloud in a low voice as if to himself, "That bitch killed my son."

Tom asked quietly if he could put his card straight on to the tray; it would catch an earlier post. The man's red-rimmed eyes focused on him and he nodded; more might neither have been said nor overheard between them. But Tom went away with the added knowledge of one more person who had reason to hate Elaine Partridge, although he didn't understand the remark about the son. Had she run a child over in her driving days? He would be curious enough to think of asking Mary Reston about it this evening, hoping they would be alone.

He went back to the hotel for tea, but spoke to none of the staff there about what he had overheard, perhaps out of a kind of loyalty to the man among his own class. There must have been gossip if the thing was true. But Mary Reston would know, and might tell him about it.

He found Mary's cottage by following the clear directions she had given him; in fact it was at the end of the other branch of the forked road which ran to Lady Bellenden and the Widow one way. It had a glass porch in front which was devoid of the usual begonias and geraniums ordinary women liked to grow. Along the front of the house was scattered a row of Virginian stock in different mauves and pinks, beginning to fade now. There was no garden. Mary herself was in the porch, wedging clay on a stout wooden table. She wore an old potter's slop marked with dried clay and paint. Her strong hands made the ox-head shape in the clay, then threw it, pummelled and finished it into a workable ball. There was a kick-wheel nearby and in the ordinary way Mary would have thrown the clay straight onto the wheel, but seeing Tom she paused, smiled, and disappeared for instants into the cool shadow of the house. When she came out she had rinsed her hands and taken off her smock. She wore a plain top and trousers of a buff colour, the colour used by the white man on safari.

"Use the clay if it's ready," Tom told her. "It must be maddening to have to stop at that point." He wanted, in fact, to see her throw something with the clay, a jar or a pot.

"It's all right; there's a bin in the house, where it's cooler," she said. "Come in." She did not sound welcoming; for the second time that day, he wondered whether something had upset her.

The room itself was plainly furnished, not with new stuff; it was comfortable but not ornate. Near the window one object caught his gaze and held it. It was a head, cast in bronze, of the blind man, Basil Oldham. Nobody could have mistaken it for anyone else. Even the tilt at which the head was carried was caught, and the features and expression reproduced faithfully.

"You'll have to make do with that," said Mary, "because Basil isn't coming today after all. Do you know what that bitch did? Because I didn't take up her suggestion – if you can call it that –

that she come up here this evening to meet you again, she rang Basil and said she had to see him urgently this evening, something she positively had to tell him that wouldn't wait and couldn't be said over the line. It was all lies, of course. But curiosity is Basil's strongest emotion nowadays and he couldn't wait to hear what it was. He says he'll come here tomorrow instead. But that'll be cut short because of chess."

"Chess? He is a player?" He watched her fetch the glasses out of the cupboard and set them on a round tray with an almost full bottle of whisky, one of gin, tonic and ginger-ale bottles and a ship's decanter of sherry.

"Yes. Don't ask me how, but he does it, to champion standard. He used to be a top-flight bridge player before the crash that blinded him, and no doubt it needs the same kind of thinking, only slower. He and Geordie from the Old Bridge pub play twice a week, rain or shine, weddings or funerals. No, I'm wrong about funerals. Basil always goes to those. He wouldn't miss them. But as you know he won't go to parties, and comes here for the news. He'll get the latest of that at any rate from the Widow – in her version."

He watched her pour the drinks and asked her a question which was none of his business. "Why don't you and Basil marry?" he said. He saw the flush spread over her neck and face.

"Why, that's exactly what the Widow asked me, but I didn't tell her. The fact is that Basil won't believe anyone could want to marry him except out of pity. It's some kind of syndrome disabled people get. It's no good trying to persuade them, they don't believe you. Elaine kindly told Basil I was fat and plain, which all helps."

Brackenbury sipped his whisky; it was a good malt. "So when she knew the coast was clear, as he thought," Mary continued, "the Widow started campaigning for him to marry her instead. Basil says she proposes to him on Tuesdays, over the telephone, having drink taken. He gets a lot of amusement out of it."

"How did you and the Widow meet? Was it when her husband was alive?" He had not commented on the situation about Basil.

Mary grimaced over her gin. "The funny part is that it was my fault. I didn't know what she'd turned into. I heard from Basil that they were here and naturally asked them for drinks. In fact she and Julius had been in the district quite some time, and although she must certainly have known I was here as well, she didn't get in touch. I know why. I knew too much."

Tom waited, not trying to direct her talk as he would have done in an interview for the paper. Here was a bitter woman glad of a listener. No doubt the as yet unencountered Basil Oldham was in like case.

Mary Reston crossed her knees carefully and began to wiggle one sturdy foot in its sandal. He had the impression that she was a creature of restless, determinedly channelled energy, unable to be idle for long if only because idleness brought frustration. "As it happens," Mary said, "we were at school together. She wasn't unpleasant – then; aggressive, a games-playing type. I saw quite a lot of her although we were in different forms. I once visited her at her home. Her father was some kind of commercial traveller, although she's told people here he was in the Foreign Office. She knew I could cross that one out if I wanted to, but that's the least of it. So is Italian."

"Italian?"

"Yes. You know that particular form of bad manners when you use a foreign word or phrase – I think it was about music – and somebody else echoes you in what they think is a superior accent? It's a habit I loathe, and Elaine has it. The joke is that she can't speak a word of the language otherwise, because when a bunch of foreign tourists got lost in the woods looking for Bigod and were benighted, she couldn't understand a word any of them said. I got that from Basil, as usual. And there's something else." She looked down at her sandal, and suddenly said, "I don't talk like this to anyone in the ordinary way. You must have some quality that makes people want to. Perhaps you're a psychiatrist."

"I'm a newspaper reporter."

"Oh, Lord." The direct hazel eyes stared across at him. "Will all this make some crummy headline?"

"I promise it won't. I'm on holiday anyway. Talk on; I'm interested."

"Well, the other thing is that some years after leaving school I tried to get in touch with Elaine by letter. She'd moved elsewhere and I'd stayed put. I expect I just took the notion to try to find out what had happened to her; we'd been moderate friends, after all. She wrote back from a new address where it had been forwarded. She said she'd taken a secretarial course, and there were long stories of all the men she'd been engaged to. In the end she said she'd got married to an Australian and walked out on him because he was a sadist. Evidently he wouldn't divorce her. That was the last I heard. When I learned through Basil that she was living not far away – he'd got hold of her maiden name and that she knew me – and was with Julius, whom everyone liked, I kept quiet, even to Basil. I simply wrote and asked them over for drinks as I said, and they came. Julius was a nice man. I didn't know what had happened about the first marriage and of course never asked. There was something about Elaine I didn't like by then. Julius said, 'Don't give Elaine too much to drink, she passes out', but it was he who almost did. Elaine got livelier and livelier, and kept holding out her glass for more. I don't know if she remembered telling me what she had, or perhaps she realised I would keep it to myself. Later they invited me back. I got the impression poor Julius locked all the drinks in the cupboard and kept the key. As you know, shortly he was found dead beneath the rockface, and now Elaine orders all she wants from the grocer and other people bring it up for her in their cars. She asked me to once, but I said I was busy. I don't know how long they will give her credit. She can't have all that much to come and go on. She tries desperately to marry Basil, of course, because he has plenty of it. As it is, she keeps asking him to lend it to her."

"And does he?"

"No. Basil has all his wits about him."

Brackenbury then told Mary about the postman. "Did Elaine Partridge ever run anyone over?" he asked. Mary shook her cropped dark head.

"It isn't that. This is quite a new piece of gossip; I got it from Basil, of course. That postman, Jerry Beale, and his wife aren't young, and they were expecting a baby this year for the first time ever. As you know – I'm sure Henry told you, he never stops talking about her – Beale had had that business to put up with as well from Elaine about the supposed rape attempt, and he made Dora, that's his wife, stop going up to clean for the Widow as she'd been used to doing before that. Dora didn't mind, because she said the Widow made her heave things like the deep freeze about and sat and watched, and she – Dora Beale – had felt some discomfort and pain at the time. The pregnancy continued, though, but when the baby was born at last it was a boy, which they'd wanted, and dead. The doctors – this is from Basil, though how he finds out about everything don't ask me, it's probably Geordie his chess partner who gets all the gossip at his pub – Basil says the reason was a slipped placenta, which might have been caused in the first place by strenuous exertion. Evidently once that happens it can recur, and anyway with one thing and another the child was dead, and they probably won't have another."

"It was Beale I saw in the wood, with a rifle, last night. Haven says he was poaching."

"If Beale has any sense he'll keep away from there except to leave mail. A second lot of trouble might lose him his job."

They talked then of other things than Widow Partridge and at last, well fortified, Tom went his way. "Before I go you must come to lunch," he said. "We'll ask our host of yesterday and Henry. I owe all three of you hospitality."

"As long as you don't ask the Widow. Driving her into town is about my limit. She came to tea here once, after Julius died and everyone was trying to be decent to her. She wouldn't eat anything, just laid hands on the honey pot and sat there guzzling it with a teaspoon. I put the pot in her handbag afterwards for her to take home. I didn't fancy using it again."

"I'm beginning to feel flattered that she only threw stones at me."

"Didn't she make a pass at you after you took her home last night? That's unusual. She's man crazy."

"After the remark she made to Hedley I wouldn't have been likely to want to touch her." He had evaded the direct question, and Mary shot a keen glance at him. Driving back to the hotel he reflected that the number of Widow-haters had risen by one to his certain knowledge. He himself would not like to make an enemy of Mary Reston. She was downright, and no doubt thorough: also, in love wih Basil Oldham.

It was too early for dinner by the time Brackenbury got back to the Lamb and Flag, and he went into the bar, where a good fire blazed thankfully; the evenings were getting cold. A solitary man sat beside it and Tom settled opposite him, having rung the bell for the barman, who was busy in the public bar through the way. Tom said good-evening as a matter of course, and the other answered with a nod, not saying anything. He was a tall fellow, very lean and ivory pale, with long features and straight dark hair of the kind that does not turn grey: it was difficult to tell his age. Tom could not rid himself of the impression that he had seen him before, but forebore to ask; in his reporting he might have met anyone anywhere, tactlessly or otherwise. On the whole this holiday was refreshing him, largely because of the lack of need to ask personal questions. In fact – he was amused at the thought – in Brennan no questions at all need be asked by anybody, it all came spilling out.

The barman appeared in shirt-sleeves and waited for Tom's order. He asked for a lager. "Have one yourself," he told the barman, and then turned to include his taciturn neighbour at the fire. "You'll join us, sir?"

"Naow. Couldn't return the round yet. I'm getting money later tonight."

"Well, have one now and stand one next time, tomorrow if you like."

"I don't mind if I do, after all. Mightn't be here tomorrow, though. Once I've settled my score here I'm leaving early." He accepted the tankard the barman had pushed at Tom, and they all three drank together. "Here's confusion to all women," said the stranger suddenly, but would not elaborate. He went out after finishing the drink and Tom and the barman looked at each other.

"Queer sort of bloke," said the barman. "He's only staying the one night that I know. He drives an Audi, it's in the garage."

They heard what was perhaps the sound of the Audi driving away. The barman went back to the public bar, where business was always brisk, and left Tom to his thoughts. He was still certain that he'd seen the man before. His "Naow" hadn't had Cockney overtones, nor had his vowels. They were more like Australian, strange perhaps. He wondered idly what the man was doing here and whether he had meant the hotel bill by talking of settling his score, or had in fact meant he had it in for somebody or other.

After dinner Tom went to bed, intending to be up early to finish his beleaguered painting. He fell asleep, then woke in the small hours; something was troubling his brain. He found himself, half awake, reaching out for Sheila in the bed, then remembered with the grim shock it always brought him that Sheila was not there, would never be there again. At the same time, as though consciousness had brought with it a wave of recall, he knew where he had seen the man in the bar before. He was Slim Joe Doherty, and the prison pallor had hardly left him; he'd been doing a good stretch for armed robbery and the crippling of a policeman. Slim Joe's trial had been one of his own first major assignments for the paper. Tom wondered again about the quoted settling of the score, and something else nagged at him; hadn't Mary Reston said Elaine Partridge had been married to an Australian and left him? It would be too much coincidence, however, that this could be the same man. Brackenbury turned over on his side and tried to sleep.

Nevertheless he rose early. The hotel did not serve breakfast until eight, and Tom filled in the intervening time by shaving, going out for a paper – the stationer's was open early – coming back to his room, looking critically at his partly-finished painting of the Peak, more critically still at the news headlines, then, carrying his newspaper, went to the breakfast-room. The sense of unease he had felt during the night had subsided with the cold light of day;

it simply left him with a curious restlessness. As soon as he had finished eating he did not linger over his last cup of tea, but went down to the car after collecting the canvas from his room.

Early as it was, the Australian's Audi was not in the garage, and he must have had breakfast already. Tom checked an instinct to go back to the reception desk and ask if he was coming back or not; then decided against it. He started up the engine of his own car and drove out towards the cottages, wondering how Lady Bellenden was today and if he should call. But she had asked to be left alone and he would respect that; after all, he was a stranger.

He got out of the car at the usual place and saw tyremarks that were not his own but broader; perhaps those of the tractor from the farm at the far end. This was almost the only turning-place until one got back to the main road. The falling leaves already partly obscured tracks, and the stony road showed no footprints. It was a cold morning, well into autumn.

He came to the place where he had been painting, ready to set up his easel. An irregularity in the ground near the rockface disturbed him. He strode towards it and then stopped. It was a dead-coloured Burberry, part covered in leaves. Under it, or rather inside it, lay the prone body of Elaine Partridge, hatless and with her greasy black-grey hair in disarray. He knelt down to make sure she was dead; the neck was at an awkward angle, and when he gently turned her head up so that he could see her face, he almost dropped it in revulsion. It was livid, the glazed eyes open and the tongue protruding from the mouth. In a kind of anxiety to look beyond, anywhere, at anything else, his glance dwelt on the stone vase at the foot of the rock where the dahlias had been. It was empty.

He decided that it would be quicker to call the police from Mary's cottage than to return to Brennan. He hurried to the cottage and knocked on the door, then tried it, but it was locked. He walked round to the back calling aloud, but there was no one in the small bedroom and the curtains were undrawn. Tom gave it up as a waste of time and went, still hurrying, to Lady

Bellenden's, not knowing what he would find. He hammered on the door and presently there were sounds of shuffling footsteps. Her voice sounded behind the door, the frightened voice of all old people who live alone. "Who is it?"

"It's Tom Brackenbury, Lady Bellenden. I must telephone the police. There has been an accident."

"To your car?" She opened the door on his assurance; she was red-eyed and pale, devoid of the rouge and wig she generally wore in public; her own grey hair straggled thinly about her scalp. She wore a woollen dressing-gown over a flowered night-dress, and felt slippers.

"No. If I may, I'll telephone first and then tell you."

"You must have a cup of tea." She pointed to the telephone and then left him and he dialled 999. Lady Bellenden could not have failed to hear his story as he told it; he was aware of her shuffling about the kitchen, filling a kettle, putting it on to boil, then silence. When he came away from the telephone he found her pale but steady.

"I heard you," she said. "The kettle will not be long. They will have to come from Llanaff. The Brennan station is not manned till nine, and sometimes they are out even then. I used to think that anyone could be murdered during the night, and not be found till after the local police were. So." She indicated a chair and took a teapot to the kettle, which boiled soon. "I am glad that you came here," she said. "I might have found it – her – myself, but I have no reason to go out for early walks any more now that my dog is dead. Do you take sugar?"

He thanked her. "I tried Mary Reston's cottage first, but she is out." The tea was scalding hot, but otherwise weak; he reflected that the English could not, on the whole, make tea; it took Celtic blood, which Sheila had partly had. Why think of that now? His mind was still occupied wih the shock of finding the body, and it was as if he came up against a stone wall when he tried to think beyond it.

It was almost an hour before the police knocked at the door; he had told them where he was. A tall sergeant with grey curling hair beneath his cap was accompanied by a dark young constable. A second constable had been left by the body until the ambulance came. "Well, Lady Bellenden," said Sergeant Lake, smiling and showing his excellent teeth, "I was sorry to hear you had a loss yesterday." It was evident, as in all country places, that the police knew everyone and heard most news. It was typical of such a situation that McGinty's death should have been mentioned sooner than that of Elaine Partridge.

Tears came into the old woman's eyes, as they had not done for Elaine. "Indeed," she said, but no more. "Will you take a cup of tea, Sergeant? It's freshly made."

"Thanks, I will." He sat down and lit a cigarette, without asking. The constable brought over two cups of tea, one for himself and one for the sergeant. "I suppose," said the sergeant presently, wiping his mouth with his hand, "that you saw as much as anyone of the late Mrs Partridge." He spoke the name with a kind of wry emphasis, and Tom reflected that the police must have heard, among other things, of the complaint against the postman Beale.

"Yes," said Lady Bellenden calmly. "I used to take her some cooked food, as otherwise she would not eat. Yesterday, however, she came here."

"Why?" The eyes behind the serviceable glasses were shrewd. Winifred Bellenden was silent for a moment. Then she said, "She told me she had come to say how sorry she was about my dog. She stayed for luncheon."

"Have you any idea as to who might have poisoned the dog?"

"I have a fair idea that it was Mrs Partridge herself. No one else would have had reason to. McGinty disliked her, and let her know it. He was my guard dog. However, he would take meat from anyone." She stared at her gnarled hands, but did not seem discomposed.

The Sergeant raised an eyebrow. "So in spite of that, you let her stay for lunch? It's more than I would have done." He glanced at the constable, who was still drinking his tea; the young man nodded. Lady Bellenden spread out her hands.

"She was a sick woman," she said. "One could not but pity

her. She was quite alone in the world after her husband died. I considered it my Christian duty to be a neighbour to her."

"Even after the business about the dog?"

"Even after that. We are told to forgive seventy times seven."

A knock came at the door. It was the second constable, to say that the ambulance men had come and that photographs had already been taken of the body. "Well, we'd better be making our way," said the sergeant, "and thank you for the tea, Lady Bellenden. If this is not cleared up you will of course be asked to make formal statements, and you, sir, having yourself found the body and very rightly got in touch with us."

Tom spoke. "I would have rung from Miss Reston's, but she seems to be out," he said. He also told them about the Australian, the Audi and the tyre marks. "It may have nothing to do with the matter, but I thought it worth mentioning, as I believe Mrs Partridge's previous marriage was to an Australian."

"Also there will be a record on Joe Doherty," said the sergeant. "You are very helpful, sir. We'll leave you now and see if Miss Reston is back yet at her cottage. Then we will report to the station in Brennan and continue with the inquiry from there."

"How long would you say she had been dead?"

"That's for the doctor, but from a brief examination I'd say that rigor had not worn off, so she might have been dead maybe up to ten hours, in other words from late last night or early this morning. The cold would make some difference."

"Would you say the cause of death had been the fall from the rockface?"

"I can't answer that, sir, until official investigation has been put under way. It may be that that was what it was intended to look like. Her husband, as you may not know, died in such a way not long ago."

"Difficult to say whether both or either fell or were pushed?"

"As you say, sir. It's time for us to go now. Miss Reston is out, you say? That's early."

"Maybe she had an early appointment."

"Who's to say, sir?" He saluted and went away.

"Well, so it's Brackenbury," said Inspector Stonor.

The two men had often met in the days when Tom was on crime-reporting assignments and John Stonor had been, before his promotion, with the Metropolitan Force, in London. Stonor looked quickly, compassionately at Tom; he said something briefly about the Harrods bomb and then, "And today, what can I do for you, sir?"

"It's rather a question of my doing it for you – if this list is of any help, that is. I happen since my arrival here to have come into contact with several persons who had every reason to do away with the late Mrs Partridge, and I've made a list with such detail as I know."

He gave a sheet of handwritten paper to the inspector. Stonor scanned the list and nodded. "It's all of use," he said. "In this case it's less a question of why, but of whom and how. The third aspect isn't in much doubt. She was strangled before being thrown over the rockface. It may have been, as you mention here, an attempt made by an ignorant person to look as if she'd fallen over."

"With crime novels as they are these days, one would have to be wet behind the ears to believe that. But her husband died by falling over about this time last year."

"Yes. You know, of course – for what it's worth – that Julius Partridge's ashes were scattered at the spot. Mrs Partridge wouldn't use the local cemetery. Lake says she made a point of buying fresh flowers from the florist's in Brennan frequently, filling a vase and putting them down there. It seems to have been the kind of extravagant gesture of which she was fond. Bought flowers are expensive."

I grow flowers. I always put them freshly on his grave. Or something like that.

"The vase was empty this morning," said Tom. "It occurred to me to wonder why she was there at all. It must have been dark when she went out."

"Enjoying the scenery, perhaps. There was a full moon last night."

"I doubt if that would have interested her. From what I've seen and learned, she was the lazy type of alcoholic; sat about the house all day, smoking and drinking brandy. I had that from Mary Reston."

"Who has still not come home. The office has called her repeatedly."

He glanced at the second constable, who was taking notes in a corner. "Have you tried Basil Oldham's?" asked Tom.

The inspector gave him a quick glance. "You've certainly had your ear to the ground if you've only been here two days. Yes, we tried Wing Commander Oldham's, and as always he was interested to a degree where he'll set out to try to find Miss Reston, or his dog will."

"At any rate, she's not available yet. The other thing was the Australian with the Audi, who happens to be Slim Joe Doherty of understated fame. He must have been only just out of gaol."

"How did he acquire the Audi? He said he had no money when I encountered him in the bar at the Lamb and Flag."

"The Audi was hired. Slim Joe has money stashed away, we always knew that, but couldn't trace it. I'll tell you in confidence – Tom, can you guarantee that there will be nothing yet in the papers?"

"As far as I myself am concerned, by all means."

"Very well. I'll tell you, still in confidence, what we've found out about Doherty. He is a strict Catholic, and would not lie to the priests. We had expected him to lose himself again at the London end, but what he did – our men have picked it up – was to drive like hell north from here across the bridge to Llanaff to try to get on the Irish ferry. He left the Audi in the park there, with the keys still in it. The port authorities have plenty to do with terrorist suspects and animal cruelty, but they are holding Joe meantime for enquiries. Also, someone, for what that is worth, used the cashpoint machine in Brennan very early this morning to draw out fifty pounds from Mrs Partridge's account on a credit card. It leaves zero in her account. The bank were very helpful. I gather the chief source of income was a series of payments from Julius Partridge's life insurance."

"For someone other than the Widow to draw money out of the night till, they must have had access not only to her credit card but also to the PIN number."

"Just so. We did, of course examine Mrs Partridge's pockets and handbag for money, but there was none. There was no money in the cottage either. It's known here that she dealt largely by credit; she had accounts with the grocer, the florist, and so on, and wasn't punctual with payments."

"Not with the butcher? I believe she never ate."

"No, Lady Bellenden will have paid for that, I daresay." The inspector had evidently gleaned all he might from local sources. He stared at Tom's list with interest. "Let's go over this," he said. "We may light on something. It consists mostly of reasons why certain persons should want to kill the Widow. This saves a good deal of time, although we will of course follow up whatever we find that's useful."

He began to read. "First you name yourself. You were looking at a view of Bigod Peak with the possibility of painting it later, when the deceased came up to you, above on the rockface, called in an offensive way to you to clear out, and presently began throwing stones."

"They didn't hurt me, but I thought I'd better make myself scarce."

"But you returned later and commenced to paint without disturbance?"

"Yes. I'm obstinate about that kind of thing. Doubtless I have a thicker skin than the full-time professional artist."

"You then went, as you say here, to lunch with Henry Haven, who is a writer of suspense stories under his own name. I remember seeing a story of his adapted for television. Very clever, I recall. He had reason for hating the Widow because she made an indecent assault on him in his car when he was driving her home from a pre-arranged dinner party."

"Arranged, if I may say so, by everyone but Haven. He

wouldn't have gone near the woman before, and certainly not after it. He makes no secret of his feelings about her."

"Partly that, and what you say about the sensitivity of artists, or at any rate of creative people, may be responsible here. It would have been possible for Haven to be there at the time of the death, as I must still call it although it is fairly obvious that it is murder, and I think we will find that the Coroner agrees."

Brackenbury broke in. "Elaine Partridge made insensitive remarks about my wife's death when I encountered her in Brennan, and also made a pass, unsuccessful, at me when I drove her home, after an appalling scene, from Bill Hedley's drinks party two days ago."

The inspector scanned the list again. "What exactly happened at Mr Hedley's?"

"In a way it was an assault on him also. First she destroyed a cherished orchid, and his orchids are his life; he was hoping to show this one which he'd grown from specially crossed seed. After that happened, as it became evident that she would have to leave the house, Mrs Partridge shouted an offensive epithet at Hedley in full hearing of the company. It was a very painful occurrence. Hedley, as you will know, had been a prisoner of war in a Japanese camp in Burma in the war, and you realise well enough what different men suffered in different ways. That that may have been Hedley's particular fate I have no evidence. But Elaine Partridge's shouting and her behaviour scandalised everyone, and may have roused deep loathing in Hedley, make him plan, cold-bloodedly enough, to kill her."

"Quite. The next person is Mary Reston, who we have not yet located. She is a potter and sculptor with strong hands. She had a motive in that Mrs Partridge was, as you put it, making passes at Wing Commander Oldham, with whom Miss Reston is known to be on a closely affectionate footing."

"Again, that could have been building up for a long time. On this occasion Elaine Partridge had done Miss Reston out of an expected regular visit from the Wing Commander because she had said to him over the telephone that there was something she herself urgently needed to tell him. The result was that he cancelled the prior arrangement with Miss Reston in order to go to Mrs Partridge instead."

"Is it possible," asked Tom, "that that something had to do with the arrival of the Australian, Joe Doherty, if he had already got in touch?"

"That we must find out, as soon as possible. It might also be Doherty who was able to use the cashpoint machine, in other words proving that he must already have seen the Widow and extracted not only her card but her private number, possibly using blackmail."

"Now Lady Bellenden," said Tom. "I don't like to include her. But her dog had been poisoned and she suspects the Widow, who had said to me on the occasion when I drove her home that she would like to murder McGinty. Lady Bellenden is a gardener and experienced dog handler, and her hands are stronger than those of many women of her age and class. She lives near. It would have been easy enough for her to have strangled the Widow and pushed or thrown her over the rock."

"Like you, I hope it's not so," said Stonor. "But we can't leave Lady Bellenden out merely because we like her. There is one more on the list; the postman Beale."

"You will know about that. He earned a reprimand owing to Elaine Partridge's complaint to the authorities that he had tried to rape her when, out of kindness, he carried her in to bed after finding her lying drunk on her own doorstep. There is also the fact that I myself heard him say, 'That bitch killed my son', when Mrs Partridge was in view in town. It's a bit far-fetched to blame the Widow for that, but it all adds up, or would do in Beale's mind."

"Anyone else?"

"Not that I've thought of."

A knock sounded on the door; it was the second constable. "Inspector, it's Miss Reston. She heard we were looking, and she's here. She drove down at once."

"Please show Miss Reston in," said Stonor. Mary appeared with her dark hair ruffled and her cheeks bright; she was wearing a nylon anorak, trousers and heavy shoes.

"I've just heard," she said. "Hello, Mr Brackenbury."

The inspector looked at her. "We hope," he said, "that you can help us with some information, Miss Reston."

She sat down in the chair. "If I can give any, I will," she told them, "but I can't pretend to be sorry Elaine's dead, and I hope she's in hell."

"It's best to be careful with statements like that," the inspector told her. "I take it you have no objection to Mr Brackenbury's presence? He is in a strong position to help us, and I would like him to hear the evidence."

"Of course I don't mind." She thrust a straying lock of hair firmly back in its place.

"Can you tell us," asked Stonor, "where you were between last night and early this morning, and in fact since? We have been trying to get hold of you all day."

"Sorry about that, but I wasn't to know. I went and climbed Bigod Peak. It was a good day and I'd always meant to do it, and I wanted some time alone."

"Is there any particular reason for that, Miss Reston?"

"Only a sense of frustration and a build-up of everything I don't like. I can't explain it any more clearly, I'm afraid."

She looked down at her hands. "I should perhaps tell you that late last night, about eleven o'clock, Elaine – Mrs Partridge – rang up and asked me to drive her again into Brennan this morning to buy chrysanthemums for Julius's memorial. I'm afraid I refused. I'd had enough of her, didn't think she cared twopence about Julius except as a meal ticket anyway, it was only the gesture she enjoyed, and I refused. I'd already taken her in that day, and I'm not made of time and petrol. She took it badly in the way she always did when she was crossed, began to be abusive and I rang off."

"So you climbed Bigod Peak today, starting in the early morning. Is there anyone who can witness to that?"

"Not a soul, at this time of year. It was glorious to be up there alone, and see the land spread out below, like coloured patchwork."

"Glorious but unfortunate," said Inspector Stonor drily. "How did you find out we were looking for you? None of the telephone calls were answered, I believe."

"Wing Commander Oldham told me. As you know, he hears everything."

"He telephoned you?"

"No, I went down to his place before going home. I wanted to see him personally about something." Her flush had deepened a little; it made her seem handsome.

"May I ask, Miss Reston, if this visit involved Mrs Partridge and her relations with you both?"

"Yes, it did. No point in disguising the fact. It certainly did." Her mouth set grimly. The second constable shifted in his chair. He had taken down everything.

After they had all parted company Tom went back to the saloon bar at the Lamb and Flag, which was beginning to fill up. Some of the crowd were commercial travellers who stayed overnight when they came this way; others were locals, and one in particular annoyed Tom by accosting him and asking in clearly heard tones if he was indeed Brackenbury of the column. He was a very young man, perhaps twenty. Evidently he was a junior reporter on the local *Prophet*, a paper with genteel family beginnings back in the 1890s. He goggled in admiration when Tom said he was who he was and then asked, without subtlety according to his lights, "Is it true your wife was killed in the Harrods bombing?" all of which would no doubt be resurrected in Friday's issue. Tom regretted his own lost anonymity; there would be no peace now and he wanted to leave. As it was he stood the boy a lager, asked what it was like to be a reporter here, and as soon as possible escaped to his room. As he closed the door the bedside telephone began to ring. It was Stonor.

"Tom, would you oblige me infinitely? I know you're on holiday, but we're so short-handed here I can't spare a man to go up north and identify Doherty and bring back the Audi. Do you think that with all expenses paid—" the inspector cleared his throat—" and with admission as a privileged visitor, you could go up by train at once? I've made it all right with the police there and the hire firm in London. Apparently they'd already got on the blower about their missing car. We can hold Doherty on that count at any rate meantime. But with regard to the established rigor of the body, I doubt if he could have carried out the murder and driven north in time."

Tom said that the task would come as a relief. "I'm under siege here," he said. "I was thinking of leaving."

"Don't leave until we have all this cleared up. I thought the *Prophet* would get on to you sooner or later. All I have against the paper is that its editor always disappears to the gents' when it's his turn to stand a round. But I appreciate your annoyance. I'll try to ensure that you are not pestered on your return. The Llanaff lot will be glad to see you. They've enough to do as it is with security and yobbos."

Accordingly Tom had a bite to eat – it had not been possible to take up Mary's invitation of yesterday and he had no doubt she had forgotten all about it, as he himself had till now – packed his suitcase, and stowed it with his painting things in the boot ready to drive to Euston, seven or eight hours' journey. He should, however, get there in good time to catch the train north. The smell of turpentine in the boot suddenly reminded him of the unfinished picture of Bigod Peak. It would probably never now be completed.

Just as he was about to reverse out of the hotel garage the little waitress, who lived in, came running. "Oh, Mr Brackenbury, it's the Commander. He's on the telephone. He wants to speak to you. Urgent, he said it was."

Tom impatiently turned his car down the steep slope that eventually led to Wing Commander Oldham's house. It seemed that there were endless rough roads here that made driving difficult, and he had wanted to make haste to Euston. But he had received a briefing over the telephone in a light dry voice that dismissed his worries about missing the train as idle. "Goodness, we'll run you into a main station if it needs to be done, and you can catch the express there." Oldham appeared to be familiar with timetables as well as his other reported fields of knowledge. Despite his annoyance Tom was interested to meet this blind man who knew everything, apparently almost before it had happened.

He saw a field with two racehorses grazing, and nearby a long low house which might have been a colonial bungalow except that it was built of the natural local stone. A freshly painted white fence contained the home field. As Tom drew up before the house he saw with admiration a long shining gentian-blue Bentley parked outside on the gravel, and a small man in a Fair Isle jersey briskly polishing it. He looked up and smiled pleasantly. He could not be more than twenty-five.

"Just sound the bell," he said, and when Tom did so it was opened, as though she had been waiting inside, by a fresh-faced housekeeper. She led Brackenbury to a white door on the right of a long straight passage.

"Come in," called the dry voice. Tom was ushered into the presence, and immediately felt himself dwarfed.

Basil Oldham was six foot two. He had blunt handsome features and his eyes, astonishingly blue and clear, stared in Tom's direction as though they could see. He wore a checked sports jacket and corduroy trousers, and his red hair, greying now and thinner on top than it had been, was cut closely in what these days would be termed military fashion, slightly outdated. A white stick lay by the chair he had evidently vacated, but in this room where everything would be familiar to Basil Oldham's touch, he had no need to use it. The black Labrador, lying in its place, raised its head briefly and then thumped its tail. Beyond the window, eerily foreshortened against the flat fields and the evening light, loomed the southern aspect of Bigod Peak. It should have dominated the room, but did not.

The two men shook hands. "Pour yourself a drink; they're in the cupboard," said the Commander. "Not for me; I don't take it."

Later, Tom was to learn that in the first despair over his blindness, the fact that he could never fly again, Oldham had started drinking heavily, had known that it was ruining his life still further, and had stopped at once. Such an effort of will must have been profound, but Tom felt that anything of that nature would be possible to Oldham. Both by his size and his personality he seemed to fill the room, looking larger than he had on the road that time Tom had seen him walking past.

Tom sat down with his whisky in a chair that gave a view of a set of superb carved ivory chessmen, set for a continuing game. "We don't start play till eight-thirty, so there's plenty of time," observed the Commander as though he could see. "As I said, we'll run you to the train if it's necessary. You can leave your car in the garage here, it will be quite safe."

He sat down. "How did you know I was looking at the chessmen?" demanded Tom, feeling that this giant had the sixth sense the blind develop. He would not dare, for instance, to filch any of the ornaments in the room, the set of toby-jugs which sat on the mantelpiece, the racing cups in silver and gold Oldham could never see, the cupboard of sparkling Waterford glass, the hunting prints and Spanish baroque mirror.

"I'm not totally without sight," Oldham told him. "I can see, for instance, a dark object against the light. There's still enough from the window for me to have seen you sit down. And I know where the chessmen are." He smiled. "I'd probably know you again, already, if we met, though not in a crowd. I don't go to cocktail parties these days, as Mary undoubtedly told you; so I missed the fun at Hedley's." His face lit up with mischief. "By God, the old Widow stirred things up! I was half sorry to hear that she'd gone; we used to have tearing rows when I went up there, and I enjoy that. I could, you know, have done her in." The blind eyes turned again to Brackenbury. "There was a moon that night. Don't rule me out of your list of suspects."

Tom suddenly guessed Oldham's secret; he must at all costs be the centre of attention, if only to avoid the kind of helpless boredom that the handicapped inevitably jettison. He said, "Why did you ask me here? Why not tell all that to the police?" They might know in any case, he thought; Stonor had not revealed everything.

"Because you seem to have met up with everyone involved, and I want to hear about it. I want to know what you think of everyone like Mary, old Bill Hedley, and I hear the Widow pelted you with stones, and poor old McGinty—" the Labrador looked up and thumped its tail loudly. "You remember McGinty," said Basil, making a fist at the dog. "You used to fight with him, and he always won. I used," he said, turning again to Tom, "to keep bull terriers m'self, before the crash. But they're too independent for me now." He caressed the black dog, who had risen and gone to him. Tom leaned back in the comfortable chair and sipped his drink. He had assumed a fatalistic outlook about time; the Commander would see that he caught his train; meanwhile they were evidently expected to chat. What would the next question be? He had a certain delicacy about talking of Mary Reston, as though it might be taking advantage of her; the Commander seemed fairly ruthless, all told. Nevertheless, the man was vulnerable. This house was full of valuable objects, and would be easy to rob.

"I see you don't lock your door," he said, by way of talk. Oldham had brought out cigarettes, offered them, been refused – Tom did not smoke – and lit his own with a small gas lighter, having fitted it carefully in an ivory holder, browned with nicotine.

"No one locks doors in the country," he said. "We aren't as suspicious as you town people. Everybody knows everybody, and you couldn't draw a chicken's neck without its being all over the countryside in ten minutes."

"I've noticed the grapevine is fairly efficient." Tom recalled Lady Bellenden and her remarks about his painting, and certain parts of Stonor's information which he would not have acquired in the ordinary way. "Miss Reston keeps her door locked," he said, recalling his own futile hammering to be let in to telephone.

Oldham laughed. "Mary won't have to lock it any more. She only did it in case the Widow came striding in. Mary likes to work in peace, covered in clay."

"I thought that bronze cast head she did of you was excellent, if I may say so."

"So do I. I've been over it with my fingers and seen it against the light, and as far as I can tell she's got my face, for what that's worth. Nobody knows themselves; most people, if you work it out, never see themselves except in mirrors, everything the wrong way round. Curious when you come to think of it."

He stubbed out his cigarette fastidiously, blew into the holder and lit another. Brackenbury noted that this was, outwardly at any rate, his only neurotic trait. Otherwise the blind man seemed normal, perhaps a trifle callous, a trifle mischievous: that might have been left over from his flying days with companions. Tom felt his reporting instincts stir. This man would make, in other circumstances, an article. Tom began ceasing to care about his train; if the worst came to the worst he could drive up to Llanaff and at least see Slim Joe, and the owners of the Audi could make other arrangements.

He asked a question. "Why, in the event, would you have murdered the Widow?"

"I wouldn't have touched the poor bitch. She could be interesting; she even had a certain charm in the right mood. She was her own worst enemy, of course. After Julius died people here would have taken her up again, because they were sorry for her stuck up there alone and unable to get away. But she kept on behaving so outrageously that everyone except Bill Hedley, who has a kind heart, dropped her. And Bill certainly wouldn't have asked her back again after that party." He laughed with a short hard sound. "I do regret missing that entertaining scene."

Tom changed the subject a little. "During the brief space of time when I was in her house—"

"When she made a pass at you. I haven't heard that; I guessed it. She used to make them at me all the time. She was man crazy."

"—she told me that her husband had been impotent. To say that to a total stranger – she was drunk, of course—"

"There was nothing wrong with Julius Patridge. I liked him; everyone did. Perhaps he pretended that he was impotent latterly and I wouldn't blame him. His life must have been absolute hell. Everyone came to his funeral."

"They never had children?"

"No. Elaine loathed them, of course. So do I. So does Mary."

"What about Haven? Why did you arrange for him to take her out to dinner? He was terrified."

Oldham gave his short hard laugh again. "Old squeaky-voice? I couldn't resist it. In any case Elaine was drinking heavily and needed taking out of herself. Chips and Maggie are socially desirable and they ask very few people; I thought she would be flattered, but evidently she behaved very badly there too, Haven's a curious case. Why doesn't he live with his wife?"

"He is a creative artist," said Tom defensively. "He's a very fine writer."

"Well, they should behave like other people. I've put up with a good deal from the Widow myself in that way, and I've never ostracised her."

"Perhaps the opposite?" said Tom carefully. He elicited the short laugh.

"You've been listening to Mary," said Oldham. "Frankly, although I've never said so to her – one doesn't, to another woman and, if you like, a rival – after Julius's death Elaine got a bit careless in personal ways. I may not be the complete stallion; I know what I can stand and what I can't."

"But you went on befriending her."

"Oh, yes, in the open air it was all right," said Basil outrageously, adding, "I'm a humanist. In my considered opinion as much as we can do for anyone during their lives and ours is what we ought to do, then that's that. The woman was lonely and I used to go and chat her up. That's all."

"And you saw her yesterday afternoon because she had something important to tell you, disappointing Mary who had been expecting you."

"I can see Mary at any time," said the Commander casually. A hard expression was on his face. "Mary's a Catholic," he said. "She even believes in angels. Nothing will shake her; it's pure superstition. She loathed Elaine in a peculiar way, none of your Christian loving-kindness, she was afraid of her – and Mary isn't easily made afraid." He fitted a new cigarette into the holder. Brackenbury looked at his watch. It was half-past eight.

"I say, I think I can get myself to Euston if I leave now," he said. "It's been very interesting to meet you and I hope we can meet again." He felt urged to say this, although his reasons to himself for doing so were not clear; this man was rocklike, and perhaps it was a temptation to hammer at the rock. Perhaps that was the way Mary Reston, sculptor, felt likewise.

"Here's Geordie for chess," remarked Oldham inconsequentially as a car drew up outside. Presently a high-coloured elderly Scotsman, seeming small by contrast to Oldham's huge frame, walked in with the ease of familiarity. His gaze went straight to the chess table and after introductions it was evident to Brackenbury that his own presence was no longer required. He left the pair to settle in, bishop against rook, and having started up his own engine outside heard the Bentley purr softly into reverse action as the young henchman in the Fair Isle pullover took it back to the garage. The Commander evidently kept his staff under strict and punctual orders; there was no doubt that the giant car could have wafted Tom all the way had it been necessary.

Driving eastwards, Brackenbury himself wondered idly why he had been summoned and then, with a stab of regret, recalled that Oldham had evaded answering the question as to why Elaine had wanted to see him. No doubt Inspector Stonor would find out.

He caught the train at Euston, enjoyed a comfortable if short night on the sleeper, and had asked the attendant to bring his tea at seven.

"Ye can sleep on till eight at Llanaff, sir," the man said. He had an incredibly black moustache, waxed like Poirot's.

Tom said he wanted to get off early, and he was in fact awake in time to hear the train jolt to a halt at Llanaff harbour, and was up, washed, shaved and dressed by the time the tea came. He drank one cup, reviled the milk, left the biscuits and departed with his suitcase down the long clear security ramp that leads to the car park and the police station. He knocked on the door of the latter at precisely half-past seven, and was admitted by a Scots constable far from home.

"My name's Brackenbury. I think they got in touch."

"Oh, aye, to get the keys and see Doherty. I'll have him brought in, sir. I was to tell ye, sir, from Inspector Stonor, that the tyre marks have been found to fit."

That would be the Audi, parked among the woods. They would have taken photographs, a cast. He was shown into a small bare office, and presently Slim Joe, unshaven, was brought in, and accommodated himself in a chair. He remembered Tom at once and smiled sardonically. "So you're the one that grassed on me," he said. "They've taken my prints again and all." He then fell back on that moral support of almost all convicts, the hand-rolled fag.

"Smoke?" he said, the weedy object dangling at last between his fingers. Tom shook his head. He was observing this man as a phenomenon. Handsome, in his thin dark way; no doubt beguiling to women with his assurance, provided they were not too particular.

"Got a match?" enquired Slim Joe. For some reason Tom was able to produce these.

"Keep them," he said. The Australian was still smiling, his hooded dark eyes bright and wary.

"You've stood me a beer," he said, "and now you hand me a box of matches. At a guess, I owe you a story. You can tell it to the narks."

Again, Tom said nothing. This character, he thought, would talk to hear the sound of his own voice; lazily, slowly, unembarrassed. He prepared to listen. There was plenty of time.

"They can only hold me so many hours," said Slim Joe. "They've got nothing on me except being in unlawful possession of a car and driving without insurance. I walked straight from the Scrubs to make a 'phone call, then I went straight on to where I have a pal in the car hire business. Told him I only needed it for a few hours. He gave me a chance – he'd been inside too – and I drove up to Brennan to see the wife."

Tom nodded slowly. "How did you know where to find her?" he asked. "You hadn't seen each other for years."

"You can say that again. I called her. I've told them as much as I'm telling you. I only had to say a few words; it was an old joke, if you can call it that, between us. I said, 'This is the Salvation Army. Got any money?' and she knew it was me, all right. She slammed down the receiver and I hit the motorway. Hadn't driven one before. They weren't invented when I went inside. Makes you think."

He drew on the small limp cigarette. "One silly thing I did right away. I'd given Fast Cars Incorporated the wife's address. Hell, I had none of my own, had I? That way the narks got me, in the end. In any case I hadn't figured I would need the car as long."

"Why did you?" It was, to say the least, instructive to listen to the workings of the criminal mind. This man would not hesitate to tell lies under oath in court, but in the meantime he had no reason for lying. Tom felt grateful to John Stonor for arranging this interview. The pieces were falling into place.

"Why did I have to hurry on? When I got there she was full of sauce, but before I left she got me to perform a certain service which takes a little time. After ten years hard a man wouldn't want to refuse an offer like that. It was after midnight when I left. I'd only hired the car till the early evening."

"You left with her credit card and number."

"Her PIN number, given to me by my loving wife. I got a cheque as well; they found it on me. I meant to cash it pronto, soon as the banks opened, or in God's country; it wasn't crossed, I saw to that. I know Elaine; I ought to. But I got pals over there." He wet his lips with his tongue. The dark eyes deepened. "Once I'm there, I'm home and dry." Slim Joe Doherty drew on the last of his cigarette.

"What made her give you money for the asking? She didn't have to." The realisation had come to him that the man did not know yet that Elaine was dead. He was interested now in the details. As Slim Joe had said himself, it was a story.

"She had to," said Elaine's widower. "For once, I used my wits. I saw she was living fine and dandy, and must be getting money from somewhere. I figured it was the other bloke's money, and she'd told me he was dead. When I said the words pension and insurance, her face went all to pieces. She said she'd give me what I wanted, but there wasn't much left in the bank this quarter. I said she'd have to ask for an overdraft. In the end she said she'd keep sending some, if only I kept quiet. Elaine hasn't got guts, not when you get down to it. It was all show, that shouting and the naughty words."

Tom leaned forward; so it had been blackmail, and a blackmailer does not in any case kill his victim. "Tell me how you found her," he said. "I'm interested." This was true enough; a man and wife parted for years, with no visits, no divorce, probably no letters.

"That's another long story. I told you one for the beer, and here's another for the matches. When I went inside there was no word from her; I didn't expect any, she walked out on me not long after our wedding. The only person who visited me was old Long Pat, the priest. He came to see everyone who didn't have anyone else coming.

"One day he asked me about all of it, seeing I'm a Catholic. Was I married? I said yes, father, a woman will swear to love and honour a man one day, and leave him the next or the one after. What went wrong? says he, and I told him some of the names she'd called me. She was nuts all right. I showed him a photograph of her I carried about in my wallet, God knows why. He said, 'I'll remember her'. Long Pat never forgot a face. I said he could keep the photograph; by then there was only one thing I wanted to do with it. Four or five years after that, before he died – we all missed Long Pat and had a Mass said for him – he took a holiday locum up at Brennan, and ran into who but my wife, with another man in the bank. You didn't know Long Pat, mister; he'd have faced up to the devil in hell; and he was tall, and all of him grey, grey eyes and hair, grey skin, looking like the Grand Inquisitor and the kindest heart underneath. He stood in front of Elaine and called her Mrs Doherty straight between the eyes. She said in ladylike fashion that he was mistaken. Pat brought out the photograph – he'd kept it ready, all those years – and said to her he knew me, and she was living in sin and all the rest. I wish I'd been a fly on the wall to see the tellers prick their ears. In the end it wasn't so much Elaine that took it bad, it was the bloke with her. He was a nice bloke, a gent, too good for Elaine. Evidently he'd thought he was the one she was married to. He turned white as chalk, and Elaine told me when I saw her lately that he'd never slept with her from that day on.

"That's all I know, sir. I reversed the car out of the woods pronto and headed it for here. They were waiting for me because Fast Cars had got on the blower. I certainly wish I could have a shave before they call me to court."

"It isn't all you know," said Tom gravely. "You didn't know Elaine is dead."

"Eh?"

"Found strangled, pushed over the high rock."

Slim Joe grew tense for a moment as though someone had given him a blow in the stomach, then relaxed: he stubbed out the fragments of the hand-rolled cigarette.

"So they want to fix it on me," he said. "They've got no evidence to keep me here, not a thing. Not this time, they haven't."

"You were in last time for robbery and violence. Why shouldn't you have done it again?" Tom knew the man couldn't have; the time factor ruled it out. When Slim Joe thought it over he would realise that. But right away, he was sullen.

"Because I didn't, that's why. Who the hell are you, anyway? At my guess, you aren't even a dick."

Tom found the Audi in the car park with the help of one of the constables, who gave him the keys. A sizeable ferry, perhaps the one Slim Joe had hoped to catch, had come into the harbour, its massive prow rising above the slipway like a blue whale coming up for air. Perhaps, after the court hearing, Slim Joe would catch the next one. They couldn't hold him for long, despite the tyre prints.

Tom drove back carefully to Brennan in the Audi, thinking over all he now knew. It shed a light on Julius Partridge's death. Had Elaine tired in any case of a man who was not her husband and would neither allow her alcohol nor sex? Had she pushed him over the rock knowing he had kept her secret faithfully – the bit about the tellers in the bank didn't count, if they had heard anything they would be discreet – and that she would now have his insurance pension to spend as she chose?

She had spent some of it on flowers, at any rate. Brackenbury remembered the dahlias.

"We haven't enough on Slim Joe to hold him," said Inspector Stonor when Tom got back with his report of the interview. "The time factor alone rules it out; he was identified by a petrol pump attendant on the motorway junction at ten minutes to three in the morning. He'll disappear into Eire, of course, and the Garda will be in touch with us if he tries to get on any aircraft from there, or even if he doesn't; they're very co-operative. It would have been convenient if he'd been guilty; a man is released from gaol, drives straight in a purloined car to meet his estranged wife, cashes her money and then she's found violently dead. However, the PM report has come in."

He handed the paper to Brackenbury and the latter glanced at the details of the death superficial: bruising caused by the fall before the body had begun to stiffen; cause of death strangulation; a few drops of congealed blood of a matched group found beneath the fingernails, together with a single strand of fibre of a blue colour. There had been evidence of recent sexual intercourse.

"Slim Joe will think I grassed on him again. He has charm."

"And evidently used it more than once. But I think that is all we have on him. His blood group is B: we knew that already. Before I forget, by the way, Brack – if you would care to stay on for a bit, I've contacted the insurance people and the lawyer who is executor, and they have no objection to your using the Partridge cottage for a week or two if you can stand it. It'll cost a lot less than staying at the Lamb and Flag, and they'd prefer to keep it occupied. I'd like to have you around, but sadly I can't pay your expenses out of police funds." He smiled.

"The atmosphere will do me good," said Tom. "What about heirs?"

"There aren't any. She died intestate and doesn't appear to have had a sou in the world belonging to her unless you care to count Slim Joe. Partridge's insurance payments and a few of his investments were all she had to live on. It's questionable whether or not the insurance people will now make a claim for refund out of the proceeds of the estate, which virtually means the sale of the house. But that will have to wait a bit."

"As she wasn't in fact Partridge's widow, the situation is, as they say nowadays, unclear."

"Just so. By the way, Sergeant Lake found a tin of phosphorus rat poison, the kind used before warfarin, in the Partridge garage. It's not easy to obtain these days. The vet has identified it as the same he found inside Lady Bellenden's dog."

The cottage was cold. Outside was a garden almost as wildly run to seed as Haven's grass park. In the sitting-room grate were still the cold ashes of the fire Elaine had lit when he came in with her. *I've lit a fire now, you'll have to stay.* Her ghost was not in the room; whatever taste she had had not stamped itself on furniture or ornaments; the place was impersonal, like a hotel, except for the grubby marks round switches and a thin veil of dust over everything by now. He could picture the Widow sitting here day after day, drinking, her mind filled with mean fantasies. There was a photograph of a man with a lean tired face in one of the rooms; doubtless the late Partridge. A coffee-table book about the Tudor Age lay as if for effect on a small table. Tom went out of the house again and looked at the garage: there were tools in it. He felt a strong desire to go into the garden and weed and dig it.

He went back into the house and cleared the cold wood ash out of the grate. There were still some logs in a basket, newspaper and sticks nearby. He set the fire and wanted to light it when he remembered that he had given his matches to Slim Joe and that by now they might be somewhere in Eire. He stared at the tidied grate and decided to stay on at the Lamb and Flag for another night at least. This place could not be lived in until it had been warmed. The cold was everywhere. It was difficult to believe that so short a time had passed since the death. The hire company had been waiting at Euston when he drove in in their car. He had fetched his own and driven back.

He would try to find a cleaning woman in Brennan, he decided. He could cope with cooking for himself. There would be a bill, doubtless, for electricity in due course; he found the meter and read it, jotting down the details. As he did so there was a rustling at the door; it was the mail, nothing large or important, all addressed to Elaine. He saw Beale the postman's back disappearing down towards the road. He was not wearing his blue scarf. *He was not wearing his blue scarf.*

Tom mocked himself. He should have remembered that, at once. He did not get in touch with the police. A certain feeling of pity prevented him.

His first visitor, once he had settled in, was Mary Reston from her cottage nearby. She arrived with a small package wrapped in tissue paper. "It's for luck in the house and an apology for having stood you up the time I asked you for tea," she said. Gratified – the episode of the invitation to tea had long slipped his mind – he opened the parcel. Inside, carefully wrapped, was a tiny jar, glazed in speckled colours like a peacock's feathers. It would hold small flowers like heartsease or, perhaps, a single rose. Tom set it on the mantelpiece.

"It makes the place feel better already," he said. "You made it, I suppose?"

"Of course I did. It's a reduction glaze. After years of searching I finally found a firm who would sell me a kiln for bottled gas. You can't get these colours with an electric kiln."

"Aren't gas kilns fairly large?" He remembered seeing one once, at an art school he had briefly attended; the great kiln had looked like a genocide chamber.

"Will you have something to drink?" he said. He had bought whisky, gin and wine at the grocer's, and there were glasses, fortunately clean, in the cupboard here. He went and fetched them and they drank together.

"Why," he asked her presently, "did you hate Elaine?"

She did not reply at once. Then she said, "Hasn't it made all the difference in the world already even to this place, not to have her here, not anywhere? I remember once Henry Haven saying that when you passed by, you always felt as if a hand was waiting to reach out and grab you. That," she nodded towards it, "is

Julius's photograph. He was the salt of the earth. Without him, she'd have been deliquescent long ago." Her voice was light and unconcerned, as if, he thought, a weight had been lifted from her.

He changed the subject. "I'd like, for my housewarming," he said, "you, Haven and Bill Hedley to come to supper here one night next week. I don't know any other women to ask, however."

"I shall be quite happy." He rose to pour her another drink and she took and sipped it. "You've improved things here already," she told him. He had rearranged the furniture; now the sofa faced the hearth, with a large solid armchair to one side. There had been no feminine touches in the house: Tom had bought a bunch of mixed flowers in Brennan and had put them in a jug on the small table beside the Tudors. They brightened the drab room. He had also wiped the surrounds of the light switches.

He returned to the matter of Julius and Elaine. He wondered if perhaps Mary had had a *tendresse* for Julius, less strong than the emotion which bound her to the Commander, but present nevertheless. "It's marvellous," she said, "how the evil has gone from here. It's like a fog lifting."

"Or a widow's veil, perhaps."

She was sitting with her chin on her hands, the unfinished drink beside her on the table. "Julius was an absolute dear," she said again. "It wasn't possible for him to visit by himself – she kept an eye – but sometimes one would meet him at the ironmonger's or somewhere, and chat. Everyone was shocked by the death."

"Put your way, he's happier dead. Do you think she did it?"

"I'm sure of it, but nothing will ever be certain now. When I heard he was dead I came in here; one or two people did, to see if they could help. She wasn't exactly crushed by sorrow; she lapped it up. She went to bed and lay queening it while the rest of us carried out her extremely precise and bitchy orders, making tea or putting through long-distance telephone calls as directed. She was in no kind of distress at all, either then or at the funeral.

She just enjoyed being at the centre of attention – and, of course, to get at the keys for the drinks cupboard. Julius had kept those to himself."

"I found them. There are still a few bottles of wine. I didn't touch them."

"I remember what it was like that day. There was an open book – it was about international finance – lying on his desk, with dust on the page. He must have sat there hour after hour, with the keys of the drinks cupboard in his pocket, not reading, thinking about God knows what, perhaps the place he'd had to resign at Cambridge, or even the chair he might have had before long. He was a very well-read, intelligent person apart from his subject, not hidebound as so many academics are. Life with Elaine must have been absolute hell."

"I asked you before why you hated her," he said openly. Her face suddenly grew stiff, masklike.

"I suppose," she said presently, "among other reasons, Elaine once told Basil I was a lesbian. That disgusted me in a way I can't explain. It's difficult to disprove the accusation, for a start. I've had men friends who were homosexual, gifted and sensitive people with whom I got on well. But the other – ugh. Basil teases me about it still. He's enough of a sadist to enjoy that. To do him justice, though, I don't think he has told anyone else; if he and Geordie had got on to it over chess, the news would be all round the countryside."

He regarded her for a moment. Then, "May I ask," he said, "another extremely personal question? You'd make good material for reviewing; you don't lose your head."

"What is it? I can't know till I hear." She regarded her own slightly spatulate fingers, the nails rimmed with grey-white dried clay.

"Why does the Commander, in his turn, dislike Henry Haven? He calls him squeaky-voice."

Mary began to laugh. He had never seen her do so before, and her square, cream-coloured teeth were in good condition. He reflected that unlike most women, laughter did not give her face charm; in fact, she had none. Perhaps one paid in that way for having creative talent, as if all the gifts could not be brought to the christening.

"Basil is a rather primitive male," Mary said. "He dislikes and resents Henry because Henry once or twice has taken me out to dinner or a film. We're only friends, but Basil knows how I feel about him and, as I say, resents any competition a lot more fiercely than he would do if he wasn't blind."

"Here's another personal question I asked before. Why don't you marry Oldham?" Now I've blotted my copybook, he thought. The smile had vanished from her face.

"You aren't the first person to ask. Everybody knows about it – my feeling for Basil, I mean. If I married him – and I'd have been glad to, at the beginning – I should be a chess widow and a doormat. And anyway, he hasn't asked me."

Shortly afterwards, she left.

* * *

Mrs Beale had been contacted through her husband and had agreed to come once more to the cottage to clean two half-days a week. "As long as it isn't heavy, sir". Tom promised that it would not be. He decided, on inspection, that to have Dora Beale working for him would be a pleasure. She seemed to have recovered by now from the loss of her baby, and not to mind, as many women would have done, coming back again to clean at Lesser Bellenden. She drove her own small Volkswagen car by now, and Tom paid for petrol and for Dora Beale's three-hour stint on each occasion. She soon had the place improved: a fire blazed in the clean grate to cheer the dim evenings; the featureless rooms were aired, dusted and likewise clean, the furniture and kitchenware polished. Dora would have hung the existing blankets out to air, but Tom disliked the idea of using the Widow's bedding. He shopped in Brennan and Penarch, and came back with not one but two Scandinavian goose-down quilts with covers and pillows. "They'll always come in useful, sir," said Dora Beale, shaking them out to fit.

"Yes, I can take them with me when I go."

"I hope that won't be yet, sir."

Tom did not know either. He had been enjoying himself

tidying the garden, though it only had to be made ready for winter; had piled up the weeds for compost and dug over some of the bare earth with the spade from the garage. Dora Beale brought him his coffee, smiling.

"Men," she said, "are terrible for buying and then losing things. Here's yourself buying these expensive duvets when there are plenty of blankets to be had, and sheets. As for the other thing, I knitted Jerry a blue wool scarf for his birthday and Christmas, and he's lost it. Just like that, lost it, and he can't say where. If you hear anything of it, sir, will you tell me, or Jerry when he comes with the post? Fisherman's rib, it was, and took me a long time. Bright blue; I sent for the wool special."

Tom made a decision suddenly.

"Mrs Beale, take my advice and don't ask any more about that blue scarf. Have you told many people?"

She was staring at him, quick nervous panic in her eyes. "Is there – something wrong about it, sir?"

A strand of blue wool found under the fingernails. Grouped blood. "It could be," he said. "Best keep it quiet."

"I've only talked about it to you, sir, and Jerry of course – I gave him a telling off – and hardly anyone else, sir. Is it – is it something to do with *her*, the death, I mean?"

"It could be. This is between you and me. You're a wise enough woman to keep your own counsel. Unless the police ask you directly, say nothing."

"The police – oh, sir—"

"Forget it, Dora." They were already on those terms. "That was good coffee."

Beale himself, red-eyed and shifty, arrived next morning with the mail. He glanced quickly at Tom, who was in the garden in his shirt-sleeves. "Sir – Mr Brackenbury, sir, about the scarf."

"About that. So Dora told you. Come in, Beale, to the fire."

He came in, and stood twisting his hands together. At last he flung up his head and faced Brackenbury defiantly.

"You know, sir, don't you?"

"Yes," said Tom gently. "I know."

"Sir—"

"I remember, you see, meeting you that first night in the wood, with your gun. Why didn't you use that?"

"Because it was too good for her, the bitch." His voice was rough and clear. "I'd thought of it. Then I says to myself, like, why let her go easy? She made it hard enough for others. Mr Partridge, he was a gentleman, sir. I'd have beaten the daylights out of her if she'd been mine. He didn't ought to have died, sir. He wouldn't have done himself in, he wasn't like that. It was either an accident or *her*. I say it was her. And that isn't all."

"There was the time you found her."

"Ay. Dead drunk she was, and snoring, across her own doorstep. I carried her inside and laid her on her bed, and put the covers over her. That nearly cost me my job after the letter she went and wrote. If they hadn't known me all these years hereabouts, sir, and if the Postmaster himself hadn't put in a good word for me, that'd have been it, and I'd have been made redundant, as they call it now."

"Then there was the baby." Tom was ruthless. He had once interviewed the mother of a battered child whose stepfather had killed it. He felt the same way now. Tears rose in Beale's eyes.

"There was that. Me and the wife had always wanted children. Dora's not strong in such ways, and at the beginning she had a miscarriage, and then we think another, sir, and it didn't seem as if we were going to be lucky in our time. It was twelve years, sir. Then last year she said she was pregnant, and we were that pleased it was like walking on the moon. Then – well, you'll know what happened, sir, you seem to know most of it. That bitch – Dora told her she was expecting, happy like, and that same day Mrs Partridge made her drag out all the heavy things and clean underneath, the deep freeze and all, and didn't help her do that or put it back. It was as though she done it on purpose, sir. Maybe she was jealous, like, having none of her own. She didn't like children. She used to say it."

He was trembling, and Tom went to the sideboard and poured a stiff whisky. "Drink that, and never mind the hour," he said. "It'll pull you together."

A ghost of a grin creased Beale's face. "You'll get me the boot for drinking on delivery, sir." But he drank it down, and afterwards his colour was better.

"Will you tell the police, sir? It'll break Dora, that it will."

"I wouldn't want to hurt Dora. Listen; I know it was murder, and that is a police matter. They say a killer always strikes again."

"Not me, sir. I haven't got an enemy in the world now, sir. It was just that I saw her coming along the drop and everything went red and I got my hands about her throat and squeezed. She got hold of me by the neck and scratched and pulled, but I was the stronger, and sober at that; I could smell the drink on her breath. I throttled the life out of her and then threw her over, the way she'd thrown *him*, and my little son born dead. They said he'd have been a spastic if he'd lived. I'd do it again, sir, not to anyone else, but to *her* every time."

He must have met her after she'd poisoned McGinty, Brackenbury thought. He said, "To get back to the scarf. A fragment of blue wool was found under Mrs Partridge's fingernails, and if the police had ever seen it on you they'd ask a few questions, to put it mildly. But I heard from Dora that she'd only just given it to you for your birthday. Have you worn it on the round?"

"Never, sir, save one cold day. We aren't supposed to spoil the look of the uniform except when it's raining, and I just put it in the back of the Post Office van when I was driving further afield, and that long stretch when there isn't any delivery I put it on, and – and – I must have forgot about it. It isn't in the van now, sir. I haven't liked to ask. I told the wife I'd lost it, and got the rough side of her tongue, a bit."

"I have told your wife not to ask or talk about it. Do you think she will?"

"Not if I tell her not to, she won't. But I wouldn't – I couldn't explain to Dora why – what I – oh, God." He began to weep openly, the tears running down his face. "Why should all this happen to a man who meant no harm, sir? Everyone in the place is like an old friend and trusts me, and then she – that devil—"

"She is dead. She can't hurt you any more."
"Except in my mind, sir. Except in my mind."

After Beale had gone Tom took the spade and went on digging over the plot of earth. What his purpose was he was not sure; it was doubtful if he would stay long enough to see the benefit, to plant snowdrops and crocuses, or allow what was already here to come up, free of weeds. The earth was tempting, rich and brown. Julius Partridge must have had it cared for in his time, by himself or another. *I grow flowers.* Tom still felt like a watcher from outside; he was uninvolved, except perhaps in his pity for Beale. That poor wretch of a postman this morning had aroused feeling in him. He knew he ought to have gone straight to the police; and he knew that he was not going to.

They had not been able to arrest Slim Joe, and a wastrel had escaped for the time. They would not hesitate to arrest Beale, an honest man who had lost a blue scarf. A harmless woman would be left unhappy, ashamed and unprotected: another inmate would join the rest in prisons already full to overcrowding, his existence confined, organised, predictable, day after day and year after year. He would be set free in the end for good conduct, soured and shamed for what was left of his life, finding everything changed outside, as Slim Joe had done. *Motorways hadn't been invented when I went inside.* And who would be the better for it all?

It was at this point that Tom leant on his spade and the spade showed a curious reluctance to set its edge in the earth. In a soft, betraying fashion there was something there. Tom resurrected a stained blue scarf, damp and dirty, made of blue fisherknit rib. It had not been buried deep.

"Lady Bellenden, I didn't want to disturb you with the telephone, so I came round. Would you—?"

"My dear young man, come in. I hear we have you as a neighbour." She looked small, ill and pale, as though the flesh had shrunk lately towards her bones. She courteously offered him coffee and he refused. She was holding a gardening tool in her hands and wore thick gloves.

"I won't stay long," he told her. "It is only that I had an idea with which I think you and certain other people can help me – or at least share the responsibility with me."

"Is it concerned with Elaine's death?" she said sharply. "If that is so, you must take your idea to the police."

"In the end it may come to that, but I want you to help me in a decision. There will be a few of us, all people you know rather better than I do. If you will, call it a conference. I have certain evidence, and if it is decided by all of us that the police should be involved, this shall be done."

"Will it lead to the discovery of Elaine's killer?"

"I know that already."

"You are a strange man," she said suddenly. "What time do you want me to come?"

"Tonight at six, if you will."

"Very well."

He went back to the cottage and telephoned Haven, Hedley, Mary Reston and the Commander. Basil Oldham was intrigued.

"I hear you've been diggin' in your garden," he said with his usual uncanny prescience. The grapevine again, or perhaps Mary.

"That is correct. I hope you will come?"

"It's chess night. What do you want me for?"

"Come and find out. It will not take long. Now I think of it, will you bring Geordie with you? As I say, it's only for a few moments."

He heard the short hard laugh. "Wouldn't miss it. What do you take me for?"

"At six, then." He had not mentioned drinks as the Commander did not take them. He had arranged for the supper party afterwards; the date suited everyone invited. He drove down to Brennan, and bought dry sherry, whisky, gin and a few bottles of tonic. It might as well be a mildly social occasion; he owed hospitality. For the supper party itself, Tom prepared a curry. He rather prided himself on his dish, with raisins, eggs, pineapple chunks and diced chicken meat. There would be only rice, lime and poppadoms to get ready later, by which time he hoped the rest would be drinking among themselves. Everything else was in order; the Partridges' knives and forks were silver, plain rat-tail pattern, heavy and good. Tom imagined Julius's hand in that; perhaps it was family stuff. He also, like Elaine, seemed to have had no other relations left in the world. Like Elaine, also, his ghost did little haunting here.

Haven arrived first, with a bottle of wine. He was jittery with excitement. "This promises to be interesting," he said. "I suppose an ouija board wouldn't help?"

"I don't think we are going to need one."

"You sound very serious, Brack. For myself, I am at the stage of near hysteria; it is all so very like *Murder in the Red Barn*." A car sounded outside, braking on the stones. "It's Hedley," said Haven. "I should think he's eaten up with curiosity too."

"I think very little will surprise Bill Hedley."

"You mean . . . is he . . . now I'm not playing the game, am I?"

"I didn't imply that. I meant that Hedley has been through so many experiences in his life that he is not likely to be taken unawares."

Tom saw Hedley get out of the car and hand out Lady Bellenden, whom he had driven up. "So kind," said the old lady, coming in at the door. She had dressed for company; she wore her rouge, and the same black silk dress she had had on for Hedley's party. A rivière of French paste encircled her withered neck and cascaded shining down over her bosom.

Tom poured drinks for all three guests. The old lady had sherry and the two men whisky and water. "I haven't laid on any soda," he apologised. "The fact is, I never take it and so I forgot to buy it."

"It's insulting a good whisky to muck it about," said Hedley. "This suits me."

"And me," said Haven's high voice. The two men settled on the sofa, leaving the old lady seated upright like a marquise in the big armchair.

"Well," she said, raising her glass, "it seems a very long time since I was in this house. You have made a difference to it."

"I am beginning to like it very much," said Tom.

"There used to be a pleasant garden under the former owners," she told him. "Later on Julius used to get a man to come and do the grass, but he himself wasn't interested."

Tom was about to reply that knowledgeable gardeners, of which he knew the old lady was one, inclined to pride themselves on tiny, almost invisible triumphs; a secret Labrador violet or gentian, never the vulgar hollyhock or rose. It came to him, not for the first time, that he would enjoy resurrecting the garden. It was perhaps at that moment that the decision to offer for the property came firmly into his mind. However, that must wait.

The purr of the Bentley sounded and then ceased outside. Mary and Geordie got out, and presently the Wing Commander's huge form filled the doorway. Behind him, Geordie peered like an elderly gnome.

"Glad to see you, Oldham. You've met—" He was considering Geordie rather than the Commander, who knew everybody. But it appeared that Geordie, who kept a good pub a few miles off, was too active a branch of the grapevine to be strange to anyone here. It hardly mattered, as Oldham's own tremendous presence caused everything to focus on him and about him. He made his way unerringly to the fire.

"No, I'll stand, thanks," As usual he refused a drink. Mary Reston's eyes never left him; he might have been her child or her lost soul. There was not quite enough seating as it was; Geordie was accommodated on a chair brought in from the bedroom.

"Now begin," said Mary. "We're all agog."

Tom stood facing the company, his feet on the hearthrug near the Commander. "Not to deceive anyone here at the outset," he told them, "I have – Lady Bellenden already knows a little of it – come on a piece of evidence which, added to the post-mortem findings, establishes, or could do if I reported it, the identity of Elaine Partridge's killer. In ordinary course this evidence should be handed to the police. I have not yet done this. I want your advice as to whether to do so or not, when I have told you a little more."

There was a silence in the room; everybody had drawn a breath. "This is compoundin' a felony," said Oldham.

"I am well aware of it. I do not think I am the only one involved."

"What is the evidence?" asked Hedley.

"I will tell you and show you. At the moment, as things are, nobody can prove that any of you have seen it, let alone touched it."

He produced the stained and sodden scarf, now drying out a little. "What the devil—?" said Hedley. Bewilderment was on everyone's face.

"A fragment of this, with some identifiable blood, was found under the fingernails of the dead woman. The blood was Group B, which is rare. Together with this it would be sufficient to arrest the owner. He is a decent honest postman whom you all know, Jerry Beale. He has been, to put it mildly, prejudiced in his work by a letter sent by Elaine Partridge which you will have heard of, as a result of helping her when she was too drunk to help herself. He also blames Elaine for the loss of his child, who was born dead and would have been spastic by reason of a slipped placenta in the mother. At the beginning of the pregnancy Mrs Beale was forced by the Widow to drag about heavy furniture and felt some pain. The condition can be progressive, in other words causing a failure of blood supply to certain parts of the unborn child at intervals through the months of gestation. The child was their first to come to term and they have been married for several years. Altogether Beale had such provocation that, meeting her when nobody was about, he strangled her and threw her over the rockface."

There was silence again. Then, "Told you you'd been diggin' in your garden," said the Commander's light dry voice. He laughed, the hard sound striking at the quiet in the room.

"But who—?" said Lady Bellenden. She had put one hand up to her mouth; her hooded eyes stared out above it like a sad owl's.

"If you want to know," said Oldham, "it was Geordie here. I'd have done it myself if I could see."

"Don't blame me, Commander. It was your idea." Geordie's voice cut briskly across the tense silence.

"Came with you to make sure you did it," said the Commander.

"So you're as much of a felon as I am," Tom could not resist saying.

"To hell with that. Beale delivers my mail last of all his round; the road ends there. He stops off for a cup of tea with Mrs Houston, my housekeeper. A few days ago, as you know, it was very cold. After he'd gone Mrs Houston came to me to say he'd taken off a blue wool scarf in the warmth of the kitchen and had left it behind. She said his manner had been strange. I expect the man was not himself by then, if the killin' had happened the night before. Mrs Houston asked me if I'd call the Post Office. I told her to leave the thing with me, and I didn't call anybody. I knew the results of that post-mortem before the police got them. The lab attendant plays darts at Geordie's pub, and Geordie had already rung me."

Geordie sat stiffly in his place, saying nothing. Tom noticed that his hands were small and precise, hands that would use bottles and glasses without knocking them over, chessmen without displacing them.

"So now half the countryside knows," he said.

"No, only ourselves. I gave Geordie strict orders, didn't I? And he fixed the darts boy. It need go no further, in my opinion. He won't transgress again." The sightless eyes were fixed on Tom. "I thought at first," he said, "of gettin' Mary to burn the thing in that kiln of hers, but I didn't want to involve her. In the end Geordie and I came round in Geordie's car, and we buried the blasted thing in Elaine's so-called garden, where it could have lain till it rotted if you, Brackenbury, hadn't started nosin'."

"That was not my intention. I didn't expect to find anything."

"I think the whole thing is most irregular," said Lady Bellenden.

Mary turned on her. "So you'll inform the police, out of your comfortable corner? Have you forgotten what Elaine Partridge did to your dog? Do you want the poor devil who killed her – in his place I'd have done the same – to be put away for life, to rot?"

"I–I am as guilty as he."

Tears started to well in the hooded eyes. Everyone was gazing fixedly at the old woman. No one spoke. Winifred Bellenden drew a harsh breath, then began to speak, the patch of rouge on each cheek standing out harshly.

"McGinty was very dear to me; I might say by now he was everything to me. You may not know bull terriers; they like to sniff about near home, they aren't great rangers. That night – it was more than a year ago but I shall never forget it – I was out, about this time of year, with McGinty for his evening walk. I see quite well at night and I hadn't brought a torch. As long as one keeps away from that steep rock the ground is safe.

"I saw a faint light through the trees and heard Julius Partridge's voice. 'I can't see it here, darling', he was saying. I moved forward and was just in time to see her give him a sharp thrust in the middle of the back, and heard him cry out and fall. McGinty was growling and by the time I got there, Elaine had come down from the high rock and was kneeling by the body. I heard her say, 'So you're dead, damn you', and she laughed. I could see his neck was broken and the torch still alight. It had rolled off. She had enough cunning not to try to touch it or put it out; it was still lit on the following morning."

"You didn't go down?" said Mary incredulously.

"No. He was dead, as she'd said; there was no doubt about it. I reflected that I had seen murder done, but it occurred to me that nobody would believe my unsupported word. I was also, I admit it, afraid; Elaine could have been violent with me also. I took McGinty away and we returned home. Next morning early I went out with him as I always did. By then it was safe to report the finding of the body in the hope that death would be assumed to have been an accident."

The old voice had grown high and quavering. "I behaved as a Christian, I believe," said Winifred Bellenden. "I did what I might for Elaine, breaking the news to her, knowing it was not news at all. I acted with deceit, I admit it. Had Julius merely been injured and in pain, I would have behaved very differently. It is like the Bible; King David mourned his child while it lived and was sick, but when it died he put off his mourning. Death allows no return. Husband and wife are both dead now; one wonders if they have met, and if so what they have found to say to one another. We ourselves will know such things in time."

Everyone reflected that for her it would not be long. "I saw McGinty's death as retribution," continued the old lady. "I had sinned, like King David, and like him had to lose the thing I loved. God disposes, in the end."

"You didn't let him dispose earlier on," said Mary Reston. "All that would have happened to Elaine would have been that they put her in an institution for diminished responsibility. I'm told they are very comfortable, those places: three square meals a day and television."

"You're hard," said Lady Bellenden. "You don't understand. Elaine was like a lost child. After that she stopped eating, and when I found that out I used to take her meals every day to see that she fed herself. I think I began to believe, with her, that Julius had really fallen over the rock. Everyone was shocked by the death, and Elaine suffered her own punishment, left alone up here."

"But with the keys to the drinks cupboard," said Mary savagely. She had grown more aggressive as the evening wore on; she sat bolt upright now, her eyes blazing, her strong hands clenched.

"And the account at the grocer's," put in Haven. He went and sat beside Mary, as if to comfort her. Oldham began to move his head restlessly, like an angry bull.

"Blast the lot of you," he said, "you've got no charity. Now what do we do? Do we tell the police about this second murder or do we leave it out, like last time?"

"The mills of God," said Hedley, speaking for almost the first time.

"I say we should keep quiet," said Haven. "Good riddance to bad rubbish. The woman was evil. Whoever had killed her it would have been a public service."

"You are all of you so heartless," said Winifred Bellenden.

Into the silence the telephone shrilled. Tom excused himself and got up to answer. He listened for a moment, made one or two enquiries, then replaced the receiver and turned to his guests. He was rather pale.

"That was Inspector Stonor," he said. "Our decision has been taken from us. Beale has been found dead, shot through the head with his own rifle. He left a note for his wife and one for the police, admitting to the murder of Elaine Partridge. So it's safe now, Mary, to incinerate the scarf."

"Don't touch it, Mary," muttered the Commander. "You keep out of this."

"I don't mind," said Mary. "I'll burn it up, filter the ashes and use them in a glaze. It might turn up something new, and they won't trace it in a hundred years."

"I think you are a most callous young woman," said Lady Bellenden. She had recovered her poise and was wiping her eyes with a handkerchief. "It sounds exactly like a medieval vengeance."

"Give it to me," growled Hedley. "I'll put it in the compost heap. Wool fibres break down to give a good fertiliser. It will give me great satisfaction to grow an orchid from it in two or three years' time."

"I think," said the Commander, "that now Beale is dead we should hand it to the police and say exactly what happened, which is that Brackenbury found it while he was diggin'. That'll settle the matter; they can't ask Beale any questions now, and they've got enough to do without askin' us."

"That lets you out," said Tom sweetly. "Very well, I'll hand it to Sergeant Lake as lost property tomorrow morning. And now, I suppose nobody feels like a spot of supper?"

* * *

Tom Brackenbury walked into the police station next day, a bulky envelope in his hand. He identified it to the constable, who took everything down, and said he would give it to the sergeant when Lake came in.

"When will that be? The whole village could go on fire and they wouldn't know about it till next time they call."

"We're short-handed, sir. And it isn't an urgent matter, or I'd telephone."

As it happened, the inspector and Lake both got out of the police car and were approaching the station door as Tom came out. He told them about finding a blue scarf. Stonor's pebble-grey eyes surveyed him.

"If that had been handed straight in it could have saved Beale's life. We could have had enough evidence then to arrest him provided the blood group was right."

"For a lifetime in prison?"

"It's our duty. There might have been mitigating circumstances. They'd take those into account."

He gave Brackenbury a very old-fashioned look indeed. "I hear," he said, "that you're buying the Partridge house?"

"That grapevine of yours works ahead of a computer. I'd only just decided to make an offer if they want to sell. It's for weekends now, possible retirement when I leave my job, if I ever do leave it."

"So I suppose all this will be reported in your column. The public must have its joke against the police."

"I promised you at the beginning that all this, as you call it, will remain confidential. It's given me an insight into a certain stratum of humanity and reawakened my curiosity, that's all. I think I'll go back to the office at the beginning of the week; my fingers itch to get at a typewriter again."

"But not about us."

"Not about you." The rather chilly eyes were still on him. Tom strapped himself into the car and started the engine. The inspector grinned suddenly.

"I was rather hoping you'd forget to use that belt and then we could at least have brought you in for something," he said amiably. "It would have been a pleasure to nail you."

"How's Slim Joe?"

"With his friends in Eire. They're welcome to him, although we'll probably hear of him again. A pity things don't work out in black and white. I'd rather by far it had been him than the other."

Sergeant Lake said, "I'm glad to hear you're buying the cottage, Mr Brackenbury. It does no good to have a house lying empty where there's been a murder. People avoid it; they'll be pleased to see you here."

"Ghosts don't bother me as a rule," said Tom. He raised a hand to them and set off down the branch road that would soon get him to the London motorway. He would arrive in the middle of the rush hour, but traffic was difficult to avoid at any time. An appetite had grown in him to get down to work, although he would keep his promise to the police; he hadn't, by and large, given them much of a helping hand. He compared himself with the wreck of a man who had driven north a few days ago. The past was past, and there was still the future. He wondered if Mary Reston would ever feel inclined to marry any man but Basil Oldham. It would be pleasant, in a way, to outmanoeuvre the Wing Commander; but there was no hurry about that, none at all. Or perhaps Dora? That might be more comfortable.

Interim

In plain fact it took a remarkably long time for Tom Brackenbury of *The Perceiver* to be accepted as a husband once again, despite his pleas. The delay gnawed at his vanity somewhat less than it might have done had he not been sent on frequent foreign assignments over the next few years, by his editor, which made the time seem shorter than it was. Once at Brennan – he visited the cottage as a rule towards the end of the week, after the main editions were out – he was surprised to see the Commander make his way in across the small garden. "Good evening, Oldham," Tom called, not too cordially; he was tired after the drive, and wanted a drink alone. Oldham registered surprise, but likewise no pleasure.

"Is nice little Dora about?" he asked. "I was passin'."

"Mrs Beale," said Tom with a shade of hauteur, "comes to clean on Tuesday and Fridays. She is seldom here when I am." Dora had told him the village might talk.

"Ha. Better come back when you ain't. Anythin' doin' in London?"

"The usual." It was a platitude, as the question had been. He resented the reference to Dora, but after all she wasn't yet his property. He turned away and went inside, seeing the blind man make his way up to Mary Reston's. Everyone knew what he went there for. The village in that instance, had given up talking long ago.

Tom had already, by then, asked Dora to marry him, and she had refused, gently but firmly, standing with her feet primly together and flushing slightly.

"Oh, Mr Brackenbury, it wouldn't be respectful."

"Then let's be disrespectful, and try calling me Tom."

"I meant disrespect to Jerry's memory. He hasn't been dead a year." Her blue eyes filled with tears, and he remembered that in Brennan's antiquated circles they kept to the good old year of mourning before anything more could happen. He apologised and said he hoped she would feel able to continue to come to the cottage; nobody else, he added, would keep it as clean.

"Oh, I'm pleased to, Mr – Tom. I like being up here by myself, with no nosy neighbours. In Brennan they know everything."

Mr Tom was better than nothing, at least for the time being; he must accustom her gradually to more exotic entitlements. He left the house and went for a walk, not going anywhere in particular, and thinking how he must be more careful, more tactful, with Dora. There were things to bridge between them that mustn't hurt her; she had been hurt enough, but he looked forward to being able to present her as an apt little hostess in London. It would be pleasant to come home to. He would persuade her in time. She knew already that he didn't want children; something or other had been said the other day, apropos of somebody else's, when he was last up.

He walked on, and realised that he was passing Mary's studio without calling in. As he went by, he heard a sound of hopeless and ugly sobbing, a woman's. He turned back.

"Mary."

She was lying on the floor, with beyond her an open kiln filled with greenware. He knew already as much as she'd told him, that the small electric kiln was for firing and the new gas kiln, which ran on bottled gas, for glazing; it turned out surprising colours like his peacock vase, and was enormous. He stared, horrified, past its looming bulk to where Mary's face, swollen and disfigured, was twisted round, her red-rimmed eyes regarding him with enmity. Her voice when she spoke was rough with tears.

"Get out. Leave me alone. I thought you were Basil."

He left, as she had asked it; there was nothing he could do for her. Oldham wasn't worth it; he had been brave, like others, in the Fleet Air Arm, but otherwise was a callous and self-centred personage, spoilt with money. 'I don't need a nurse', he had once said openly about Mary. That happened with maimed people; offered love, they took it out on the lover. *If you love me, there's something wrong with you.* He'd heard it often. In addition to that, being told that his mistress was dumpy and plain, Oldham would feel foolish; and, in turn, would have spared Mary nothing. 'You couldn't get a man who could see you, could you?' Something like that. He himself must be careful, with Dora; already he'd said a schoolmasterish thing about knives and forks. *You're turning into a pain in the neck, Brack.* He could hear his editor's voice.

On return to the cottage, Dora had left a note. *Your editor rang. He wants you to get in touch about a foreign job.*

Well, there it was. He would go, and then return, perhaps mellowed a trifle. He was sorry not to do more for Mary.

* * *

A faint echo of Elaine Partridge reached Tom on his travels. The foreign job, as Dora had called his assignment, was to Australia to investigate the financial state of the wool farmers whose goods were rotting in warehouses in Fremantle since the EEC. Tom's editor, known throughout the industry as 'A.B.', was a passionate anti-European, maintaining that the EEC was the biggest con trick since the Tudors. "The man in the street doesn't like it, but he wasn't asked. It's all big business," and A.B. named a certain politician who had done very well out of the whole thing, adding nostalgically that in point of fact there had been very little wrong with the British Empire in the first place. Tom, who sometimes wondered why his chief got the sizeable sales he did, refrained from argument and caught the first available flight to Perth, Western Australia. Having viewed the sad, stuffed and silent warehouses beside the great port nearby, he booked a place on the long silver snake of a train winding across the subcontinent to Sydney; there had been a cancellation and while he was here, he wanted to see the ghost towns from the gold rushes last century. A.B. could use a piece about those as well, in his Sunday supplement.

Tom visited the lost glitter of the abandoned towns, rejoined the train and, over breakfast, listened to the laconic drawl of Australian men and the everlasting domestic chatter of the women. At the next stop a fat man in spectacles got in. He was American, as it turned out. After a few moments' survey of Brackenbury he said, "Say, didn't you report on that Partridge case some while back? The Partridge doll was at school with my sister in England. Her name was Purkiss-Thomson then, does that tell you anythin'?"

"It tells me what her maiden name was. I hadn't found out."

"Well, that name says somethin', I can tell you. My sister didn't like that school, came home to Oz after two years, but there were worse things than Elaine Purkiss-Thomson then. It makes you wonder why they end on the bottle."

Tom asked politely why they lived in Australia rather than the States.

"Oh, we live in Sydney. Nowhere like it. As I was sayin', this woman's mother married a poor guy named Thomson, and made him add on Purkiss because she said it showed descent from Imperial Rome."

"That seems going a bit far back."

"You can say that again, but this woman talked big." The American began to clean his teeth of shreds of meat using a small silver toothpick. "My sister – she's married in Darwin with four kids, and writes often – said when she saw the papers that this woman Purkiss-Thomson, Elaine's mother, used to talk about Marcus Porcius Cato the Censor and how he never touched a drop of anythin' and they were descendants. Maybe the girl heard so much about her ancestor she took against water altogether. There's no sayin' what causes it." He himself turned out to be an accountant, married to a lady he called Honeybee.

Tom's correcting apparatus was busy; Cato the Censor had been long before the emperors. A mother with faulty knowledge who talked big, perhaps gave her daughter false notions of what was what, made the young Elaine in the end pretentious, a liar; maybe. Nobody now would ever know. Tom heard the American drone on about something else and not for the first time, remembered his own photograph shown by custom at the top of his column. It was difficult not to be recognised. However, he had learned a little by the conversation, not that it would matter to Elaine Partridge where she was now.

He watched kangaroos, across the entire dull puddled breadth of the Nullarbor, then towards Sydney, just as the low brush started, a pair of emus waggling their immense backsides and scampering off into the shallow growth. There didn't seem much life; the sheep farmers had meted out brutal treatment to the kangaroos as pests for generations. Tom recalled the full-blood aboriginal he had met in Perth, unusually so far from base; innocent and friendly, with the coloured threads of his tribe wound round his head above a white Benedictine mission habit. He closed his eyes now to silence the American, and thought of the Pope's recent message to the aborigines and its hope that in time, things would be again as they had been; the soft-footed kangaroos permitted the vegetation to grow, while sheep destroyed it. *We brought rabbits, sheep, cats, half-bloods and trouble*. Maybe the Dream Time should return.

In the end, he faxed an article of that sort to A.B. The man could fire him if he liked; he, Brackenbury, could always make a living. However a fax came back:

'SALES MARKEDLY INCREASED. CONGRATULATIONS. EXACTLY THE RIGHT LINE. RETURN SOON. OTHER ASSIGNMENT PENDING. A.B.'

Tom would have preferred a few days' relaxation near Dora. He wanted increasingly to find himself in bed with her. He told himself sexual deprivation was what was the matter with him; if only Dora would have mercy, he would again be a pleasant and normal individual without obsessions, fit to know. Dora, Dora . . .

* * *

On his return, Tom was instructed to wage war on the declining use of English, and as a result found himself becoming mildly professorial, correcting juniors in the office till they ducked and ran when they saw him come in. At the end of three months of writing the series A.B. said to him, "Look, Brack, old boy, you'll have to watch it. You're turning into a bloody pedant. Think of something else."

The something else was Dora, who other? With an unexpected joy he finally heard her accept his proposal six months after his first attempt. It was as a result of that, that Tom Brackenbury became again involved with the British police when he met them in the course of his second honeymoon. The case in question was so bizarre that it could hardly have been foreseen that the events tied up with former ones at Bellenden. Subsequently, these were once more stirred up in his memory, and when at last old age overtook him, Tom expected that the two would long since have run into one in his recollection. Otherwise, they were quite dissimilar.

Part Two

Five

Tom and Dora, since yesterday his second wife, were driving north. With Dora seated beside him in the car in a state of interested speculation and wearing a becoming scoop-necked dress he had bought her the day before, Tom was able to reflect on recent events, the traffic being by this time minimal.

He recalled with tolerant amusement his editor's outrage at a request for time off for a week's honeymoon at the peak season, even with the offer thrown in of covering the bicentenary games at Insshe. A.B. had brushed this red herring aside as editors will.

"Damn it, Brack, you didn't have to *marry* the woman. She's been up with you at your cottage at that place – Brennan, isn't it? – for years now. I want you to go out to Pakistan to report on the nuclear crisis."

"It's too hot in July, and there's always a crisis." He did not add that there was also always a peak season. "Send George," he suggested. George was an up-and-coming bright boy with the hide of a Tamworth Twin who would feel neither a rise nor a fall in temperature, the stock market or any other matter provided he got front page headlines. At this moment, for many reasons, Tom did not want to leave Dora by herself. He put it in firm tones to A.B. that their lives at the cottage had resembled driven snow, that Dora herself was still, despite fifteen years of childless marriage and the sobering experiences that had ended it, prim, highly moral and still quite naive, which naturally increased lewd appetites in roving newspapermen.

A.B. – his full name was increasingly famous – had stared balefully into his computer, as usual resembling an angry Aberdeen Angus although his inner nature was that of a dove and at home, his own wife mastered him without difficulty. "If you aren't damned careful," he growled, "George will get your job. I remember that last Brennan double murder and suicide case. It must be the only thing that's ever happened there till now. Take yourself off to Insshe or to hell, take a week, cool off, and if anything crops up north of the so-called border I expect you to cover it." He added congratulations.

Tom did not expect anything to crop up in particular. The initial furore concerning Insshe had, after all, happened two hundred years ago and should now, even in the remote Scottish Highlands, have been allowed to subside more or less in the collective memory. It was in any case a better place to take the shy, uncertain and homeloving Dora than, for instance, Spain in the fiesta. At present she was still, or had been till last night, in the state of shock which must eventually have induced her to marry him at all after several turned-down proposals.

He had come upon her last week perched primly, with a small suitcase, her dark curls ruffled, in the porter's alcove in the block of grimy flats where Tom for the moment had his being, although he had already found a pleasant light apartment in Docklands and would move in when the carpets were down. If they had been, Dora might not have found him, or he her. That might well have been disastrous. He had just returned from work in *The Perceiver*'s offices, and observed at once that although Dora appeared calm – he had never known her to be flustered, no matter what befell – her speedwell-blue eyes were wide with distress and her pretty colour had gone. It was not till next day that news was faxed through about the body in the kiln. Meantime he asked no questions till he got Dora upstairs, then poured two stiff whiskies, one for her and another for himself.

"I shouldn't be taking spirits," said Dora. However, she sipped the stuff almost absently, the operation bringing back a little of the colour into her cheeks. When she smiled these had two deep dimples, one of the things that had attracted him, and still did. However, she was not smiling now.

"I rang from Penarch, but there was only that answerphone," she said. "I couldn't stay in Brennan, with all the talk."

"What were they talking about?" She then told him about the postman's gruesome discovery, Tom was shocked: he had known Mary Reston and at one time had half considered marrying her. It was difficult to think of her as dead, no longer efficient, no longer wedging and throwing and moulding clay. He wondered why the talk should have affected Dora, but Brennan always talked. Everybody knew everyone else's business, or thought they did; and the outlook there in general was still what it might have been elsewhere before the Second World War, or even the First. The last major excitement in those parts had been the nine days' wonder of the suicide of Dora's husband, the late Jeremiah Beale. Everybody had sat in judgment about the whole thing, and Dora had suffered then. Tom put his arm round her now.

"What happened?" he said. "What made her do it? Was it Oldham?" Mary Reston had been known to be doggedly in love with the blinded ex-Fleet Air Arm officer who lived in his secluded house beyond the end of the village. She had been his mistress, according to Brennan; but the old Commander hadn't married her. Tom recalled Mary's stocky body, square hands with rims of dried clay forever beneath the fingernails, and crew-cut to keep her hair out of the way. The late Elaine Partridge, who not surprisingly had got herself murdered later on, had been careful to inform the blind man that Mary was physically unattractive. That hadn't helped matters.

At any rate, even Brennan had long ceased to speculate about the relations between himself and Dora, who after Jerry Beale's death came up to clean, and to cook as well when he stayed there, at the cottage which Tom had bought for a small sum after the murders; other offers, as usual in such circumstances, being sparse. Mary Reston's studio had been not far off, among the small group of houses on the postman's last round.

"It was my fault," said Dora. He became aware that she was trembling. "The Commander's housekeeper, that old woman who was with him for years, died, and he asked me to come and keep his house. I said I couldn't all the time, because I was doing yours, but that I'd help out till he'd found somebody. He had to be particular, being blind. He said if I'd come and stay, his man would drive me back and forth to your place whenever I liked. I said it was all right, I'd drive myself. I was packing a few things at the cottage – you know I keep some there – when Miss Reston appeared. She'd been crying and she looked ugly. She put both hands round my throat and said if I went down to the Commander, she'd strangle me. 'I have strong hands, as you know,' she said. 'Tell him you can't go'.

"Well, I wasn't going to give in, but it shook me a bit. I went round to Mr Hedley's house for a cuppa with his housekeeper, Mrs Houston, you know her, and felt better. That must have been how it got back to the Commander that Miss Reston had threatened me. He hears everything in the end. When I got down there, I heard him on the telephone. He was shouting at Miss Reston and telling her not to come back. 'I wouldn't take on a bitch like you for life for all the tea in China,' he was saying, in that icy voice he has, you know, and then I heard him say he'd cane her bottom for her if she ever came down again, and that would be all that would happen to it. He put the receiver down then because he saw me coming, and greeted me as if I was the Queen. I got on with cleaning the carpets. I was frightened of Miss Reston for a bit, and didn't go up to your cottage. Then I heard she must have gone away, because nobody had seen her. I went back up to clean round, and Bill – he's a nice chap, the new postman – said she hadn't had her letters forwarded, because they were lying behind the glass door. I said it was odd, because she never went away as a rule, because of the Commander, everybody knew that. In the end they broke open the door and went in and there was still a smell of gas, with all the doors and windows closed. They found her inside the closed kiln, and she'd been dead for ages." Dora wiped her eyes. "Poor thing. I felt awful. If a window had been left open they mightn't have known even then, because bottle gas comes to an end. They might still have thought she'd gone away."

She was shaking. Tom kissed her and then behaved as he ought; he rang the Penarch police – there was still no round-the-clock manning of the station at Brennan – told them where Dora was, was assured she wasn't involved or needed for questioning, and then went back to her.

"Now," he said firmly, "what else happened, Dora? Between the time she must have shut herself in the kiln, I mean, and now. You were at the Commander's meantime. Why did you leave and come here? I don't mean I'm not delighted to see you. Why didn't you just go to your own little house?" She had kept on, since Beale's death, the council house in which they had lived together in the village, but had had to work since then to pay the rent. Basil Oldham's part-time job should have suited her in that way, although he was happy that it hadn't; he himself could persuade her, he knew, this time, to marry him. She wouldn't have come otherwise.

Dora had flushed a little. "He – he – I think he thought he'd get me to do what Miss Reston used to for him. You know what I mean. I wasn't going to, and I told him so. I – I packed a suitcase and drove to the station, and here I am. They were saying in Brennan that it was my fault she'd killed herself. In a way, I suppose it was."

She then burst into tears, destroying any logic that might have pertained to the situation. Brackenbury kissed and comforted her, then proposed for the sixth time. "What's happened to your car?" he asked, in the middle of everything.

"It's still there, at the station. I didn't think. They'll see it and talk."

"Let them," said Tom. He made arrangements for her to stay meantime at a quiet nearby hotel, went out, and arranged for his second marriage.

The whole thing suited him admirably, because for a long time now he had been edgy, wanting Dora. It had grown upon him that she was desirable, then very desirable, then that he could not do without her, then that he probably had to. Now, here she was; and though he was sorry about poor Mary Reston, sorrow was not his prevailing emotion. Mary had no doubt assumed Basil Oldham would marry her when the old housekeeper died, and he hadn't. Tom bought flowers and remembered the small vase with its reduction glaze, in peacock colours, that Mary had given him when he bought the Brennan cottage.

Then he forgot about her. Dora was a dear little thing, he wanted to go to bed with her, and although he would never forget his wife Sheila, dead now four years, a man had physical needs. Also, he respected Dora's shrewd common sense, which only seemed to have deserted her on this one occasion; and she was a meticulous housewife and a good plain cook. He had, in fact, been worried lest the nice chap Bill got in first, or some other; but no doubt Dora would have said the same to all comers at Brennan, namely that she couldn't forget poor Jerry's death. Well, he himself couldn't forget Sheila's, killed as she had been in the Harrods bombing. He resolved, to exorcise the horror still in his mind, to take Dora shopping there to buy the wedding dress.

She had demurred, after being made aware for the first time of the glories of Harrods. "You shouldn't be marrying anyone like me," she said solemnly. He laughed.

"Why not?"

"I've said it often. I'm not your class. Take me to M&S." Tom refused.

"Stop talking rubbish, Dora darling. There's no such thing as class any more, and anyway we're all descended from Adam. We can enjoy the good things of life in what is a rapidly approaching middle-age for both of us."

"I'm thirty-eight," said Dora.

"And I'm forty-seven. If you persist in feeling inferior we can be like a Victorian couple and I will beat you."

After last night, he thought, their relationship would come more easily. He turned off the motorway now with confidence. There were certain items of marital finesse Beale, decent man, hadn't known about. Dora's innocent and entranced acceptance of them had added to the physical satisfaction Tom had known he would feel in any case. Now, here they were on the A9, and still happily married.

Six

Whilst driving further north, Tom took leisure to reflect on existing circumstances. In his way, he felt like Pygmalion, or perhaps Professor Higgins. There was no doubt that, now his ambition had been achieved, he would have to do a little unobtrusive educating of Dora. It must of course be done without hurting her feelings. Cinderella, after marrying her prince – not that there was any comparison – must have had to adjust. Certainly Dora would do a certain amount for herself, but he must keep an eye and put in a tactful word now and again, though not too often.

This honeymoon in the north was precisely what was needed to transform Dora gently and lovingly from one milieu to another. Up there they would still be Brennanish in their notions, though less uncharitable and certainly more aristocratic. Dora would be able to witness, and copy, what at the moment she called posh manners. Tom told himself with some complacency that after a week, she would have picked up a good deal of what needed picking and which hitherto had not come her way. In the new flat in Docklands she wouldn't have to clean carpets, there was service. She—

"This is the killer road, you said," remarked Dora as he sped on. "Be careful."

"I'm always careful."

Dora blushed. She wouldn't have said so last night, though he'd long ago made it clear he didn't want children. That was for her sake, he said. At her age, and last time, with the Partridge business, she'd had the stillbirth later on after Mrs P. made her drag the deep freeze across the floor, and before that, at the beginning with Jerry, a miscarriage – well, there it was, and a lot of people besides poor Jerry had wanted to kill Mrs P. To be honest, it was difficult to remember Jerry now she was married to Tom. She glanced shyly at his craggy profile. He wasn't what you would call handsome, though rangy and long in the leg, and with thick hair of a nondescript colour, not going bald like Jerry without his cap. Tom's eyes were shrewd, missing nothing. Dora felt slight discomfort, but supposed that was why he made a good reporter. The police often called him in. That was, after all, how she'd met him; he'd been on a painting holiday at Brennan, but never got the painting finished.

It was sad about his first wife. Sheila, that was her name, had been lovely, with silver-fair hair. Dora had often polished the frame of the exquisite profile which still sat on Tom's dressing table. Sheila had been clever, an architect. It made Dora wonder why, after the dreadful bombing, he'd fancied a person like herself; it was like marrying a sparrow after a bird of paradise. She switched her thoughts to how odd it was of Tom to go to Harrods to buy her wedding dress; it was the last store she'd have chosen, in his place. He admitted it was the first time he'd been back there. They'd both stared at the avenue of teddy bears leading to the downstairs bank. That was the kind of thing Tom was used to and she wasn't. She must try to live up to it.

They saw a roadside café approaching. "Let's stop and have something to eat," said Tom.

They had tomato sandwiches and coffee and cakes, the last fresh and home-baked. Dora knew she could have done as well, but Tom told her Scotland was a famous place for cakes. "They used to call it the Land of Cakes," he said. "When I was a boy they had tea rooms with piled cake stands on the tables, but not any more."

"How did they keep an eye on who took what?" asked Dora.

"I didn't ask. I used to be sent up to visit a great-aunt, and she had an aspidistra. She used to take it on train journeys because she felt lonely without it. She was considered a bit odd by then, because it was after the days when if you didn't have one, you weren't considered respectable. By now, they're a status symbol."

"We'd better get one for Docklands then," said Dora, who was beginning to be amused by Tom's eccentricities.

Tom paid the bill, and they continued north-west. The country had grown darker and more mountainous, with peaks incredibly high, and long sad glens. Dora was used to the sight of Bigod Peak towering over Brennan, but Bigod would be lost here. She thought the whole place a bit creepy, but didn't say so. However, Tom seemed to know what she was thinking, in the uncanny way he had. He turned to smile.

"It's a bit forbidding," he said. "Presently we come to level country again."

"Well, I expect it brings the tourists," said Dora.

After some time they turned off the trunk road to a branch one, then on to where a hidden clachan lay at last in its green hollow. Passing through there was nothing much to notice except the church, the manse and some cottages, and a former school, which like many such had now become a private house but would never look quite like anything except what it had once been. There were geraniums in tubs cheering up the bleak irredeemable space of the former playground. "I'll get out to ask where the sign for Inshtochradh is," said Tom. He had a map, but there were several narrow roads like rivulets and nothing to say where any of them went.

He made towards the newsagent and grocer combined, and met a woman coming out with her shopping bag full. She gave him the direction, repeating the name slowly; it rhymed with Dora. As they drove off she stared after them as though his query had been slightly improper. He explained to Dora what the name meant.

"It's the dower house for Great House of Insshe, which has been closed except to tourists since the last laird died eight or nine years ago now. His daughter and her husband run Inshtochradh as a private hotel."

"Like Bellenden," Dora said, remembering the death not long ago of the last owner of the big house beyond the cottage. Old Lady Bellenden had never recovered from losing her dog, he was all she'd had left. "Do they have any children?" Dora asked idly.

"I have never enquired and I don't care particularly, except that if there are they will be noisy. There must be some reason why a late booking was available for the games. Perhaps few people trouble to find it."

"Perhaps they can't pronounce it."

"Remember it rhymes with your name. These Gaelic spellings often look more difficult than the word sounds. I believe it means Dowry of Insshe. There was an older house on the site, but they pulled it down, of course, and built something much uglier and more grandiose in mid-Victorian times. At least there's plumbing."

"Nobody has the money to keep up these big houses any more," said Dora. "When Lady Bellenden died her house was on the market for quite a long time, then a hotel chain bought it, as you know. The trouble with that is the late night drinkers. I used to hear them going home past the cottage if I stayed overnight, revving up their cars and blaring the radios."

"Well, here's the sign at last," said Tom. It wasn't very professional, perhaps deliberately not so: painted white by hand on a black board as much as to say that everything beyond was individually attended to. Moreover, the handmade ethic, if that was what it was, included a badly potholed drive which was death on axles. Tom drove slowly, evading the holes where he might. They passed a dilapidated lodge in which nobody lived; half the slates were off the roof. "I hope the hotel's a bit brighter," said Dora. "Goodness, it's bumpy. They can't have enough money to mend the road."

"Either that or they have so much they don't care if nobody comes up it. What they charge for two guests for the time we're staying here would take them to the South of France for the winter. Probably they go there anyway and close down till the season."

"Why did you choose it?" asked Dora, who found it creepy, like the mountains they'd passed.

"Partly because I would be left in peace with you, but also

because I'm a snob and liked the subtly conveyed atmosphere. The Insshe title lured me."

"You can't be a snob or you wouldn't have married me."

"Dora, you sound like a record that's got stuck. Look, here's a Humber Pullman. I didn't think they still existed outside car museums."

The stately equipage, approaching slowly because of the lamentable road, looked as if it ought to be chauffeur-driven but was not. A long-nosed young woman with an unhappy face sat at the wheel, making no sign of recognition as Tom drew aside to let her pass.

"Might have said thanks. She didn't look too pleased with life, whoever she thought she was," remarked Dora. Waspish as the remark sounded, it was made in her soft voice, which was one more thing Tom cherished about her. Mary Reston's had been harsh, almost a man's. Poor Mary; she would never speak again. He supposed the funeral was over. There could have been no doubt about the verdict.

There was time to think of all that again, as the drive was long and Dora's company restful. Tom was still angry with Basil Oldham for his arrogance, his refusal to think of Mary as anything but a physical convenience, his driving her at last to despair and death instead of continuing happily in her craft. She'd been a fine potter and good sculptor. Also, Oldham had evidently had the impertinence to think that Dora – *Dora*, the soul of rather too much respectability for too long – would let him knock her over like a ninepin. Instead, she had got on the train to London and himself.

He turned now and smiled at her, his dear little new acquisition, his Galatea, or, more probably, his Eliza Higgins. After dinner they'd go to bed again. Meantime the road wound fearfully, a rocky snail-trail, and there was still no sign of the house. "I think that may, judging from the nose – which is a sure sign of overbreeding – have been Lady Charlotte Norton-Insshe, hereditary laird of Insshe and Great House and its Palladian attractions and its artwork. If so, she is the wife of the proprietor, whose name was formerly Norton. That he is now Norton-Insshe, not the other way round, tells one a certain amount."

"I don't know what you're talking about," said Dora.

Tom did not answer. He remembered the bleak announcement of the engagement in *The Times*, no pictures, and the wedding held in private. Shortly thereafter, the bride's father, the late peer and diplomat, had died.

"She married big money," Tom replied after delay, "or at least one supposes so. She herself is the last of the cadet line. The main line perished at Culloden, which up here is like yesterday."

"Well, she didn't look as if she enjoys life much."

"The burdens of the one-time great must begin to weigh them down. She was probably on the way to Great House to dust round ready for tomorrow and then hoover up the silver dust from baroque tapestry chairs, or something. I am told the public leave an incredible amount simply by filing past behind guide-ropes."

"Can we go and see it?" Dora liked houses.

"Certainly you shall see it, and pick on every fault in the housekeeping and run your fingers along the red ropes to make sure they're free of dust," he said. Dora didn't know whether he was serious or not, and hoped she wasn't like that all the time. She asked again about the prospect of children at the hotel. She heard him sigh.

"Even a newspaper reporter can't remember everything in the news, darling, or he'd go mad," he replied. "I think I recall now there was a son, and something happened." He remembered perfectly well, but wasn't going to mention dead children to Dora. The less said on the whole subject the better; in any case it was unlikely that, even though she wanted a baby, at her age, and with her medical history, Dora would conceive again.

Meantime, here at last was the hotel – grey and incomparably ugly, rearing at the end of the trees which from the beginning had darkened the lunatic drive. There were pepper-pot towers at each corner of the regrettable edifice. Outside, in a bleak gravelled car park – there seemed to be no garden unless it was located round the back – stood a small modest Morris and an odd vehicle lacking number-plates. Tom stared at it with passing interest, but this was at once deflected by the appearance of the proprietor.

He stood on the steps, a figure incredible in its lack of authenticity. Am Insheach, as he evidently called himself without any specific right to do so, introduced himself with beaming professionalism as their host. He spoke in a voice which was intended to convey the rhythmic intonation of the Gael, but failed to do so. He was thick-set, possibly nearing fifty, and wore full rig in the manner of a clan chief: kilt, sporran with a glass-eyed beaver's face and fur tassels; calf-high socks in which reposed the customary black knife or *sgian dubh*, its silver-plated top giving away the whole thing immediately, as real ones are plain. The socks had red tabs. When out of doors Am Insheach undoubtedly wore a round bonnet or, on formal occasions, one with an eagle's feather. As things were, the tartan was too bright to be other than recent, bringing to mind certain nightmares containing Balmoral. The man nevertheless had a sleazy charm, though the red face and coarse features were not enhanced, above a thick neck, by a pair of eyes like currants set in dough. They rested on Dora with appreciation. Tom decided Norton-Insshe ought to have been a grocer, and perhaps had.

"*Slainthe*. Welcome to Inshtochradh." The laird then lifted Dora's hand in a practised manner and set it to his lips, stating thereafter that their luggage would be brought upstairs for them by the porter once they had kindly signed the book. It turned out that the porter was himself. So, as they were to discover, was the cook.

They were shepherded into a large high-ceilinged hall with a roof-light above which pigeons evidently roosted. Such light as filtered through – there was enough – revealed walls studded copiously with the stuffed heads of slaughtered stags in their antlers. Over a tortured mahogany balustrade, leading upstairs, was draped certain evidence of clan identity in the form of several dozen yards of Insshe tartan. Despite the ancient nature of that clan itself, the tartan had not been thought separately necessary till the nineteenth century, and looked it. Again, the too-bright colours were spurious.

Tom could not resist protesting about the tartan. "I understood you shared one with the Clan Kay," he said wickedly. Nobody was quite certain who the Clan Kay had been, unlike the Clan Chattan, and he wanted to see if this man knew. The two clans had done battle long ago on the North Inch of Perth in the seated presence of a very old king of Scots. Tom had forgotten which side had won. The laird, at any rate, made a non-committal reply while Tom and Dora signed the book as designated. They were then shown personally up to what proved to be the west tower room, and were told it looked out on the river.

"You will have had your lunch?" enquired the laird hopefully. Tom replied with truth that they had eaten something. It had been back on the A9, but he had already decided that they would go out somewhere else to look for dinner. There would be plenty of less exalted hotels round the nearby loch into which the river emptied itself. It meant negotiating the fateful drive again, but it couldn't be helped. Disappointed, the laird made it clear that he cooked everything himself. The brochure had assured them of gourmet food, and it was possible; but Tom was adamant. "You must be coming down, then, before you go, and see the drawing room and all the rest. There are twenty different kinds of malt whisky in there." He added that they were very busy in the evenings. That explained, no doubt, how the hotel paid.

"I'm so glad he's gone," said Dora when the sounds beyond the door had died away. "It's a lovely room, though."

It was certainly very agreeably decorated throughout, in peach. There was a large four-poster, with draped peach curtains, occupying half the space. At least all of that could be looked forward to, thought Tom, experiencing lecherous stirrings now the drive was over. However, Dora had disappeared into the small triangular bathroom which opened off, and here there had already been glimpsed a peach-coloured lavatory and bath and peach-coloured bath gel and shampoo. The towels were thick, copious and, predictably, peach. Tom went to look out of the window at the view of the river. Money, he was thinking, had been spent on the dower-house hotel for those who cared to find out. The only thing lacking in the room was tea-making facilities. He would have liked a cup of tea, but no doubt shortage of space did not allow.

"It's a lovely loo," said Dora, coming out.

Tom didn't reply, his mind still on the curious set-up they'd entered. No doubt there were reasons for Lady Charlotte's unhappy face. It didn't seem a suitable marriage. The emptiness of the hotel might be accounted for similarly. This man would be disliked by the neighbours; in the Highlands there are few fools. The Games and the clan bicentenary would mean that all other hotels in the district were overflowing, but here he and Dora seemed to be the only guests.

"Will this be posh enough?" enquired Dora of the Harrods dress. Tom had decided that they would dine early, to avoid the crowd, at one of the new lochside hotels which they could see in the distance from their tower window. He replied that of course it was posh enough: in fact, Dora looked enchanting. Her figure, though plump as a small bird's, was neat, the scoop neckline stressing the curvaceous allure of her bosom. Her waist was trim and her legs short but shapely. She had a clear skin, the two deep dimples in both cheeks when she smiled, good teeth, and her little soft hands and white arms and neck pleased him greatly.

They went downstairs, to find the ubiquitous laird in attendance, evidently determined to show them round whether they liked it or not. He pressed a drink on them, which Tom refused somewhat curtly.

"No, thanks, I'm driving." The excuse was unwelcome as a rule, but now he was glad of it. He wanted to get Dora out of here; she declined a drink also. They were shown the famous drawing room, a miracle of gloom filled with chintz-covered sofas and, as Norton-Insshe had stated, numerous brands of malt whisky, snouts down. There was a bar counter.

"You will help yourselves when you are ready, and sign," said the bogus Highland voice, adding that the glasses were under the counter. Tom reflected that the price would, without question, be double that charged in most places, but there were some interesting brands; the fellow knew his business. Later, when they got back, he said, he might indulge. There was no need to sound ungracious, after all; Norton-Insshe was doing his best.

"My wife is at the Great House still, getting it ready for the bicentenary," confided Am Insheach. He indicated a portrait which hung over the fireplace, not knowing they had already glimpsed Lady Charlotte on the drive. The painting had been made some years ago, and showed what was hardly more than a girl, in a pale-blue dress with eyes of a still paler blue, and a nose like a heron's beak. Her hair was a dull colour, which might have been fair in childhood. The whole effect, whether the fault of the artist or not, was anaemic. It was a face that would be easily dominated, despite the long nose. Below and a little to one side, the wedding photograph itself was displayed on a side table. It showed Norton-Insshe slightly less heavy of flesh than he had by now become, though still not young enough for the bride. Lady Charlotte looked miserable even in her going-away hat. Perhaps she was merely one of those persons rarely known to smile.

The writing room had to be viewed, then the breakfast room. "I make the porridge myself from our own oats," announced the laird proudly. "All our vegetables are home-grown likewise, and the herbs." There was something appealing in the way he talked, almost as if he was baring his soul, and had one after all. There was no sign yet of any staff; no doubt they came in for a half-day and left early. At last Tom and Dora found out otherwise, being led out into the hall again and into a small side room which was a souvenir shop. At the sales table sat, incredibly, a Morningside spinster.

Even Tom, who saw most things in course of his work, had only set eyes on one of these once in youth, while visiting his great-aunt. They are now seldom to be met with, but used to be typical of their type and could be mistaken for no other. Tom registered, with the appreciation of one surveying a rare antique, the classic severe expression, the wartime roll of neatly bestowed grey hair, the metal-rimmed spectacles on their prudent chain, and, most of all, the diagnostic long narrow shoes with curly heels, almost as vintage as the Humber Pullman and, by now, as unobtainable. Tom wondered for how many years the good lady had polished them. This, of course, had been scrupulously done. She sat with her feet together, a genteel two-piece disguising her prescribed lack of bosom. She was made known to them as Miss Walshe.

"Miss Walshe will sell you souvenirs," stated the laird, his inference being gently obvious. The spinster sat quietly among tartan whatnots and caddy-spoons and mugs with the Insshe device, this last being a spring of rowan, and T-shirts displaying the same thing and anchored on display by teddy bears in mini-kilts.

"Many of these will be sold, of course, at the Games," remarked Miss Walshe drily, as if less anxious than her employer, which one supposed the laird was, to appear to sell anything too eagerly.

Tom and Dora escaped at last to the car. "That seemed a bit counter-productive, or was it disguised sales talk to make us covet everything and anything?" murmured Tom. Dora said she didn't know.

"She's like a retired schoolmistress, the way they used to be," she said. "Why are there teddy bears everywhere now?"

Tom said he didn't know that either. "That's probably her Morris," he said, looking across the gravel. The little car sat modestly waiting, late as it was. By now, there might not be a table to themselves for dinner. They climbed into the car and drove off. Dora was still thinking about Miss Walshe.

"How do you suppose she got the job?" she asked. "It doesn't seem her sort of – well, you'd expect her to be doing something else."

"And not up here. She was probably Lady Charlotte's old governess, and has turned souvenir-person rather than part with her charge." No doubt the faithful retainer drove herself, with careful precision, up the appalling path from the gate and back each day.

"There's that man again now, with his dog," said Dora. "He can't seem to leave us alone."

Their host came striding up a side path, wearing his predictable round bonnet and in company with a large deerhound. He called out, "*Slainthe.*" as might have been expected, and they waved and drove without further incident down to the gate and out.

"What a great big dog that was," said Dora. "I wonder where Miss Walshe lives? Perhaps it's in one of those houses in the village."

"The clachan." Tom smiled over the wheel. "Perhaps. But after that performance, I do not think we are going to get our dinner unless we drive fast."

He accelerated, once out on the flat road. "He didn't show us all of the house," said Dora. "There's the part they must live in, he and Lady Charlotte when she's at home."

"Well, it's private, no doubt," Tom answered, remembering the key in his pocket. The laird had pressed it on him at the last moment to unlock the door again if they were to come back late. There was no doubt that Norton-Insshe was trying to be helpful.

Seven

They found not too bad a dinner at the first hotel they tried, leaving the car parked among many others within view of the shimmering loch. The hotel called itself The Rowan Tree, doubtless in homage to the clan. They were shown to a table with a view of the long water, but after the first course the waitress came. Would they be minding if Colonel and Mrs McIntosh were to join them, as they were fery busy with the Games coming on and the hotel was full of folk?

"Of course not," said Tom, thinking how in England they wouldn't have been asked. A middle-aged couple arrived, the wife garrulous, the husband silent and wearing a kilt. Tom remembered that the Clan McIntosh was one of the few known components, with the Campbells, of the old Clan Kay. He threw this gambit into the talk, which was otherwise about Mrs McIntosh's opinions of the weather and its prospects for the Games.

"Yes, the Insshe Games are in fact the annual gathering of the Clan Kay," remarked the Colonel, speaking for the first time. He and Tom began to discuss the old, old battle of the North Inch, going into all its known techniques with caution. The ladies were of necessity silent. Dora ate what was by now her lemon soufflé in silence, glad Tom was enjoying himself but, also, relieved not to have to make polite talk with Mrs Mac. That lady she had already named thus and disliked slightly; too nosy, like Brennan, and with a voice everybody could hear. She leaned across the table now in mid-battle and asked where Tom and Dora were staying.

Dora managed to pronounce Inshtochradh. The Colonel's lady threw up her hands in metaphoric distaste while continuing to eat *poulet royale*.

"Nobody goes there," she grated. "The only customers they have go up at night to drink the whisky. They certainly have to be able to afford *that*." She eyed Tom as if he might be worth knowing at that rate. Dora didn't say the tower room was nice. She had sensed that with this variety of female, it was best to say as little as possible. Luckily Mrs Mac liked the sound of her own voice best.

"That's a dreadful man," she said. "They should never have allowed the marriage. It was for money, of course. He – N-I, as we call him – sold some hotel chain or other at a large profit. He ploughed that back into the Insshe estate, and no doubt it saved Great House from becoming one of these youth hostels. Charlotte—" Dora suspected that the too-casual use of the Christian name implied a better acquaintance than existed in reality "— Charlotte is very proud of her ancestral home, and of being the Lady of Insshe, so she puts up with him. He is a first-rate cook, I'm told. We ourselves have only been there on one occasion, haven't we, Tosh?"

"Surprised you remember it," growled her husband. He was dissecting out his chicken with a fork, and the battle was, for the time, over. Tom still wasn't sure who had won, and he gathered the Colonel didn't know either. There was a certain tension to be felt across the table, as if the pair had some matter they would rather not talk about. However Mrs Mac broke what silence there had been.

"Every year in life that man takes his place at the head of the procession," she said. "It's Charlotte's right, and he shouldn't. However, she is very shy, poor thing."

"Are there any children?" Dora asked, as she still wanted to know. Mrs Mac was providing some information at last.

"Not after poor little Ronnie. It is a mercy, perhaps, that things happened as they did. That type of child—"

"What happened?" Mrs Mac for once dropped her metallic voice a little.

"Why, of course you might not know," she said. "He was drowned last year, in the river."

"How horrible! How?" asked Dora. The river, she'd seen it

from the tower room window, looked quite narrow and small, though you never knew. Mrs Mac explained that Ronald had been a Down's syndrome case. "N-I was very much ashamed of it," she said. "Nevertheless he is proud of owning Charlotte; one can't call it any less. They say," and her voice dropped still further, "that he can't leave her alone. He won't give her more children, which is perhaps understandable, but—" The eyes rolled up expressively to her plucked eyebrows. She had a shallow face, perhaps pretty long ago.

"How old was the boy when he was drowned?" Dora asked. If the laird had been ashamed of his child, that was dreadful. She disliked him more than ever.

"Ronnie was eight," said Mrs Mac. "His father used to try to teach him to swim, and on fine days they would go down to the river. One day the child went too far by himself, and got into difficulties. The dog Diarmaidh tried to get to him, but it was too late. That's all we know." The voice sounded smug.

"Why didn't his father get to him? He must have been able to swim if he was teaching his son." Dora was becoming angry. Mrs Mac looked both bored and wary.

"We don't speak about it much," she said. "There it was, there were no witnesses, and it was generally acknowledged to be the best thing. Charlotte has never recovered from it; the little boy used to go up with her to Great House each day and stay with her and the dog while she saw to things there. It's a lovely house, full of art objects. You must go during the Games; one can't watch them for ever."

"Wait for the procession, though," put in the Colonel. "That's worth seein'."

"Who is Miss Walshe?" asked Dora, who had attained a certain mastery of the table. Tom watched her with some admiration. "She doesn't," continued Dora, "look right in that souvenir shop." She didn't know why she had asked, except that she wanted to get away from the thought of the child's drowning. Later, she would talk about it with Tom.

"Oh, she's the sort of old soul nothing has ever happened to," barked Mrs Mac. "She used to be Charlotte's governess. If you ask me, that's why Charlotte is so shy. It would have been better to send her to school, to mix with other young people. She has always been dominated by somebody; her father, the governess, and now that husband."

Dora noticed that no mother had been mentioned, but before she could start asking about that Tom turned to her and said they ought to be on their way. "We have a lunar landscape to negotiate," he said. However, nothing would stop the Colonel's lady from a last jangling chord out of tune.

"Lord Insshe, of course, was in India in the days of the Raj," she said. The Colonel broke in.

"That couldn't continue, Cis, as you know, because of the wife's behaviour. I see no reason to shield the memory of Sonia Insshe. For a diplomat to have to resign—" He shrugged, and turned to Tom as if to dismiss the subject. "I heard you say, Brackenbury, that you were stayin' at Inshtochradh. I don't want to put you off – you will get an excellent meal there – but it is not a place anyone cares to stay in longer than they have to. After tomorrow you will undoubtedly be able to find room in another hotel. Many of us leave, though not all, immediately after the Games and the AGM."

Dora saw a lot of the clan tartan come and go, muted from the Inshtochradh version, in the restaurant: the men in kilts, the women wearing scarves or even a ribbon pinned to their dresses. It was obviously an occasion. She dared to say so to the Colonel, as she hadn't spoken to him yet and it might look rude.

"It is a particularly memorable one this year, young lady," said he, having opened up somewhat with a penultimate brandy, also stimulated by the discussion of generally long-forgotten military tactics at the North Inch. This feller Brackenbury was knowledgeable; a pleasure to talk to an intelligent person. The Colonel did not look at his wife. He smiled suddenly, and lifted his glass.

"The whole thing's phoney, increasin'ly so with the years," he said. "The old clan have died out, except for Sawnie. The Games by now are a tourist gimmick fostered by the so-called laird. God, it makes you sick." His small bloodshot eyes gleamed with detestation, like a cornered wild boar. "The present Lady of Insshe and her late father, despite his peerage, were descended from the much resented fourteenth laird, who was an Englishman."

"Oh, Tosh, you need a black coffee," said the Colonel's lady. Her husband thumped the table.

"Dammit, there's a livin' heir," he bellowed. "His forefathers were out with the Prince, and after Culloden took to the heather, and their descent became tinkers. There exists a character you will undoubtedly see tomorrow, taking the ticket money at the gate. He's honest, poor old Sawnie, but not too bright in the wits. The estate and title went, under the Hanoverian Government, to their own man, who married the grand-niece who was left after proscription was at an end around the seventies. The present line descends from that marriage."

"So Lady Charlotte still has her drop of Insshe blood?" said Tom.

"Indeed, and is very proud of it. I think that is why she tolerates the marriage. There was very little money left after the old lord's death – he took to drink, I remember, not surprisin' – and this man has enough of it, as you've already heard, to turn Insshe into a payin' concern. He hasn't quite got as far as the fourteenth laird, who brought in so many unpopular measures it's a wonder he died in his bed, but this one manages the estate and the farms, and the hotel for what it's worth, and of course masterminds the Games sellin' souvenirs and whisky. That'll bring in plenty tomorrow, I expect; they come from the States and all over."

"What is it a bicentenary of?" asked Dora.

"It is exactly two hundred years since the fourteenth laird built the Great House on the old foundations," replied the Colonel solemnly. "I could tell you a thing or two about him that ain't pleasant, but I won't. If you care to, you can go up when they lay a wreath in front of his statue up on the hill as part of the jollifications. It's got an inscription round the base sayin' what good he did and how he was a father to his people. He didn't do any good at all, rather the reverse, and they weren't his people. In fact they hated his guts the way they hate N-I's."

"Oh, Tosh, let's go and have our coffee in the lounge," said his wife. "You're getting impossible."

Tom declined an invitation to join them and said they must be getting along. As they parted the Colonel turned to Dora, whom he thought a good-looker. "You'll see a remarkable sight tomorrow, m'dear, lady pipers for the first time," he said. "Feminists, I dare say. Shouldn't think you're one; don't have to be." He winked broadly at Tom, and the party broke up for the evening.

"She said lounge," remarked Dora in triumph on the way back. "You said I was to call it drawing room."

"She said a number of things no lady would say. I think the poor old Colonel married out of his class, as you'd put it. Look what happens to men who do." He smiled down at her.

"What are Highland Games about? I've never seen any, except on porridge oats."

"Oh, dancers and pipers and a procession – the procession is the important part and everybody arrives in time for it – and tossing the caber and running and doing the long jump and dancing on platforms in shoes with long black laces, and a narrow bonnet. It isn't porridge that makes them do as much, it's drammoch."

"What's drammoch?"

"Oh, my darling, that takes too long to tell. Let me relate it over breakfast. After the porridge made and grown by the laird, I think we'll make tracks, Dora, and find some other hotel. They're available, evidently, after tomorrow."

"He'll make you pay the bill for the full booking," said Dora. She had rather been looking forward to life in the peach-coloured room. "I'm sleepy," she said, and yawned. There had been a moon reflected in the loch, alongside the lights from the different hotels.

"It's the Highland air. I'll go down and try one of his famous whiskies, then come up to you, my darling. What did you think of that couple tonight?"

"They were just like Brennan in the end."

"Most people are. However, if there was no gossip I'd be out of business and unable to take you to the best hotels. Nevertheless, I won't make an article about Inshtochradh and its inhabitants. I shall simply cover the Games and the procession."

"Not the AGM? It sounded important."

"You make a good reporter's wife, Dora. If they let me I will try. I can picture N-I in his clan chain and the Colonel, who is of course Chairman, running the show and hating each other, or perhaps the laird doesn't even realise he is disliked?"

They drove back safely despite meeting a few lurching headlights returning among the potholes. It had grown dark, with an owl hooting in the tree not far off. Tom parked the car, let Dora out, then, having unlocked the door with the laird's key, saw her inside and upstairs. After that he went into the drawing room.

Eight

The room showed signs of recent revelry since his earlier sight of it. The sofa covers were rumpled, the whisky bottles emptier than they had been; squashed cigarette stubs in the ashtrays made the air foul. Tom made no delay about finding a brand he knew, helped himself using a clean glass from under the counter as instructed, signed on the block of paper left for the purpose – other signatures must have been supervised and removed – and decided to go out for a few moments again to breathe the clear air. There were no cars left except for their own, and the strange monster lacking number-plates. It occurred to Tom to wonder if the Humber Pullman had come back; no doubt it was kept under cover. He strolled round to the back of the house, sipping his whisky. A former stable or coach-house had, as expected, been converted into a garage, where the Pullman loomed silently beside a Volvo in some dark colour identifiable only in daylight. Lady Charlotte had returned from tending her inheritance. She obviously only came home to bed.

"Your tits aren't much, never were."

The alien sound seemed to smirch the clean night air. Tom realised there was an open window above, belonging to what must be the main house bedroom. Norton-Insshe's voice had lost its pretence to a Highland lilt and had become no more than an ordinary lecher's, with an accent which might have come from anywhere or nowhere. He and the Lady of Insshe were evidently engaged in the marital act, and from the sound of things, she didn't like it.

"Stop, please stop now, I'm tired." The voice was high and piping, a schoolgirl's.

"It's your own fault, Charlotte. You take a hell of a time to bring on. In the end, I make you come. Coming yet, eh? Is it?"

"No. I don't know. I wish you'd stop."

"I can make you come, I tell you. I can fuck any woman till she comes. I can fuck a little stubborn mule. Coming yet? Is it coming, or not? Say which."

The voice had thickened. Tom wondered how much of the man's own whisky he had imbibed; perhaps none, they said it stimulated desire and reduced performance. The laird was performing adequately, from the sounds he made; but there was still an unresponsive silence.

Presently, "Come on, Charlotte. Come *on*. We've both got to work tomorrow. You're at the sales booth the day after, while I lead the damned procession. I've got to get the tartan stuff down early."

"I'm tired, I told you. I wish you would leave me alone." Suddenly she told him in Gaelic that she loathed him, evidently afraid of saying so in words he would understand. Tom knew a little of the tongue, which was enough.

"Never mind all that. What are you holding back for? Are you afraid of another idiot child? I'm wearing these, aren't I? I made you put the cap in as usual, didn't I? Come on, you skinny bitch."

"Ugh."

"All right, you don't like it, but you'll do as you're bloody well told. I've bought you, my dear wife, like a little bitch dog with its name on its collar. If it wasn't for my money the slates would be falling off Great House like they are at the lodge. I keep it like that so that every time you pass it in your damned Pullman, you'll think of what the rest might be like by now."

"You keep the lodge like that to keep people away, and the road too." Her voice had sunk to a whisper, which Tom barely heard. The other voice rose.

"Don't give me that, or in two more days, after all this is over, I'll leather your bottom like last time till it can't sit down, in the Pullman or anywhere else. The Lady of Insshe regrets not being able to appear today, she can't sit. That gave you a hot little tail for once. We could have stayed in bed after that for days. Give me a bit of that now, eh? Eh?"

"Ugh. Ugh. I think it's coming now. *A reachd.* Please—"

"Thought you'd better sing for your supper after all, eh? I bring you your supper, don't I? I pay for it, pay for everything. Don't I? Don't I?"

"Yes, yes, you pay for everything. Oh, now, please—" There came the high, inadvertent sounds of a frigid woman's finally elicited orgasm, like a bird's twittering. After a time it ceased. Then, "Not again. I am tired, I tell you. I have worked all day at the house."

"Tired? You've been tired since you were born. Anyhow you're serviced, like that bloody Humber of yours that was your father's and eats petrol the way he drank booze. I pay for that as well. I paid for him, paid his debts. I've done a lot for you all, and you can bloody well do your duty."

She did not answer, evidently still under him. The man's jeering laughter came.

"Given you your hot tail by now, like I said, haven't I? Want it again already, don't you, eh? Little whore . . ."

Tom had left the place below the window. It was no doubt his heartless reporter's instinct that had let him listen for as long. The owl hooted again in its tree, not far off. He was assailed by a great desire to get to Dora, erase the ugly recollection from his mind, find again the warm familiar things Sheila had once meant and Dora would come to mean in time. He let himself quietly in with the key.

He found that he was shaking, and needed a second whisky after what he'd heard. He went back into the drawing room, switched on the table-lamp and poured a different brand, leaning to drink it against the ring-stained counter. Somebody, no doubt the laird, would clean up in the morning. Tom knocked the stuff back, found he felt better and could use a third. He took it, remembered to sign for both and then went out of the room and upstairs past the by now ghostly draped tartan and arrayed stags' heads. He felt reckless, even to a certain extent in sympathy with the vulgarian laird. After all, the man had only been taking what one supposed were his rights. Tomorrow . . .

Tonight.

Dora had had her peach-coloured bath, and lay waiting in the four-poster. Tom was taking longer than she'd expected. Presently she heard him come upstairs and turn the handle; she hadn't locked the door. There was a bright moon outside, shining through the partly-open curtains. She saw him stumble towards her, shedding his clothes as he came. He slid into bed.

"Sheila. Sheila."

It gave Dora, briefly, a chill at the heart, even though she could smell whisky on Tom's breath. Jerry hadn't ever touched spirits, only beer with the lads on Fridays. She supposed that if she was thinking of Jerry while they were like this, it was all right for Tom to think of Sheila. All the same, it would have been nicer if he'd known who she was herself.

He was handling her soft warm flesh when he realised the difference. Sheila's breasts had been slim, almost boyish. These, now, were breasts to fill a man's hand. This was Dora, little decent, plump Dora, and he'd said the wrong thing. He began to cry against her, the tears soaking into the front of her flimsy honeymoon nightgown.

"Forgive me, Dora love. I'm a swine to have said that. All men are swine."

She kept her arms round him. The moon outside had risen high, seeming by now what used to be called a silver sixpence. Dora stared up at it, with Tom's head lying still between her breasts. He was asleep, breathing heavily. Tomorrow they'd be somewhere else. In a way, she'd liked it here. She'd buy a souvenir to take home from the Games from old Miss Walshe, or perhaps from the Lady of Insshe herself. It would be something to keep and remember. That was what souvenirs were for.

Tom had a dream just before waking. He could hear Sheila's voice saying, "Don't worry, Tom darling. It's perfectly and absolutely all right".

He couldn't think at first what it was that was supposed to be all right. Sheila had never fussed. He found himself suddenly back in the cottage at Brennan, staring at the silver-framed photograph on the dressing table. That was the only studio photograph she'd ever had taken, by his request, soon after their marriage. As a rule she was too busy, like himself. The ceremony itself had been a hasty affair owing, as usual, to A.B.'s sudden demand for an overseas assignment. Only one evening newspaper recorded TOP REPORTER WEDS LADY ARCHITECT, and there hadn't even been time to photograph them together, then or later. That time, Sheila had worn a black lace hat perched on her pretty silver-blonde hair. She seldom wore hats. He himself didn't photograph well, then or now.

At the cottage, he recalled, Dora dusted and polished the photograph each day in its frame, and kept it shining. He couldn't at first remember the other connection between Dora and Sheila, then it came to him again that he was now married to Dora. There had been a second object on the dressing table, where he'd put it so that he could see the peacock colours on first waking; Mary Reston's pottery vase, perfected in the new gas kiln she was so proud of. "It's for your house", the harsh, mannish voice had said. Mary was dead. He remembered everything now.

Oldham had made use of Mary. Oldham had tried, and failed, to make use of Dora. It all began to come back now he was awake. He smiled. Oldham wouldn't have been lucky enough even to be able to look at Dora, as he himself was looking now.

She lay, still asleep, on the peach-coloured pillow beside him, her short dark curls glossy and clean. The long lashes lay on her cheeks and her breaths came evenly. She didn't snore. He was increasingly protective of her, remembering with shame at least certain parts of last night. The nights from now on would no longer be lonely.

We'll gather lilacs in the spring again. Well, perhaps not quite that; cheerful little nasturtiums in the Indian summer, perhaps. Dora had planted them two years running now in the garden of the Bellenden cottage, yellow colours and golden and flame, with spurs, and a smell of pepper.

He would have liked to wake her with a cup of tea, but again noticed the absence of any facility such as one would expect at the price. It didn't matter; except that the taste of last night's malts still made his mouth dry and, probably, unsavoury. Poor Dora. He'd go and brush his teeth. He tried to leave the bed carefully, but Dora woke, blinking her eyelashes. She smiled.

"I've thought of a better name for N-I," she said. "It's much better: McNorton."

"I won't kiss you, my darling, till I've cleaned my mouth out," he told her. "It feels foul." He did not comment on the name, but grinned slightly; it suited the laird.

"So it ought to," said Dora, showing dimples in both cheeks. "McNorton had better give us a good breakfast."

Nine

They went down to breakfast at the appointed hour, eight-thirty till nine-thirty. The sun shone outside the windows, promising a fine day for the bicentenary. Dora had hung the Harrods dress carefully in the built-in wardrobe in the tower room, and had put on a denim dress and sandals. Tom wore his checked shirt. The first sight they encountered on the way down was the laird himself, ascending the tortuous staircase with a breakfast tray. The large deerhound followed in douce fashion. Norton-Insshe had a white apron wrapped round himself over a slightly less commercial kilt than last night's. He nodded with assumed Highland dignity.

"My wife does not come down for breakfast," he explained. He asked if they had spent a comfortable night.

"The bed was excellent," replied Tom, feeling like an echo of Lord Peter Wimsey. Dora blushed, and to hide it bent down to pat the deerhound. Despite its size, it seemed good-natured. Norton-Insshe, however, assured them that Diarmaidh would remain upstairs with Lady Charlotte till they left for Great House.

"He is a part of the procession today, and I myself have a great deal to see to. I do not, of course, permit the dog to remain in the kitchen while I am preparing food for guests."

He might have been explaining to Egon Ronay in person. Tom and Dora continued down to the breakfast room, which was empty of anything except a number of small handmade tables and matching chairs, set as for two per table. Only one was set for breakfast and they took it. A small, square old-fashioned side window looked out on the nearby car park.

"Ours is still there," remarked Dora, unfolding her napkin.

"I would be worried if it wasn't. There is no other way of getting out of here." Tom had observed a large lacquered copper pot containing porridge with its ladle in it and the whole contraption standing on a glass stand, inside which burned a small night-light. Presumably, the steaming porridge had been heated by other means. A closed door no doubt led to the unseen kitchen.

"I assume we help ourselves." He got up and went to the copper pot, taking a plate from a heated pile there and ladling out some for Dora and for himself. There was a jug of thick cream, mercifully fresh. There must be a dairy herd somewhere. He returned with the porridge and the jug, and seated himself. "You asked me," he said, "yesterday, how to make drammoch. The first thing needed is a horse."

Dora spooned porridge and cream into her mouth. She didn't know much about Scotland, but if he wanted drammoch, whatever it was, she'd better find out how to make it, horse or no horse. Last night he had astonished her by arousing in her sensations she'd never known existed, certainly not with Jerry, who had been kindly but humdrum: a kind of glow, a rushing sweetness inside herself. She'd heard sounds coming and had realised they were her own. It was like a wider world opening up. This porridge was very good, smooth and with no lumps, and the proper amount of salt. Dora already knew enough not to ask for sugar with it, like they did in England.

Tom was going on about getting on the horse while wearing your sporran. "Obviously women don't make drammoch unless they have to. A kilt isn't needed, however. In fact, the fewer clothes the better, because then you won't be identified except by your face. You find the little hollow between the horse's shoulder-blades, and wait till it's begun to move. Then you take out of your sporran – this is the entire reason for wearing one – a poke of oatmeal and a little flask of Scotch. Any brand will do. "Then," he continued, "you take the whisky flask in your right hand – this is important, unless you're left-handed – and open the screw. If you have any foresight you'll have loosened it already. After that, bring out the poke with your left. All this time you have to control the horse with your knees, because both your hands are busy. You then pour, very carefully in case the horse tosses its head and spills everything, the two at once into the little hollow between its shoulder-blades I told you about. Then you sit back, take up the reins again and leave the rest to the horse. By the time you've got ready to steal your neighbour's cattle and take it back over the Border to turn into the roast beef of old England, there's a nice little ready-mixed pudding called drammoch sitting there between the horse's shoulder-blades, exactly right to dip your finger in whenever you feel hungry. It can keep you going for days."

"Well, it's just as well I haven't done horse-riding."

Tom smiled and looked up, disguising a grimace of pain. "Lord, here's our host." Norton-Insshe had appeared suddenly by way of the kitchen door; it must have a second exit to the upstairs quarters.

"What more would you be liking for your breakfast? We have bacon from the home farm, free range eggs, local mushrooms, sausage—"

The list went on. They chose bacon, egg, mushrooms and tomatoes, probably from the greenhouses. Tom had already reflected that there was none of the usual display to be found in hotels these days which charged almost as much as this one; grapefruit, prunes, figs, cereal, yoghurt, orange juice: everything here was, on the contrary, strictly Scottish and baronial. They ought to have asked for devilled kidneys and kedgeree, like Edward VII. The quasi-Highland voice sounded once more; would they be liking tea or coffee?

"A great many folk prefer coffee nowadays, because so many of them do not themselves know any more how to make a good cup of tea."

They chose tea.

The laird brought their breakfast, and Tom handed back the porridge plates, cleaned appreciatively like Oliver Twist's bowl. He said, "I thought the proper way to take porridge was walking up and down, but there isn't room here, is there, with the tables?"

Norton-Insshe did not reply, and Tom knew with some triumph that he'd nettled him. The bacon and eggs were, however, first-rate and fresh, the tea hot and properly infused. The laird had his moments after all. They finished and went upstairs. There didn't seem to be any evidence of staff yet, and Tom wondered if Insshe-Norton did all the washing up and cleaning himself. No doubt Miss Walshe helped out.

He suggested that they might drive about and find the field where the Games were to be held, but Dora said she'd eaten so much that if she sat in a car yet she'd be sick. "We'll walk it off, then," he told her. He got out the local map Norton-Insshe had sent when he made the booking, and saw that in fact they could walk in a circle and arrive back at the hotel without negotiating the potholed drive, provided there was a ford in the narrow river, which was probable.

They set off, after Tom had told the laird they would be back for lunch. He was beginning to dislike the man less, the memory of yesterday evening having faded by now, and his cooking was quite something; he deserved, as it were, to be encouraged. Norton-Insshe however said he hoped they wouldn't mind if lunch today was cold.

"I have to get ready the things for the clan tent table," he said. "It is outside the great marquee where there will be the annual general meeting, with chairs and tables inside. The souvenirs will go outside unless it rains, which we hope will not happen. My wife will preside there while I lead the procession with Diarmaidh. It is what the public come to see."

"That and the lady pipers. Cold lunch will be a good idea on a hot day." An echo of the McIntosh gossip drifted through Tom's remembrance; this man hogged the publicity for himself. He was explaining that lunch would be fresh-caught salmon with their own home-grown salad, and a syllabub and cheese with the coffee. It was astonishing that there were not the usual gourmet recommendations or badges displayed at the front door.

"He really does try," said Tom to his wife as they strolled together across green fields.

"I still don't like him," replied Dora.

They found the Games field, which was below Great House, rearing on its eminence, its neo-classical portico seen from far off. Below, the field was already filled with activity like a hive of ants. Marquees, one larger than all the rest, and a few humbler tents as well, were being erected round its edge, their ropes attached by pegs hammered into the turf by enthusiastic volunteers of the kind who miraculously appear for such occasions and then are not seen again till next year. There was a pervading scent of mown grass, crushed and sweet. The central showground itself, where the procession would take place and the caber-tossing and Highland dancing and all the rest later, was being roped off already, and piled plastic chairs from somewhere or other were being carried to be disposed, if it didn't rain, to support the posteriors of those persons who might arrive early enough to get one. A final rope was being passed from hand to hand to surround the field itself and prevent anyone from getting in for nothing. They had just come up against this deterrent when Tom and Dora became aware of being watched themselves.

An extraordinary figure, whose garb left the laird of Inshtochradh's well in the shade, was standing a few feet away on the nearby bank, staring at them with mad light eyes beneath a round much-worn and felted bonnet, from which trailed a long and exhausted heron's feather. The man's face was long also and lean, with straggling nondescript hair to his shoulders but no beard; either he shaved himself or else was one of those who had none by nature. His kilt had faded colours, and that and his saffron jacket might have come out with Bonnie Prince Charlie. His shirt was filthy and they could smell his presence from where they stood.

"You will not be able to stand there tomorrow as you are, and get in. There will be an entrance fee."

The voice had the true sing-song of the Gael. Tom nodded amiably and said they would pay their way tomorrow. "Mind you do," said the apparition. "It iss to make some money they are doing all of this, the clan. It iss the only money they make in the whole of the year."

He turned away with dignity, and they saw his thin bare legs, smeared with dirt, shamble off; he was wearing down-at-heel brogans. "He probably sleeps rough in some cave," said Tom.

"You meet all sorts. There are the McIntoshes, spying out the land like us. Let's go and have a word."

"I bet Mrs Mac will know all about that smelly man with his feather. Ask her. I'd like to know."

"He's probably a local character."

Mrs Mac, in pink trousers which didn't suit her short legs, knew all right: the man's name was Sawnie Cattanach and he thought himself the true heir to the Insshe estates.

"A kind of Master of Ravenswood," explained the Colonel, who was wearing his kilt of last night. He added foreseeably that he himself was the clan Chairman and would preside at the AGM. "You can report it if you like," he said. Tom had said last night what his occupation was, which had perhaps been unwise.

"Ooh, the papers," said Mrs Mac now. "I expect they'll be all over the place, with the bicentenary. They're going to place a wreath on the fourteenth laird's statue, though not everybody is in favour."

Tom glanced up at the remote statue, seen staring like some tiny stone soldier on its far hill. He'd try and cover both aspects after the AGM, which anyone could attend provided they didn't vote. "Who is the President of the clan?" he asked innocently. The Colonel winked.

"Who do you think? It wouldn't be his wife. Appearing in the chain of office, with the dog, in the annual procession is one of N-I's big moments, more so this year than any other."

"Oh, Tosh, don't be so small-minded," said Mrs Mac, explaining in a loud aside to Dora that he'd have liked to be able to wear the chain himself. Dora, however, wanted to know more about Sawnie; she had a certain sympathy with him, he was an outsider, like herself.

"Oh, he comes every year, and never looks different, let alone washes himself. He lives in a shanty, a *bothan*, he built for himself, up on the moor near the laird's statue. He used to be a shepherd for old Lord Insshe when he was young, but now he's on social security. He says the government owe it to him for taking away his birthright."

Going back, Dora said to Tom suddenly "There's that man Peters; you know, the one who used to carry in logs for Mrs Partridge. He vanished at the time. He's come a long way."

Tom saw only the back of the man's head, as he sloped off: Peters looked shabby and grey and not notable in a crowd. No doubt he was casing the joint for tomorrow. Tom decided not to do anything about it; if anything went wrong, it was the job of the local police, not his; he was, after all, on his honeymoon. The distances covered by the gypsy fraternity had long ceased to surprise him: no doubt the man was here for some rich pickings at the famous bicentenary.

Later, forgetting Peters, Dora mentioned to Tom that there seemed a great deal of underground ill-feeling one way and another. "Mrs Mac's husband heard what she said about wearing the clan chain, and he didn't like it." she said. "He puts up with a good deal from her."

"And you do from me, Dora," said her husband. "All couples are like that. They rub along, and I hope so will we. Let me tell you, till we get to the river ford, about what happened here under the fourteenth laird and why he is so unpopular; half the nobs want to put the wreath up on the statue's base and the other half are against it, and some even say the statue ought to be taken down. It's the same story as happened in Sutherland at the time of the Clearances, when they drove out the clansmen and their families and burned down their houses and covered the hills with sheep. This laird was an Englishman as well, though not quite as bad as the Duke of Sutherland and his factor, which last they say shut some of the crofters who wouldn't leave to emigrate, or go down to the coast to learn fishery as prescribed, in a church and burnt it down with all of them trapped inside."

"How horrible," said Dora. "I suppose the sheep meant money."

"Money, that was it. A lot of the clansmen, that is as many as were left alive by then after the Jacobite risings of former generations, made a living afterwards in Canada, and some of their sons made fortunes; that's why you find so many Scottish names out there, and in New Zealand, I believe. Australia at that time was for convicts. The English government had a lot to answer for."

"You talk as if you didn't like England."

"I do, and wouldn't live anywhere out of touch with London. The Scots, though, have had a pretty rough ride, and I have Scottish blood. To continue about the unpopular laird; perhaps he meant well, but he made the women and children who were left in the houses he'd built in the clachan – with a school, nice and proper – work in his mill he'd founded; to spin as well as clip and weave the sheep's wool and make more money, for himself, of course. He paid them hardly anything, and made it a condition of a roof over their heads that they work so many hours in his mill. Soon they set it on fire, and he concentrated after that on plain quiet untroublesome sheep on the hills, and died in the end of old age. He didn't raise a regiment like they did in Sutherland, to use the men that remained for fighting their English wars, as was said then and later.

"Nobody asked any questions about what he was doing; it was supposed to be for the people's welfare, and in London they were too far away to care. The irony is that if you climb up to the base of the statue, there's an inscription carved there saying what a father he was to his people. It's the kind of flattery they gave then to the rich, and he'd got very rich and called himself the laird, though he'd only married the grand-niece of the older ones and the true heir by then was somewhere in the heather, like many of them who stayed in hiding and bred sons. No doubt that's where Sawnie's ancestry comes from: many of these Jacobite descendants became tinkers, as I heard the Macs say last night, and you still used to meet them up here on the roadsides boiling kettles on their fires when I was a boy. Once one of them died somewhere far off across the hills, and next day there wasn't one of them to be seen: word had come down, passed from one to the other, and they were gone for the funeral in the north by morning. It was a kind of resistance movement, although they'd forgotten by then what it was they were resisting. Only one or two such as Sawnie are left.

"Here's the river," finished Tom. "Now we look for a place to cross."

There were sycamores and limes along the bank, and they soon found a place where pebbles let the water purl along in a shallow race. Beyond was the back of Inshtochradh, and what must be the walled kitchen garden where Himself probably grew his herbs. Tom gallantly picked Dora up and waded across with her.

"You needn't have," she said, her arms round his neck. "I could have managed it."

"I wanted to. Now I want payment."

On the further side were mossy banks. He laid her carefully down on her back, shaded by green leaves from the sun. The little river ran on, making its quiet continuous singing over the pebbles.

"Not here, Tom," Dora protested. "It isn't proper."

"Then let's be improper. It isn't time for salmon yet, and nobody knows where we are."

This time, at any rate, he knew who she was. Soon there was no sound but the purling of the river, and Dora's happy sighing.

Presently, however, the alien churning of a motor began, nearing. Dora started up, pulling down the denim dress.

"I told you," she said. "It's that man in his crazy machine. He's coming towards us across the field."

"Don't worry, he can't have seen us," said Tom, preparing to help her up the near bank. "Say again what I told you that time in French."

"*Je suis bien foutue*." He kissed her, laughing. "Tell me what it means," she said. "It's all very well to laugh."

"You ought to know by now. Here comes the laird." Norton-Insshe was advancing towards them, with dignity, in the high driving seat, having divested himself of his copious white breakfast apron. What he was driving was, Tom at last realised, the kind of amphibious vehicle which can be driven across rough ground and shallow water. They cost a great deal of money and must be strictly for use on the estate. A trailer was piled with souvenirs for sale at the marquee: they shone variously in the sun.

He and Dora began to walk towards the laird, an encounter

being inevitable. Their host drew near, a fleshy god in his machine. The amphibian vehicle was loaded with tartan objects, tea-cosies, caddy-spoons, painted trays, mugs, teddy bears, and T-shirts still in their polythene. Tom hoped to pass by the vehicle, but Norton-Insshe beckoned from the high seat.

"There is a fax for you," he called. "I have brought it with me." He must have seen, after all, where they were; he had an omniscient faculty, perhaps, or else used field-glasses. Tom hoped Dora wouldn't put two and two together, held out his hand for the fax message, then frowned quickly in irritation. It was from A.B. and should have been delivered earlier: "BEAUTY QUEEN ALLEGES RAPE BY MILKMAN, URGENT, INVESTIGATE." There were directions given for an address in Edinburgh. A.B., like most southern dwellers, had very little idea of Highland distances.

Tom swallowed lunch, hardly taking notice of the excellence of the salmon and new potatoes, having skipped the starter and ignoring the pudding, and knocking back his coffee while it was still too hot. The McIntoshes, alerted, had given them both a lift back to the hotel. It would have taken too long to walk back across the field or, alternatively, to wait for a lift in Norton-Insshe's equipage; he would in any case take some time to unload his wares for tomorrow once he was over the river.

"I hate leaving you for the night, but it'll have to happen now, I'm afraid," Tom told Dora. "I don't want to give my old boy cause for complaint; he gave me time off to marry you, but we don't want to end up on social security like Sawnie."

"It'd pay better," said Dora, who had noted the astronomical price mentioned at the bottom of the handwritten menu. She waved Tom off outside, then turned disconsolately back into the house. It would be difficult to know what to do with herself until tomorrow, but Tom would certainly be back by then to cover the Games.

She was not to be left alone to repine. Their host appeared shortly, having disposed of his load and returned. He evidently considered it his duty to entertain her.

"Please don't trouble yourself," said Dora, who had returned to the dining room and poured herself more coffee and drunk it; it was still hot. "I'll go for another walk till dinner," she said. She supposed she would have to have that here. In any case, Tom hadn't left her any money. She recalled that he'd said the only way to escape from here was by car; well, he'd escaped and she couldn't. There was no reason, after all, to want to. The sun shone, the surroundings were pleasant if one avoided the creepy horror of the front drive, and her host was assiduous in insisting that she walk round with him, if so, and be shown the kitchen garden and a few other things most guests didn't see.

"Do you have many guests?" asked Dora. It was not as guileless a question as she knew it sounded. She wanted to see if he would tell lies.

"Those that come, we treat as royalty," said Norton-Insshe, evading the issue. Dora was certainly impressed with the kitchen garden, and its herbs in neat rows. "Parsley, mint, borage, fennel, summer savory, dill, sage, lettuces, chives," recited her host compulsively. There were a few small pale roses on a bush near the wall and he picked one on a long stem and gave it to Dora. "Sweets for the sweet, my dear," he said with gallantry.

Dora politely switched to some old story of Jerry's about the devil not getting into parsley if it survived with you nine days; did Norton-Insshe know it? He appeared not to be particularly interested and presently guided her by the elbow back into the house.

"Let me show you my kitchen," he said. "I'm very proud of it. I'm like the Duchess of Windsor's cook, who was only allowed to use one copper pan, but the resulting food was superb."

She could have said she had an omelette pan at home like that, but didn't; and surveyed the gleaming object on the wall, the plastic electric kettle, and the Aga stove on which reposed a second kettle.

"The electricity here is by diesel, of course, so I cut down on that," the laird explained, adding that the solid fuel Aga heated water very well and there was plenty of that from the river; had there been enough for them upstairs?

"Yes, it was nice and hot." A soak in the peach-coloured bath had been refreshing. Tom had had one afterwards. She wondered where Tom was by now and how soon he could get back. He could drive fast when he had to, but she hoped there wouldn't be an accident at that rate; you heard things about the A9.

"Come upstairs, and see our part of the house," said the laird persuasively.

At least it would keep her from worrying about Tom, Dora thought, so obeyed. Stairs from the kitchen led straight up to the private quarters. She wondered why he'd had to appear on the front stairs carrying Lady Charlotte's breakfast tray that morning; it was as though he'd wanted to be seen.

Norton-Insshe then flung open a door to reveal a large four-poster, even larger than the one in their tower. It had a crested tester and counterpane, with lozenges in which reposed sewn sprigs of rowan. "That is the clan device," said her host, behind her. "This is where I sleep with my wife."

The voice was smooth with satisfaction. There seemed no reply, and Dora made none. She'd noticed already that besides the bed, which looked as if a duchess slept in it, the room was filled with objects to prove that Lady Charlotte did. There was a second wedding photograph like the one downstairs; a photograph likewise of the Games in some earlier year, with Norton-Insshe in full regalia and a chain over his shoulders, leading Diarmaidh in the procession. There was also one of a little boy in a white sunhat, holding a stuffed toy.

"Is that your son?" asked Dora, once again not totally guileless. She wanted to see how Norton-Insshe would react, to tell Tom later. Mrs Mac had implied that the drowning hadn't been an accident. Dora went over and picked up the framed snapshot. It wasn't easy to see, from beneath the shade of the hat's brim, whether the eyes were those of a Down's syndrome child or not; and the hands clutching the toy could have been any child's.

"Yes. He is dead. My wife likes to have the photograph there. We do not speak of it."

He sounded coldly angry, and Dora made it an excuse to get to the door. She hadn't liked being in the room alone with him.

Once outside, she made polite talk as best she might, asking how old the deerhound was.

"Eight. That means he is getting on now. He was a present to my wife from the clan society when our son was born, but he prefers my company to hers. He seldom leaves me unless I shut him in, but he is with her today at Great House. The Pullman is a large car and he likes to sit in the back of it."

He'd mentioned the boy again, although he hadn't had to. It was as though it was safe to do so now the photograph was out of sight. Dora was, for some reason, afraid.

"I think I will go and lie down for a little," she said. "Thank you for showing me the herb garden." She still held the rose in her hand; upstairs, she'd put it in water. She didn't like to see things wilt.

"You would like tea brought up in a little while, perhaps?"

"No, thank you." She didn't want any tea. She simply wanted to be left in peace. She'd lock her door with the key. Tom wouldn't be back till tomorrow.

"I will send your dinner up if you like? Miss Walshe will bring it, as I myself will be back down at the tents."

That was a comfort, anyway. Dora said she'd have some dinner. He'd have read the fax, anyway, so knew Tom was in Edinburgh. No doubt there was a good deal to do down at the field. Norton-Insshe's presence made her uncomfortable, probably for no reason. As Tom had said, he really was doing his best.

Ten

Tom put his foot down hard on the accelerator. It was relatively safe to do so, as there was nobody about on these roads at this hour. He had left the purlieus of Edinburgh behind long ago, A.B. having no notion that it wasn't exactly round the corner, and had evaded the Eurolorries which no longer thundered along in these remote northern parts. He was returning somewhat earlier than expected, having wrapped up the case as quickly as possible and faxed the result to the London office. There had been no need, he decided resentfully, to send him in person; anyone would have provided the necessary, reporters usually being willing to oblige each other provided it wasn't an exclusive. This one had been cats' meat; the beauty queen must have got where she had by sleeping with the judges anyway, and the milkman had such an honest face he was certain to be guilty although no court would wear it. Tom had assembled his impatient thoughts to concoct an article fit to print; after all he didn't want the royal push quite yet.

In fact, he was thinking of freelancing soon, to have more time to spend with Dora, somewhere in the country which wasn't Brennan. The cottage up there could be sold to the Bellenden House hotel despite Mary Reston's suicide, which would undoubtedly induce them to drop the offer still further. However, they wanted the cottage for an annexe, and would bite in the end.

He thought of that while speeding on, headlights blazing as it was too late even to crash into homegoing drunks, the police themselves being in bed up here. His opinion of Norton-Insshe had risen, he knew, because the man was a good cook: that wasn't logical, at any rate as regarded character. Dora didn't like the man, and Dora was shrewd. For that reason, here he was himself, hurtling through the night instead of spending a comfortable one on the expense account at the Old Waverley. He was anxious to get back to Dora, and it wasn't only sex. By the time he reached Inshtochradh again it would anyway be almost porridge hour, if not quite. After that there were the Games. He wondered idly if Norton-Insshe had set out all the bits and pieces in the marquee for the AGM; presumbaly the tartan objects for sale would not be left on the table overnight in case they were removed by some trigger-happy tourist who had climbed over the rope. It would be diverting to write up the bicentenary Games alongside the first known public ebullience of lady pipers.

Thankfully at last, he saw the headlights pick out the Inshtochradh potholes, negotiated these without mishap, and parked the car on the gravel outside the front door. He remembered to turn off the headlights, locked the Renault, and fished out the laird's key from his pocket. He let himself in soundlessly; like everything else about the place the lock was efficiently oiled, and didn't creak.

The laird himself was encountered then, suddenly, in the dawn's light, in his dressing-gown, descending the stairs from the tower room. At sight of Tom he hurriedly stuffed something in his pocket, then came, smiling blandly, down as far as the stairs' turn.

"I always go round the house about now to ensure that things are as they should be. Burglars are not unknown, even in these parts, and with the bicentenary anybody may come."

He continued on his way, smiling. Tom, whose heart had stopped, went up a few steps to where the man had first been seen, and checked. A small pale object had inadvertently been dropped when Norton-Insshe stuffed the rest into his dressing-gown pocket. It was a peeled-off condom.

The laird's efficiency had failed him for once. The thing was to get first to Dora. Tom shot upstairs, unlocked the tower door – the brute had remembered to lock it again – and saw her lying in disarray in the growing daylight, her face swollen with tears. At sight of him she flung her arms round his neck, and burst out sobbing.

"Oh Tom, it was horrible. He – he came in soon after midnight with his key. I'd been asleep and thought it was you, back early. He came into bed and began. I knew at once it wasn't you, and I began to struggle, but he held me down. He was saying dreadful things, over and over. I think he's mad. He told me I was a nice little armful, that he'd spotted me at once, that it wasn't worth telling you about it because he'd deny ever being in here. He stayed for, oh, I don't know how long. I couldn't call out by then. Oh, Tom, I don't want to meet him at breakfast. I don't want to set eyes on him ever again."

"We won't wait for breakfast," Tom said grimly.

He knew he must control the primeval urge to kill at once. For one thing the man would be back now with his wife, saying he'd been round to check for burglars. There would be a witness and, hence, headlines: REPORTER'S WIFE RAPED ON HONEYMOON, MURDER ALLEGED. That would almost put the beauty queen and the milkman back on the sports pages, and A.B. wouldn't take much more. All of it sat like separate ice cubes in Brackenbury's brain as he ran a hot bath for Dora, saw her into it, dried her afterwards with the damned peach-coloured towels – somebody had changed them – and told her then to start packing his things and hers. To give her something to do was better than putting her back to bed to lie there, while he couldn't even make her a cup of tea. She said in any case she felt better after the bath.

"I felt dirty," she said. "His hands were all over me, squeezing."

"Forget about it. Go and dress, darling, and pack. We want to leave as soon as I settle the bill." By that, he didn't mean signing any cheque; what they owed could be posted, later. If it was still difficult to find anywhere to stay tonight, the Games themselves could be covered by some other reporter who'd lend him the details, even photographs; he'd after all done the same for others in his day. The main thing, after what he intended to do first, was to get Dora away from here. They should, of course, never have come.

Something in his curt orders and set face alarmed her. "Tom, you look quite white," she said. "Don't murder him. It's over, and – and if we go away nobody need know except you. Don't get yourself in trouble. Let's just leave."

Trouble. It would be worse, he knew, for her than for him. Apart from the rape – rape after all made news every other day – it would mean raking up the five-year-old Brennan murders, Jerry Beale's suicide, perhaps Mary's; and in that case Dora herself would have been known to be down at the Commander's. The media would then proceed to turn Dora into a sex kitten and make her life hell. Much as he himself would have liked to hold down Norton-Insshe's head in his own boiling porridge, he would refrain from quite that; it was less spectacular in the end to smash the man's face in. At least he wouldn't decorate the bicentenary procession to quite the extent he'd expected.

One ice-cube had melted. Tom got ready while Dora busied herself packing, then quietly left the room and went downstairs. By now, it was firm summer daylight. He found the front door still locked, unlocked it again with his key, went out to the Renault to open both doors and the boot for a quick getaway, then went into the breakfast room to wait, having left the outdoor key tidily on the reception desk in the hall.

Norton-Insshe was already about in the kitchen, carrying the pot of oats to the stove. "I am afraid breakfast is not served quite yet," he called through. "A special arrangement can be made the night before; I soak the oats then, but they will not now be ready for ten minutes."

He went on talking, presumably half to himself, perhaps not yet aware that he had dropped his condom or that Dora had said what had happened. Tom stalked into the kitchen; the man turned then and saw his face. "I—" he began, and got no further.

"You will send your bill to my London address. Meantime—" Tom's fists shot out, left and right. One landed on Norton-Insshe's nose, squashing it like fruit. The other hit his jaw. He went down like a sack of potatoes, screaming like a woman. He lay there writhing and sobbing. Tom resisted the temptation to kick him where it hurt most. From behind the shut further door, the deerhound began scratching and howling, then beating with its full weight against the panels. Shortly the woman's voice he had formerly heard came, high and childish, speaking in Gaelic to the dog.

"*Diarmaidh, samach. Samhach, tasnach.*" She did not come out.

Tom turned on his heel and went, calling to Dora, who was already at the top of the outer stairs carrying two suitcases. He raced up to take them from her, they got to the car, and drove off. There seemed no pursuit from Inshtochradh.

It was still very early, but when driving towards the outer gate they saw the small Morris come.

"Miss Walshe surely doesn't arrive so soon as a rule," remarked Tom. "It must be the great day of the Games that brings her. And now, love, talk to me."

What she told him was even more sickening than he had expected. Last night, Dora said, Miss Walshe had brought up dinner on a tray to her room and had taken away the used towels. The laird had sent his apologies concerning the tray, but as Mrs Brackenbury was aware, he was busy down at the tents.

"I think Miss Walshe helps out in other ways than in the shop," Dora said. "Afterwards she came back again with coffee and fresh towels, and a complementary drink of malt whisky the laird had said to say was a gift to me from Inshtochradh. I didn't want to drink it, but thought it would be polite. Miss Walshe took everything away then. I quite like her."

It was certainly hard to think of Miss Walshe in the role of procuress. Dora had then taken her bath and had gone to bed to sleep, hearing the key later on in the lock as she'd already said. "He has duplicates for the whole house, of course," said Tom. The recent past already seemed unreal.

"You see, Tom – when he came into bed – he, he behaved the same way as you had the night before, with the smell of whisky. Oh, the things he did I can't tell you. They were vulgar and beastly. He's a beast." She began to cry. "One of the first things he said at the beginning, after he'd made sure of me, was, 'Every night I fuck my wife till she comes. She's a lady, and I make her come. I can make you at that rate, darling duck, can't I?' Then he said he knew I wasn't a lady as soon as I came in at the door, anyone could tell, and probably I wasn't married to you at all. Then he said again I was like a little plump duck, and he could fuck a duck till it quacked." Dora had stopped crying and her face was scarlet. "He went on that way, saying fuck, fuck, little duck, quack, quack, quack. It – it went on for a long time. He said, I told you, that he'd deny ever being there, that he'd say I was making the whole thing up, like that beauty queen who was getting herself into the papers after your fax. He said he'd get me into them the same way if I said a word, because he knew who you were. I didn't think at the time of answering that it would be bad publicity for his hotel. There aren't any guests there. Probably that's why."

"You're right; he's known. Otherwise they would have descended for the bicentenary like a swarm of bees."

They had long passed Miss Walshe, who had driven on. She could think what she liked about their early departure. Dora by now was looking less calm than she had done when she brought out the cases; she was shivering, no doubt with delayed shock, and Tom was concerned with getting her to a hotel for some breakfast and, if possible, a bed to lie on quietly for the day.

The Rowan Tree, to which they went first, was sorry, but not only was it full up with guests but the staff were going off early to the Games and everything was closing down till dinner time. Two other lochside hotels they tried were the same; there wasn't even coffee available, everything was geared up for the annual jamboree. Driving Dora about would do her no good, and Tom suddenly had an idea: there was the garden at Great House, Taigh Mór itself. She could at least sit there while he went to try to get hold of a plastic cup of something or other hot from a tent as soon as things were open. What must be happening at Inshtochradh by now gave him a certain satisfaction. At best, the laird would be wearing sticking plaster across his nose.

Eleven

The fourteenth laird, in his unhallowed time, had caused Great House garden to be placed so that the sun would fall on it in afternoons, in order that he and his family, the ladies' sacques trailing gracefully beneath their high-dressed powdered hair, might walk there in private convenience and pleasure. By now, the trees he had had planted were two hundred years old, rare in type and thick in leaf, and beyond was the formal knot-garden. Tom placed Dora in view of this on a seat beneath a fine Spanish chestnut, with a meticulously planted *Taigh Mór Am Insheach*, if that was the way round it went, nearby in an oval arrangement of tiny lobelias and alyssum. Hardly noticing this dubious horticultural triumph, Tom went up to the door beneath the portico to see if anything inside was open yet; if so, there might be a refreshment room which sold tea. However, 'Taigh Mór House open 10.00 a.m. till 5.00 p.m.', was pinned firmly on the door. It was not yet ten o'clock. He rejoined Dora rather than leaving her alone quite yet to hunt for coffee. There was hardly any activity down on the field; nothing would be open there either. Round the corner, within view, was a car park where they'd left the Renault, but he couldn't see from here who else might have arrived since, if anyone. The movements of the Lady of Insshe were as always mysterious, but no doubt she'd stayed to patch up her 'afflicted' spouse, although his screams had not brought her out instantly into the kitchen. Perhaps those failed to move her, or even made her glad.

While he hesitated about what to do, he saw the small Morris creep mouse-like into the car park. Out then stepped Miss Walshe, carrying a neat holdall made of striped handwoven linen. It hardly looked as if any disaster had been discovered by her at Inshtochradh, but it could scarcely have been avoided. She was evidently a personage who remained forever cool.

She saw them, smiled, came round and approached them both, still appearing perfectly collected. She then dived into her holdall – it could almost have been called a reticule – and brought out, miraculously, a flask and an extra cup.

"I was aware, when I saw you both on the drive, that you could not have had any breakfast before leaving, and knew you were unlikely to obtain it today in these parts," she observed. She then joined them, after invitation, on the seat, prim and with her narrow-shod feet together. Perspicacious old girl, Tom thought gratefully, pouring hot coffee for Dora and himself. No doubt the good lady had been coming up here in any case to help out. He would ask no questions whatever. Silence was golden, and the coffee was hot.

He saw Dora sip hers cautiously. She couldn't be feeling too well, and didn't look it. Miss Walshe sat quietly without troubling anyone, but Tom guessed very little would surprise her. Perhaps she was, in her well-bred way, congratulating him on having punched up the laird. A lady of the old school, he had already decided; and was no longer as certain about Mrs Mac's remark that nothing ever happened to such persons. They had after all been known to ride elephants across unknown parts of British India, and camels before that in Arabia; Miss Walshe had that same ambience now that she was seen in the open air, away from the souvenir shop at Inshtochradh. He wondered what her past had been, decided she must certainly have had one, and heard her talking evenly now Dora had finished with the cup.

"It occurred to me also that you will probably be quite unable to find accommodation for tonight. The Games and Annual General Meeting are taken very seriously; many clan members have travelled long distances, and will perhaps stay over for a day or two. I have a little house in the village of which you might care to make use; I myself am seldom there at present." She did not say clachan, Dora noted. "There will be crowds of tourists up here presently, and one has to keep an eye on the valuable objects inside," she continued. "I myself am dealing with Great House, as in any case Mr Norton-Insshe has had a slight accident with his motor and will not after all lead the procession; Lady Charlotte must therefore do so, while he presides at the sales booth and, later on, the Annual General Meeting in the great tent. I am, accordingly, in charge up here."

No staff were yet apparent here any more than at Inshtochradh. Tom suspected that Miss Walshe and the Lady of Insshe did most things themselves with a vacuum cleaner, perhaps even a manual planter for bulbs. Meantime, he thanked Miss Walshe devoutly, said it was indeed kind of her, and they would gladly make use of her house as she had been good enough to offer it. "It's always a bit of trouble having people to stay, but I assure you we will tidy up after ourselves," he said, smiling.

Miss Walshe assured him that it was no trouble whatever. "I am in fact glad to have an eye kept, as they say, on my house on the bicentenary occasion," she replied. "In a village they know everything, and it is of course known to be empty at present. One can never be certain about breakers-in. You cannot miss it, it is in the main street, with geraniums outside in pots."

She produced a small bunch of keys and handed them to Tom. "Personally," she went on, "I think it is a great pity village communities are no longer what they were. My house used to be the primary school; now the poor children are herded on a bus and driven several miles to the comprehensive, which now boasts its own primary department. Some of them do not travel well, and it means a double journey. Education authorities and planners never consider the human factor, as they themselves call it, nowadays. In my time . . ." She smiled, and made off to the house door, sharp at five to ten.

"I'm going to be sick," muttered Dora, and vanished into the car park. Coming back presently from the small neat hedge and wiping her mouth with a tissue, she went to where Tom had tactfully returned to their own car and opened the offside door ready for her.

"All right now, love?" he said. "Would you like to sit for longer in the garden?"

"No. I want to get to her house and brush my teeth."

He drove off with relief; there had been moments when he had wondered, having a certain talent for the macabre, if Miss Walshe had doctored the coffee in some form of quiet revenge. However, he himself felt all right and smiled, ruefully, feeling the atmosphere of rage and suspicion which had built up within him over the past hour subside. He was also, probably, suffering from delayed shock. He'd likewise grazed his knuckles on Norton-Insshe's chin. "We'll get you with your feet up in the house first, then I'll go to the grocer if he's open today, and buy some food," he told Dora. He'd find some somehow, and meantime make both of them a pot of tea. Miss Walshe was bound to have some.

They found the little whitewashed former schoolhouse once again, with the date carved over the coping-stone of the door, 1787. That must have been when the fourteenth laird started his unpopular English improvements. Nobody likes being forcibly improved. The playground still had its modern tarmac, which would probably cost too much to remove, and instead Miss Walshe had placed her white-painted wooden tubs of bright geraniums here and there to hide its ugliness. The former bicycle shed had been turned into a lean-to garage for the Morris when it was at home. Tom parked considerately out of its way; there was plenty of room.

He unlocked the door; there was, immediately, a room which must have been the main classroom. There was a chaise-longue and, incredibly, an aspidistra; those alone were worth burgling, he'd heard that those prestigious plants were worth somewhere near one pound per leaf. "They're more or less impossible to kill," he heard himself saying. "You go and lie down on that thing, Dora darling, and I'll go and hunt up the grocer and make him open up if he's shut." He hadn't noticed one way or the other as they drove in, being too intent on finding the house entry.

"I'll come with you," said Dora.

They found the grocer open, and he said his wife had gone down to see the parade and the lady pipers, but that he was staying open in case there were tourists. "Very sensible," Tom told him.

They bought ham, rolls, margarine, a box of free range eggs and some milk, and returned to the schoolhouse. Once back there, they refreshed themselves, and Dora said she felt much better.

"I'd come with you to the Games, if it wasn't for the likelihood of seeing *him*," she said. She was lying with her feet up on the chaise-longue.

"You will stay precisely where you are, or make up a bed and get into it if you feel inclined. I'd do it for you, but I'd better get away; the traffic will be piling up." They could hear cars increasingly in the street already. "Whatever you do, don't answer the door to *anyone*," he told her.

"How stupid d'you think I am?" She looked up at the wall, which although white-painted now like the flower containers, still somehow kept the classroom atmosphere.

"Anyway, rest," said Tom.

"What time is the parade?" asked Dora suddenly.

"Twelve, but you aren't going to look at it."

She put out a hand. "There's time to tell you something. Tom, I'm a sinful woman."

He burst out laughing. "Oh, Dora, darling Dora, not now." It was like she'd used to be at the very beginning of their acquaintance, bright, cheerful and impeccably respectable, married to decent Jerry Beale. The shock must have brought it all back.

"Don't laugh, please," said Dora. "There's – there's something I haven't told you about last night, with that horrible man. If I'm left here thinking about it, I'll go mad. It won't take long."

He was contrite at once. "What is it, love? I won't be angry. Tell me. Damn the parade. It doesn't matter and you do."

There were tears on her lashes, She said then "You remember what I told you he was saying about a duck. I won't go over all of that again, it was disgusting, but the worst part was that I – Tom, I *did* enjoy it, in the end. You know, the noise I make with you. It took a long time, but I did. I couldn't help it. He said he could make me, and – well, there it is. I was so ashamed I couldn't tell you in the car. You may not want to – to touch me again, but you know now. I decided I'd rather you knew."

Tom sat down on the chaise-longue's edge and took her in his arms.

"My precious love, all women at that rate are whores," he said. "Don't worry about it any more. If Caliban raped Miranda and held on long enough, she'd make the right sounds for him as well. It's a matter of endocrines. Your morals are perfectly sound." He kissed her on the wet eyelashes and in several other relevant places. "I won't start talking about Caliban now because you saw enough of him last night, but one day I will take you to Stratford to see a certain play performed in which he appears. As regards endocrines—"

"Stratford. That means Shakespeare wrote it. Perhaps there's hope for me yet." She was smiling again, the dimples deep and happy in both cheeks. He traced one gently with a finger.

"You will cause me to be late for the parade if I start talking about endocrines or even start up yours. They are mostly, but not all, inside your head. If any of them are missing or in short supply, the person isn't normal. There are in fact very few normal people, but you are one, Dora, so don't worry about sin." He rose. "I'm off to the parade now, my love. It's after all what we came up for."

"Oh?" said Dora. "Go away, then!"

He kissed her finally, let himself at last out of the schoolhouse door, and drove the Renault carefully out over the former child-proof tarmac and away. Dora heard the car drive off, lying on the chaise-longue and staring at the aspidistra.

Tom's fears were realised; he was caught in a relentless queue of cars. Having survived such things in London and on motorways he knew the only thing to do was relax and think of something else till it was time to move a few inches. He thought of Dora.

He had astonished himself by the rapid altering of the quality of his feeling for her since the marriage. He'd begun by liking her and admiring her courage at the time of Jerry Beale's death after the loss of their baby; then the way she'd kept his cottage spotless and welcoming whenever he chose to appear, which in the nature of his occupation was bound to mean a moveable feast.

Gradually, as any feeling he'd developed for Mary Reston began to turn towards its sad, dead end, he had begun to notice, and gradually to desire, Dora physically. He'd still thought of her, no doubt, almost as a little cuddly pillow to hug in bed. He had certainly known, quite soon, that he wanted to take her there.

Now, with that achieved and perfected – he'd soon make her forget last night with that unspeakable brute – he had begun to appreciate her company. She was restful, but never abject; had plenty of sense, as he'd known, and wit, and an intelligence which he hadn't taken much time to find out about till now. At the Brennan cottage he had liked to relax in front of television if it was raining, or else go out and walk, or climb or paint if it wasn't. Dora hadn't obtruded, had certainly never flaunted her attractions at him. It had been an undoubted surprise to her when he proposed the first time. All she had replied was that about poor Jerry not being long enough dead. That was the way Dora had been taught to think; and it had taken the Commander's unwelcome pass to bring her to him at last. Tom didn't think that, by now, she regretted being brought.

The cars began to make slight progress, moving at the traditional rate of tortoises, directed by not one but two perspiring policemen wearing luminous yellow tabards. Suddenly one of them depressed his hand, and everything stopped just as Tom glimpsed the downward slope which led at last to the field and its roped-off car park. The news, "It's the pipes", made itself manifest in a kind of agreeable anticipatory hissing. A further sound was wafted far off, but growing ever closer. It was the mighty sound as of all the winds of heaven rolled into one, best heard, as is well known among the English, across a mountain range, but if necessary to be endured near at hand, which is no doubt why those who play bagpipes keep moving, out of consideration.

One of the policemen walked over meantime and made himself known again, having spotted Tom at his open driver's window. Why a London Metropolitan cop should have been posted up to these far parts Tom didn't ask; perhaps the man had wanted a transfer. The pipes were growing imminent, and talk became inadvisable, then impossible. Everyone watched, listened and sat still.

The pipers approached close-packed, a darkly intent schiltrom like the foremost phalanx at Bannockburn, with a few men still left here and there; a drum-major swung his baton with panache and expertise, showing red flaps in his busby and on his socks, above spats stiff with whiting. There is no worse sight than a knock-kneed man in a kilt, and there were none such to be seen here. The pipers followed, blowing proudly on. Behind them came the commissioned ladies, cheeks full of air, their stomachs swinging in time to their own performance and the regular beat of the drum. They wore round bonnets with dark green feathers, green jackets, the kilt, and spats. Tom shuddered, and glanced beyond these baroque wonders to where the lone figure of Sawnie Cattanach could already been seen, no doubt preparing to take the ticket money. The mad eyes, visible even from here between eyelids red with ingrained dirt, registered a certain cold disapproval. The pipers passed by, and, one's eardrums having survived, there was talk to be heard again, and the cars started moving. Tom had been able to lean out of the window and gleefully photograph one low-swung kilted female bottom as it passed, in a swirl of protesting pleats, swinging, swinging, ay, hooch ay, above short plump legs like Mrs Mac's own.

The tune they were playing floated back to him; *The Flowers o' the Forest*. It was true that the ladies played well enough, and there had only been women left to weep after Flodden. Then, as Tom and the rest progressed downhill in their cars with funereal dignity, there was a pause, to allow for the shaking of spittle, male and female, out of the narrow ivory tubes and mouthpieces. Then, after a deep breath, *Stand Fast, Craigellachie* began. In the brief silence, however, Sawnie Cattanach had prophesied aloud.

"It iss the silly pitches they are," said he, to nobody but the sky. This fortunately was blue, and in the Highlands a fine day is a very fine day indeed. Everyone on the field sweated invisibly under heavy kilts and plaids and shining appurtenances, especially a very old chief of some other clan who had been invited to make the speech before the prize-giving by Lady Charlotte, but was long past remembering whatever it was he had been meaning to say. He wore capercailzie's feathers and his shoulder-brooch gleamed in infinite superiority to any findings ever likely to be made at Sutton Hoo.

The noise continued further off, while Tom was jammed in his slowly moving downward fellow-traffic into what looked like more hell to get out of again than in. He was glad Dora had a second key to the house; it might well be late before he got back to her. Her courage over the whole ugly business of last night roused his renewed admiration.

The known policeman, whose name Tom remembered as Rowbotham, beckoned him at last into the park, having himself moved down. Despite his northern name he had a Whitechapel accent, sounding like a foreign language up here.

"Thank Gawd, the noise is gorn nah. 'Ere y'are, guv'nor, in between them vans there, left." Tom turned left obediently; it wasn't too bad a place.

"Thanks," he signalled, and the Cockney winked.

"Get it all inter the pipers, eh?" He meant the newspapers, not the ladies.

"How long are you on for?" Tom asked him.

"Get tea and a hot dog after the parade. World stops after the parade, first I've seen and 'ope it's the last. Gawd, that noise. I can't 'eat nothin' yet, worse than jets flyin' in over 'ead at 'eathrow."

It had started again, the piping, the band having formed a new square at the far end of the field, where the marquee was and near where he and Dora had stood yesterday. Out of the great tent itself there came a small quiet figure in a pale grey well-cut suit, leading Diarmaidh on a short lead. It was the first time Tom had set full eyes on the Lady of Insshe.

The sun shone on her hair, eliciting fair highlights. More Tom could not perceive until after *Belphegor* had blasted forth, rather unsuitably, and the march began. The small lady and the large dog did their best, Charlotte valiantly taking the place in the procession which was, after all, hers by right. Battered husbands, Tom thought, and a good thing too. The slow march continued twice round the field, backed up by the great drum's beat, beat, thump, thumpity thump. There was a pleasant smell of trodden grass in the sun. Music played, kilts swung, cheeks male and female blew out full of Highland air to send down the narrow ivory into the bag and blare forth. Tom was out of the car in time to take a photograph of Lady Charlotte close at hand as she came round at the head of all. Photography, for Tom, was automatic; at the same time he felt a shock. If this was the much-mated Lady of Insshe, her face, expression and narrow body closely resembled, unless it was a trick of the sunlight, her own governess in youth.

There was always ice-cream for sale in the tents, and as soon as the parade was over everyone would move thankfully towards them. There were filled rolls and hot dogs and beefburgers and chocolate and handloom weaving and pirated rowan mugs and tartan scarves and canvas bags and sunglasses and sneakers. There was free whisky in a secret tent erected by an uninvited pirate clan, and those who knew about it disappeared for the afternoon and were no more seen. The ignorant would sit on the grass instead, licking their ice-cream cones or else queuing up to relieve nature at the Portakabins, two of which stood end to end and for which there was a charge, so some people as a rule merely went behind a tree. Others would sit on seats if they had got one in time, waiting for the Highland dancing to start. Potential dancers were lacing up their traditional black lightweight leather shoes and adjusting their beribboned narrow bonnets. Tom went on with his photography as shots occurred, immortalising twirling dancers and caber-tossers and long and high jumps waiting to be taken when the parade had finished, likewise stolid ponies who could be trusted not to unseat excited children who had never ridden one before. Tom glimpsed the man Peters in change of some of them. Everything and everyone on the field waited, while the pipes and the Lady passed by for the final time.

Suddenly, the great hound wrenched from its owner's grasp and streaked towards the great tent door, outside which souvenirs had been waiting for custom with the laird behind them.

But the grey hurricane, lead flying, stopped all that. The pipes died down to a wail. Lady Charlotte stood abandoned on the field, seeming uncertain what to do, as if nobody had told her this might happen; she was no doubt used to being directed. She would never manage to appear fashionable; her coat and skirt, though they fitted well over her slender figure, might have been cut for the last generation. Her thin legs were encased in fawn medium-weight stockings and she wore sensible shoes. Altogether, she resembled a small, immature crane. Tom took in all such details before a voice cried out in Gaelic; there had come also by then the howling of a dog, the long, long coronach for a soul escaped from the body.

"Police! Police! The laird has been stabbed with his own *sgian dubh*! Am Insheach is dead!"

Twelve

"Press," yelled Brackenbury, and shouldered his way in past those who watched already by the dead. The dog was being taken away, held by its collar.

There, slumped forward in the chair at which he had been about to preside over the sales table of souvenirs *malgré lui*, was the body of Norton-Insshe, with the shining silver-plate and ebony *sgian dubh* missing from his right stocking. Instead, it was sticking deep in his back to the left, below the rib-cage. There was no doubt whatever that he was dead. Blood had stopped oozing from the wound, and flies had begun to gather in numbers, like the Camerons after flesh. The sticking-plaster which had prevented Norton-Insshe's presence this time at the head of the procession could just be seen across the late laird's nose, sunk sideways as it was to the right against the table. Several of the objects there had been upset: a rowan mug had parted from its handle; nearby one of Miss Walshe's handmade teddy bears was lurching crazily, its expression unchangingly bland.

Tom noted at least one unusual thing and pondered it: the clan president wasn't wearing his great chain of office, as might have been expected; the AGM was to have been immediately after the prize-giving. The marquee behind – as it was a fine day the sales table had been placed just outside on the grass – was filled with precisely arranged benches and tables for the purpose, with sheets of paper and copies of the minutes set out ready. The meeting would presumably have to be postponed. Tom pictured Colonel McIntosh's chagrin; or would the reason please him?

Within the hour, a helicopter had landed on the field and therefrom debouched two Yard men, a sergeant, a pathologist and two technicians. The DI – called Dixon Hawke – contrived to look as might have been expected. Tom knew him already.

"Hallo, Brack. You here?" remarked the DI without surprise.

"As you see." He hadn't met Hawke's colleague, and didn't much think he wanted to; Inspector Allen was blunt of feature, with a fishlike eye that missed nothing and an entire lack of humour, which last asset had got him where he was.

They lost no time in getting under way. Tom had taken a photograph of the dead laird but was asked not to release it. "I can stay, can't I?" he murmured to Hawke.

"Provided you don't release the evidence yet." Their voices remained unheard in the buzz of the now restrained crowd, the local police having already roped off the area and told everyone except Tom to go to the other end of the field and stay there meantime. Tom owed his undoubted status in this respect to his acquaintance with Constable Rowbotham. The other reporters who had been present at the Games looked sour, but went as instructed.

"The only people who couldn't have done it are the pipers and Lady Charlotte," remarked DI Hawke not long after his arrival. "We can't keep everyone here like the feeding of the five thousand. Rope in as many as you think proper and take down the car numbers of the rest." The local policemen, whose own hot dogs had been rudely interrupted by the murder, hastened to do as bidden. Soon enough the field at that end was deserted and the body measured, photographed, chalked round about and covered with a sheet. It was then carried meantime into the marquee. Decidedly, the clan AGM would not now take place. The prizegiving, likewise, was abandoned, among those not questioned having been the man Peters, who had, in his usual way, sloped off unseen.

"At least we have the exact time of death," said Hawke. "The dog knew the instant it had happened." A dog's scent would smell blood across the smell of close-mown grass, the smells of cigarettes and ice-cream and humanity. It seemed the only living creature that had cared for the dead man; it had been led, protesting and whining, back to Lady Charlotte to go up to Great House meantime.

"I could have done it," said Tom. "I got a photograph of Diarmaidh streaking across the field, as I was down at that end. It's a scoop for A.B., with the bystanders falling back and about like ninepins as he hurtled through."

"Where had you been before that?" asked Allen suspiciously. He and Tom had taken an instant dislike to one another. Tom said he'd been taking photographs all round the field.

"Brack has often helped us with enquiries," put in the DI gently.

"That doesn't prevent him from having done it. What you need is motive, and with all these hundreds of people present—"

"I'm still not going to arrest Brack to save ourselves further trouble. The man who called out the news, at least, is here; the local boys took him in."

The voice in the wilderness turned out to belong to a nondescript old man with wild white hair and a lurcher sidling by him: the pair lived in a ramshackle caravan at the loch's end whose non-existent state of hygiene continued to alarm the proprietors of the cheerful new nearby tourist hotels. There had been several attempts to get Joe Jolly re-housed, but he had eluded all of them.

"So you called out as soon as you saw the laird's body? Tell us exactly what you saw," said Hawke. Everyone noted the distinction between lord and laird, as understood even up here.

"A laird is more like a squire, I take it?" enquired Allen, after Jolly had been allowed to go, having told them nothing about the killing they didn't know already.

"Nobody is left to protect him now from the county planners," said Tom. "They'll have him in sheltered housing before the year's end, and the lurcher put down."

"And he will make the housing stink as badly as the caravan ever did with tins that haven't been thrown away, and choked-up plumbing," remarked Hawke, who knew his world and its blanket of the dark. "The resistance to enforced civilisation is clearly seen in what is happening to the genuine gypsies. They are never happy under a roof."

"Well, let's get on," muttered Allen impatiently. "Who's next?"

It turned out, after much sorting of sheep from goats, that so many had disliked the laird without knowing why that if one individual could be found who did not, he or she was probably guilty, like the beauty queen's milkman. Tom kept quiet in Allen's presence. He was not necessarily going to mention their stay, his and Dora's, at Inshtochradh; that would no doubt be discovered when the police went there and found the signatures in the book, but he was by no means going to involve Dora unnecessarily.

Thirteen

Great house had been offered as a convenient venue for questioning, as the forensic boys were busy down at the marquee. Once inside, Tom gazed up at the rococo ceiling, which had been newly gilded and decorated with pale eggshell pink. Money had been spent on Taigh Mór inside and outside, not always in the best of taste; no doubt the Lady had been governed by her husband, who was paying the bills. Nevertheless, Norton-Insshe's personality was totally absent; he could be remembered chiefly with the white cloth tied round his middle, cooking oats on the Aga at Inshtochradh. There was a print of that abode in earlier days, labelled in copperplate, on the wall; it had once been a pleasant unpretentious dower house of the seventeenth century or earlier, with a rowan tree in front.

Down at the field, the Games, like the AGM, had been abandoned out of respect; the silent pipers, male and female, had gone home. The sound of the emptying car park could be heard from up here. Taigh Mór was built on a fair eminence; Tom wondered if there had been an earlier castle here, on the high rock by way of protection against rival clans. The fourteenth laird, understandably, had chosen to live in classical isolation, to protect himself.

Sawnie Cattanach had, of course, been picked on at once as a likely suspect, but had given relative satisfaction as far as that went, despite having absconded early from the ticket-booth.

"Have you ever been in trouble with the police?" Allen asked him, most unfairly. The mad eyes stared over, a caged animal's, taking the Englishman in.

"Nobody iss in trouble with the likes of them that does not have a car. I have no car and never had."

Hawke, who was at his most dangerous when sounding amiable, asked, "How did you get here today, then? Where do you come from?"

"I got here on my own two feet, and where I come from the likes of you would never be knowing."

Tom murmured that this was the lost laird. His statement was somewhat hindered by the pervading odour of lice. The red-rimmed gaze flickered across to where he sat.

"Nor would you, for you are English like the rest," Sawnie stated with contempt.

Tom would have denied the total impeachment in other circumstances, but as it was he didn't want to rouse Allen again. He smiled a little, and Hawke let Sawnie go soon because, as he said afterwards, the man had had his own black knife in his belt. It was unlikely that he would have taken the trouble to pull out Norton-Insshe's from the top of the late laird's stocking and use that rather than his own. "In any case, the police here know where to find him. He lives in a bothan on the hill."

Colonel McIntosh had already been briefly interviewed, still carrying the folder of papers he had intended to read out at the AGM. He had a buttoned-up look and had prudently left his wife beside their car in the sun. On being asked, he stated that the meeting would probably take place at some date to be arranged elsewhere. Asked if he was aware of any circumstances that could have led to the death, he said he knew of none in particular except that Norton-Insshe was generally held to have retained the position of clan President far too long.

"How long has he held it?" It handly seemed a reason for murder, although one never knew.

"Eight years, ever since the marriage. Lord Insshe proposed him at the time, and in those days one didn't argue because of the old lord's state of health. Insshe died, in fact, shortly after."

"What is the normal term of office?"

"Three years. Several of us resented the fact of Norton-

Insshe's refusal to step down, but owing to the convenience of the clan Games and Taigh Moŕ, nothing was done; you know how such things continue."

"Where was the president's chain of office kept?" asked Hawke idly.

"Oh, he kept it himself. He kept everything of the kind. Something was to have been said this year. I myself have been in touch with several committee members."

Hawke didn't ask where the chain was now. The laird had not been wearing it when found, and it was unlikely that he would have failed to bring it with him from Inshtochradh, even with his nose covered in sticking plaster. It was, as it would appear, one of the perks of being Am Insheach. The man had evidently given out that he'd injured his face with his motor. It was a curious place for an injury. The pathologists would have more to say, no doubt, given time. Meantime, it had been obvious that the good Colonel had a personal grudge. No doubt he had hoped to be elected president himself in proper course, but murdering a rival was hardly, these days, a practical solution.

A tray of tea and biscuits from Taigh Mór refreshment room was then carried in by Miss Walshe. Having poured it for them, she sat down in a chair, folding her hands quietly in her lap.

"I want to save the police further trouble," she said. "I killed Willard Norton-Insshe. As you can see, my hands are quite strong. I am anxious to avoid needless expense to the taxpayer. You ask why I did this? He was exceedingly cruel to his wife, who had been my pupil. Also, as I have known now for eleven months, he killed their son."

The world does not immediately stop turning because of a random confession, and routine questioning of a general kind continued for some time down at the field entry. Rowbotham, struggling with not being understood by anyone very quickly, took details from those he might or might not allow to pass through, while his colleague noted down the respective numbers of exiting cars. By the time forty-four persons had sworn they had been queuing up for the Portakabins at the time Diarmaidh had put over his act of detection, fifteen more assuring the police that they had been taking a little nap by the river after eating hot dogs on a hot day, and so on, Constable Rowbotham was beginning to want a hot dog of his own; he'd been interrupted, after all, just as they were about to enjoy them. Several more couldn't exactly remember which part of the field they had been in, but were certain it hadn't been anywhere near. The sun grilled down, and it was a relief to be instructed to lay off and return to Great House: there might be an arrest. A WPC was said to be on the way from Inverness.

There had been a moment's silence in the great hall at Taigh Mór. Then Allen spoke, his workaday voice intruding into what had seemed a bizarre situation, perhaps certain madness. It was the more grotesque in that Miss Walshe continued to look, and speak, like the retired headmistress of a genteel girls' school.

"Did you see it happen?" asked Allen ruthlessly about the boy's drowning last year.

"No, I must be truthful; an observer told me, one whom I trust. It happened down at the pool in the river where Willard used to take the little boy on fine days to try to teach him to swim. Ronald was a handicapped child and I was surprised that Mr Norton-Insshe continued so long with his attempts. He was not otherwise a patient or a kindly man. He liked to see what he called results."

She brought out a carefully ironed handkerchief, and fastidiously applied it to her nose. *Come on, woman. Come on.* Brackenbury heard the voices sound inside his head.

"It would hardly have been a reason for drowning the child unless it had happened sooner. Who was the observer?" Allen continued. His eyes, pale and prominent in the blunt high-coloured face, were fastened on her impersonally. Like Tom and the DI, the thought was no doubt in his head that she might be fantasising; these old girls who'd had uneventful lives sometimes did.

"I decline to say who my informant was," replied Miss Walshe with spirit. "I am giving you the facts of this murder, not the last. I admit today's. I have likewise been informed that I have inoperable cancer, so it was advisable enough to do as I have done, as well as an historic occasion on which to do so, and it is of little importance what becomes of me for as long as I have to live. I decided to tell the police, as I have said, to save time and expense for the British taxpayer, who already pays far too much for bringing these everlasting traffic offences to court and not enough for having an eye kept on genuine offenders in other spheres."

"I am glad, Miss Walshe, that you consider your fellow-citizens," broke in the DI with a certain irony. "All the same, you took, if I may say, an unnecessarily long time to kill Mr Norton-Insshe, if so. You should have had ample opportunity apart from the bicentenary. I understand you worked in his hotel souvenir shop?"

The report had come in by telephone by now from Inshtochradh; Tom knew his own signature would have been found on the whisky receipts as well as his and Dora's in the registration book. He spoke up; silence might seem over-cautious now.

"I recognised some of the souvenirs on the table outside the tent," he said. "What will become of them now?"

"I – I—" She passed her tongue round her lips, evidently nervous for the first time. "I helped out with several aspects of the hotel, as staff were hard to come by," she said. "I used to see to the laundry – there was a machine, of course, and a tumble dryer – and change the towels and bed linen if guests happened to be staying overnight. This did not happen often, though there were always late night drinkers who came and went in their cars. I did not, of course, wait to see *that*."

"Why were staff difficult to obtain, Miss Walshe? One would have thought the local people would have been glad of employment."

"My – Mr Norton-Insshe did not offer a high wage. He preferred to see to everything himself. He – he was a perfectionist, as he used to say. That may have been one reason why he perfected the plan to drown little Ronnie. He used to go down with him every day till there was no longer any question of his good intentions."

"Also, Inshtochradh is, I believe, remote?" said the DI smoothly. They must have described it to him over the telephone, Tom thought.

"Yes. My – Mr Norton-Insshe preferred to be out of the public gaze. Also, Taigh Mór is expensive to keep up and it has been turned into a show place for the public, especially at this time of year, with the bicentenary."

The questioning went on. Tom had grown restless, and while still able to overhear the talk, went quietly to where the reception desk stood for issuing tickets to see over the house, presumably without any kind of security search; there weren't enough staff here. Doors opened at different places off the great outer tiled hall, leading to other rooms and, no doubt, the kitchens below and the service attics above. There was a framed map hanging on the wall with instructions of where to find the kitchens down their chilly flagged passages, below ground level and the rock; there hadn't been much consideration in those days for servants anywhere. Cans of hot water had had to be carried upstairs to guests, food delivered and kept hot also by some means, slops emptied, whims and tempers met, ironing done, fires stoked, logs carried. Attic bedrooms near the roof, one's mistress down in the drawing room large or small, the gentlemen in the billiard room, that was by last century; the folly in the original garden was long since defunct, and a refreshment room was included at the east end of the house, where there was a firmly announced Caracci.

That, and what Mrs Mac had called the *objets d'art*, were mostly reproduced as postcards on sale near the door. Tom decided to take some back to Dora; there would almost certainly not be time to show her over Taigh Mór in person, they must get back south now for several reasons. Tom turned the revolving stand of cards while still listening to the police enquiries. It would end, evidently – the WPC had arrived, and with her a constable who said he spoke Irish Gaelic – by letting Miss Walshe stay here overnight in the room she from time to time occupied, with the policewoman on guard. Hawke didn't seem certain yet about making an arrest; there must be more people questioned.

Brackenbury absently chose the reproduced Caracci, a Reynolds of the heiress who'd married the fourteenth laird and didn't look too pleased about it, though she was handsome enough with her hair up on a frame; and one of the fourteenth laird himself, cold-eyed; it was easy to picture him making profits from the mill and the everlasting sheep. There was also a more modern portrait, a de Laszlo, Tom assumed, and found on the card's back that he was correct. It was of a handsome long-nosed man of the previous generation, stated on the caption to have been James Insshe, third baron. This must almost certainly be the present Lady's father. There were none of Charlotte herself to be had; no doubt she hadn't wanted to sit here selling reproductions of herself as shown in the pale-blue dress over the fireplace at Inshtochradh.

Tom paid for the postcards, with commendable honesty as there was nobody at the desk. He put the money for safety in a drawer, and on opening it saw two things. One was a photograph of a small boy in a white sunhat clutching a toy rabbit. Tom had more time than Dora to study the features, and could make out the eyes beneath the hat's tactful shade; the strange diagnostic thumbs were concealed in the toy's softness, no doubt the reason why they'd taken him in that pose, poor Master Ronnie. Down's syndrome, certainly: and drowned last year. People still spoke of it; he'd heard one woman say earlier today that she wasn't going to let the twins go down near that river, it wasn't safe for children.

The second object in the drawer was a plain notepad. The top remaining page had been filled in with yesterday's date and an exact account, in small neat immature handwriting, of how each separate hour had been spent between nine-thirty and six-thirty. The remainder of the pad was blank, as though each sheet had been duly filled with entries day after day, thereafter being regularly torn off, read and disposed of by whoever was interested.

Tom rejoined the police at their questioning, knowing it would be very late before he got back to Dora; but he must at all costs stay now.

Fourteen

For some time after his departure Dora had done as Tom told her, and had stayed resting on the chaise-longue. She heard the increase of traffic outside and then it ceased. Either everyone must have arrived at the Games or else there was a traffic jam, as had used to happen yearly at the agricultural show in Penarch; they couldn't ever all seem to get into the car park at once.

She looked about her; Miss Walshe's house could do with a good clean, there was that slight film of dust on everything with not being lived in. She felt quite well by now. It would be repaying hospitality to brighten things up for when Miss Walshe returned, whenever that might be. Dora supposed she had some other place at which to stay, perhaps Great House itself; it certainly wasn't at Inshtochradh.

"Ugh," Dora said, aloud, remembering the laird; and, realising that she couldn't stay alone all day thinking of what had happened last night. She went to Tom's suitcase, packed by herself that morning, and found the local map. It showed several of the branching minor roads round the clachan, one of which led to the Games field. Tom would be cross if he saw her there, but one of the little further roads round the back would show enough to see the procession, perhaps, and Great House again on its high rock. She'd go for a little walk by herself, and say nothing about it.

She put on her sandals. The denim dress had the advantage of two deep pockets, and into one Dora slipped the key from the hook on the wall, having tested it first to make sure it was the right one and she wouldn't be locked out after all. Then she let herself out of the door, shut it, and was gone for quite some time.

When she returned it was still bright day. She let herself in, found the cupboard where dusters and brooms and the vacuum cleaner were kept, and got to work. If Tom came in he would find her busy. Dora smiled. She felt quite all right by now.

She dusted and polished round till everything in the room was as clean as a whistle, then, as Tom still hadn't come home, made herself a cup of tea. After that she decided to get to work upstairs; after all, Miss Walshe had said to make themselves at home.

There had been other things upstairs, besides the books, that told you a certain amount about Miss Walshe. Evidently she made lots of little tartan souvenirs and things for the Inshtochradh shop herself. No doubt they paid her; the things were very well made, tiny dressed dolls and teddy bears in tartan kilts or bonnets and aprons, or, once or twice, tartan trousers.

She put the brush and shovel resolutely back in their cupboard before marching once again upstairs. If there was a dictionary she'd find it. If there wasn't, she'd find something else to read till Tom came back. There wasn't telly here. Whatever a lady like Miss Walshe chose to read would broaden the mind, as poor Jerry used to say.

There wasn't a dictionary on the shelves, but there was a large Bible. Dora took the great volume down and opened it at random. The Bible opened naturally at a photograph, which fell out. It was brown and faded; that of a handsome man with a long nose. Dora knew she'd seen the face, or something like it, somewhere before, but for the moment couldn't think where. She picked the photograph up to replace it and stared at the large sprawling writing across the bottom: '*For my beloved Mavis, with all my heart, James Insshe*'.

Insshe. Perhaps Miss Walshe was really part of the family, although the wording was a bit strong if so. Or perhaps Mavis was somebody else altogether. The photograph was, after all, quite old. It would probably have faded more if it had been left out in daylight. However, there might have been other reasons for hiding it.

There was something attached, folded in behind; stuck on by the torn-open flap of an envelope. Having been pressed together for so long had made what was left of the delicate glue adhere; probably it had been kept for a long time somewhere damp. The writing on the envelope was in thick black ink turned brown, the same as the message on the photograph. It would be wrong to pry, but the letter was clearly addressed to Miss Mavis Walshe, at an address somewhere or other in India.

Dora would not have been human had she failed to read the first line, which was all that showed of the letter jutting up slightly from its envelope. It had been read, perhaps many times, and put back again; then at last put in here, with the photograph. She wouldn't take it out to read the whole thing. It was a love letter. Still, the first line made you think. It began, '*My dearest Mavis, my own dear heart*', then, '*Our child must be born safely. I will arrange—*' and that was where the paper came to an end, and nobody could say she, Dora Brackenbury, was nosy. She put everything back exactly as she had found it, and closed and replaced the Bible.

She wondered how much to tell Tom. He might think she was like that gossiping Mrs Mac at the Rowan Tree, whose husband Tom had said he felt sorry for. She'd wait and see. That was what to do. Jerry had always said, 'When in doubt, do nothing'. She wouldn't even mention to Tom where she'd been today, let alone tell him Miss Walshe had had a baby somewhere out in India and that its father had been called James Insshe.

The cars had roared past again for some time now beyond the windows, but Tom still hadn't returned. Dora hoped nothing had happened to him. For the time being, she'd make more tea and boil herself an egg, then go to bed if he still hadn't come in. It was beginning to get dark, but after all at Brennan he'd often arrived very late indeed, reporters had to be like that. If no word had come by tomorrow, she'd perhaps ask the police.

She had her supper, and before drifting off to sleep recalled where she'd seen the long-nosed face before. It had been Lady Charlotte's, first of all driving the ancient Humber car down the drive when they first went to Inshtochradh, and after that in the drawing room there above the fireplace, in a pale-blue dress among the whisky. Then . . .

It might, after all, be the Insshe clan face. Tom had said once there was a Campbell one, with light eyelashes. Things like that were passed on, distinctive characteristics; a living hallmark . . .

She slept.

Fifteen

"Why didn't you make the arrest?" asked Inspector Allen crossly over dinner at the Rowan Tree, now miraculously emptied of clan members; only the officers were staying there, likewise the McIntosh couple by request.

"Because of several things," Hawke said. "Firstly, I share your opinion that she mightn't after all have done it. For one thing, she was somewhat too quick in destroying certain evidence we might have used at Inshtochradh."

"What was that?"

"I would have told you sooner, but I think you have your knife in Brackenbury."

"I don't have knives in anyone. We're investigating a murder. I want the job tied up, that's all."

"But not to the extent of allowing a self-confession to apply when it may be made to shield somebody else. As Miss Walshe herself stated, it doesn't greatly matter what happens to her if she hasn't long to live." She had struck him, watching, as suppressing a certain degree of pain; he had admired her courage in any case. They had sent her up to her room for the night at Taigh Mór, with WPC Marshall sitting outside; that young woman was reliable, nothing would go wrong. Lady Charlotte, whom he'd seen briefly, said she also would stay in Great House with Diarmaidh: it was understandable that she didn't want to return to Inshtochradh. Colonel McIntosh had been asked not to leave till tomorrow. He and his wife had meantime taken dinner elsewhere.

"Did you know Brackenbury was married?" Hawke asked Allen. The other shrugged.

"Hadn't thought about it one way or the other. Thought his wife was killed, wasn't she?" Allen had a precise memory and forgot nothing, a faculty which had earned him promotion to a certain extent, but not beyond it.

"That was the first wife. He remarried only the other day, and they came up to Inshtochradh for their honeymoon and for Brack, I daresay, to cover the Games and the bicentenary."

"Well, what was the evidence you spoke of?"

Hawke surveyed his fingers. "I might not have put two and two together if the receptionist here hadn't mentioned, by way of chat, that a couple from the murdered man's hotel had left early without any breakfast, and had called in for coffee here she wasn't able to produce. It seems odd that they left so early. The forensic boys have been over Inshtochradh, naturally, and have examined the sheets on the late laird's bed. I instructed them to look for allied semen in the tower room occupied by the couple, but Miss Walshe had whipped the sheets off the bed and put them straight in the machine to wash. That's what I mean by removing evidence."

"You mean the dead man was a lecher," said Allen primly.

"He certainly wasn't popular in the neighbourhood, although we've been unable to find evidence of lechery except in the marriage bed with Lady Charlotte. I've hesitated to question her so far as she is, as you know already, one of the people it couldn't possibly have been. Perhaps tomorrow."

"Why did you detain McIntosh?" Allen asked, with growing respect; he had previously thought the DI somewhat inept, and that he himself would have wrapped the case up much faster. However, perhaps there was more to it than a mad old girl.

Hawke met his gaze with grey eyes difficult to read. "Because we can't locate the clan chain of office, and the good Colonel seemed to desire it rather unduly. That's a thin clue, I know, but I haven't forgotten it."

"Probably nothing to do with the case," remarked Allen, and poured himself more coffee. That clucking McIntosh woman had irritated him as much as Brackenbury, for some reason, also did;

a matter, no doubt, of personality clash, like two positive electric poles meeting with the inevitable explosion.

At that moment a real explosion rent the summer night. The two officers rushed to the window to observe in the last of the daylight the fourteenth laird's statue, high on its hill, topple and dissolve into shards which gave off a dim red light from here, soon fading to a grey evanescent cloud. Activity manifested itself immediately from the hills and the hotels; everyone rushed outside to look up at what was no longer there, leaving a bare green mountain.

"The bicentenary celebration," observed Hawke drily. They couldn't have been expected, after all, to foresee everything,

The police rushed to the scene which, however, involved climbing the steep hill by torchlight. There was nothing they could do when they got there, everything having been done already. The remains of the fourteenth laird lay about in a settling cloud of dust. He had evidently been blown up most efficiently by means of a detonator attached to a long plastic fuse, whose further end was discovered a quarter of a mile off among boulders over which the police tripped and cursed, but found no other evidence. The whole exercise resembled a mild horror film. Arrangements about the fuse had been made some time before and any identification of the culprit, or culprits, was in any case rendered unlikely by the effects of weather, which had made everything muddy. More might be discovered in daylight. The torches were switched off except one, to guide everybody back downhill, except PC Rowbotham, who was ordered to remain on site till dawn.

"Bloody shithole," muttered the Cockney, left alone in a creepy situation and for once glad of his luminous traffic tabard. Apart from warning off potential thugs it kept him warm, and the night air grew cold up here even in summer, especially at this height. The whole business gave a bloke the crawling 'orrors, particularly as there hadn't been any open curiosity shown by the locals; it was almost as though they'd expected the ruddy explosion: either that or they were keeping out of the way on principle. He thought once he saw Joe Jolly's lurcher slinking along by itself as lurchers do when ordered by their owners to make themselves scarce, but that didn't prove anything. A light across the hills at Great House had burned in the upper room for some time, but by now had gone out. There was only darkness on the hills, and the silence of remembered wrongs. Even the Englishman felt it.

Cor, he thought, he'd ask for a transfer back south as soon as might be. At least the Met hadn't left a bloke on his own half frozen up the slope of a bleedin' mountain in the small hours. There had always been a cuppa to go and have back at the station.

Dawn came, and Rowbotham was relieved by other personnel. The fourteenth laird lay shattered, his pretensions revealed for what they were. It had been, in its way, the Day of Judgement at the bicentenary.

Sixteen

Before all of that, Tom had stopped on his way to rejoin Dora and had bought himself an evening paper at the clachan. He was gratified to see, on the front page with a large sub-heading, his kilted lady piper presenting her bare bottom to viewers below its swirl of pleats, with a white spat in the lower background marching away from the camera. THE FEMINISTS' REPLY? the headline said, and put in Tom's byline. Grinning, he took the paper in to show to Dora. He found her sitting upstairs in bed, having heard his key in the lock.

"Have you had anything to eat?" she asked. He said he had; they'd brought up the remains of the tent stock during questioning.

"Why were you so long? Has anything happened?" It was growing dark. He went to her, put his arms about her and told her about the death. "Ugh," was all she said. Then, "The police will find out we were at Inshtochradh. Tom, I'm scared."

"Nonsense." He showed her the kilted female to make her laugh, but Dora only stared at it. She was disturbed, he knew; so was he, and to take her mind off things he brought out the postcards he'd bought at Taigh Mór. "There won't be time for you to see the house, it's full of cops for the next day or two," he said. "These are some of the people who lived there."

Dora exclaimed at sight of the late Lord Insshe. "That's the man in the photograph upstairs in the Bible," she said. "I was going to tell you." She told him, also about finding the letter.

He frowned. He'd better tell Hawke tomorrow. There was

more and more to this case than met the eye. Luckily Hawke's eye saw past immediacy, even if Allen's didn't.

He would have left Dora alone that night, after what she'd been through, although the made-up bed tempted him, with its fresh sheets found by her in Miss Walshe's cupboard. "I'll put them through the washing machine first thing tomorrow before we go," Dora said. "Bed-and-breakfast people must do it every day."

Tom smiled, and began to take off his shoes. He could see her small sandals lying neatly placed beneath the chair, and to divert himself took one up in his hand to measure against the shoe he'd removed, and compare sizes. She'd been wearing her high heels this morning, he recalled, with the suitcases; she must have changed to—

There was crushed newly-mown grass trapped in the place on the sole where the flat heel joined it. It wasn't even yesterday's grass; they hadn't stood together in the mown field then, only on the bank. *Dora had been down at the field today*. He wouldn't ask her about it; she must tell him herself. He replaced the sandal, and took off his other shoe. He finished undressing and routinely, still in late shock, bent to kiss her formally goodnight. A hand, flower-smooth, laid itself against his cheek.

"I want it from you, Tom," she said. "I want it. Please. I'm all right now, except that I'm afraid."

At least, he thought, they could be afraid together.

Chimeras rose then, circling slowly in his mind like demons. What was in hers? *You may be a killer, Dora, held in my arms. You may have killed before. It may have been you, not Jerry who took the blame, who killed Elaine Partridge that time up at Brennan; she'd made you lose your baby. Later on Mary Reston killed herself; why was that? She'd known for long enough Basil Oldham didn't love her. Did you tempt him on purpose? Did you lie with him*? There'd been a rose in a tooth-tumbler today at Inshtochradh; had she invited Norton-Insshe into the bedroom while they knew he himself was away? She'd been secretly down at the field today, and still hadn't told him. She'd made sure, after all, that he hadn't seen her there. Perhaps this passion for keeping everything clean was the known sign of guilt criminals had. *I don't know you, Dora, at all.* Tomorrow the police might come here, having guessed.

Nevertheless, he still wanted her, his little duck, as she wanted him now. Fuck, fuck. Quack, quack, quack. A great many things had changed.

He heard the explosion in the distance when it was almost dark. A good reporter would have got his clothes on again and rushed out to see what had happened. He didn't want to go back there yet, however; not yet. He was still afraid, for her and for himself.

"What was that?" asked Dora drowsily.

"Nothing. Go back to sleep."

* * *

In the dawn he rose and dressed himself quietly, took the car and drove up to the hill. The remains of the fourteenth laird were lying about like Ozymandias. *Half sunk, a shattered visage lies, whose frown and wrinkled lip and sneer of cold command* . . . That was what the head looked like, now he could see it close and split in two. A shadow darkened the morning and he saw a second reporter, one who'd been at the Games yesterday with the rest; they greeted each other.

"Know who did it?" Tom asked. "This, I mean."

"The police think they know; they've gone to bring a man in. Care to let me share your photo?" Tom had taken a snap from a good angle.

"Take one of your own," snapped Brackenbury. He wasn't feeling charitable.

"Oh, all right. I told you what I knew, though. They'll all be here soon, I expect. This place is the hub of the universe for once, innit?"

He took one of his own with a flash lens, scowled and made off. Tom went downhill to fax his photograph and send a few words to A.B. He left the two vast and trunkless legs of stone not standing in the desert, but blown into eight or nine pieces on a Highland hill where once there had been crofts and living folk.

The word PATER stared up ironically from the surviving shards. The fulsome inscription – he wondered what had happened to the wreath that was to have been laid – at the former statue's base had been in Latin on one side and English on the other, but no Gaelic. He didn't suppose they would bother to mend the fourteenth laird up again. There had been ill-feeling about the presence of the statue for a long time. It might have been blown to smithereens by anyone, or more than one. Quietly, he wished them well. He supposed he'd better go back to the house for some breakfast.

Seventeen

"They can't all 'ave been queuin' for them Portakabins, though that's wot all of 'em says," remarked PC Rowbotham later that day in tones of gloom. "We'll be 'ere till ruddy doomsday at this rate."

The newly arrived constable, whose name was Finnegan and who understood Irish Gaelic, for which reason it had been decided to send him along with the WPC from Inverness, stuck his head round the door.

"There's a lady outside, sorr. She's wantin' to speak with yez."

Tom's heart stopped; was it Dora, in whatever fashion? He'd forgotten that the Irishman had not yet set eyes on Miss Walshe, who walked in again calmly, followed by the WPC in her pony tail. "I greatly wish, Inspector, that you would take the rest of my statement," Miss Walshe began. "It will save time and trouble for *everyone.*"

"Madam, we have not yet taken a statement from you in any formal way. That may come, but there are others to see; you heard last night's explosion?" DI Hawke looked weary.

"Not before time; the statue was much disapproved of by everybody," replied Miss Walshe evenly, adding that the hill looked much better without the fourteenth laird's presence in any case. "I should like to continue as regards my killing of Willard Norton-Insshe," she said. "There is a great deal more you do not yet know."

At this point the door burst open and two more local traffic police entered in their yellow tabards, manhandling between them a struggling Sawnie Cattanach, attired as usual except that he wore the Clan Insshe chain of office. It gleamed across his shoulders as by right, if a trifle askew. He shook off the two policemen and stood thereafter alone and with dignity. The police had already taken the black knife out of his belt; Rowbotham held it uncertainly, as if it might sting. "We found the chain on 'im, sir, up at his shack."

"Why should I not be wearing the *slabhraidh* of my own society?" enquired Sawnie with hauteur. "It was time that I, Alasdair Insshe of Insshe of the old line, was the clan's president myself. Give me back my *sgian dubh*; you have no right to it."

"That depends on what you do with it and on how you got hold of the chain." Hawke told him. "Tell us what has happened." He was familiar enough with the minds of the solitary, the eccentrics and outcasts of society, to speak in a way they understood. Alasdair – the English, he reflected, was Alexander, the diminutive being Sandy or Sawnie – ceased to regard the pale pink rococo ceiling and instead addressed his audience.

"It was I who destroyed the false laird, wass it not? I took the *slabhraidh*, the clan chain, from the dead man's body and put it round my shoulders. He will not wear it again. He had no right to it. He wass a usurper, being a Sassenach, in the first place." The word was spat out as explaining everything.

"Are you talking about the stone laird or the dead one?" Hawke went on.

"Stone is stone and flesh is flesh. After the false *dhiolain* had been killed, I took it from his corpse, his *marbhan*. You fools did not know yesterday that it wass lying inside my shirt."

He grinned, showing deplorable teeth. "Oh, Sawnie, Sawnie," said Miss Walshe sadly. She had been quietly weeping since they brought him in.

He cheerfully admitted to having laid the fuse and blown up the statue. "It wass time," he said. "He did black deeds among us." He had dug the fuse in over some months along the hill, cutting the turf with his knife and replacing it afterwards. "It should have gone off at midday, the fuse, with the procession and the pipes," he said. "The damp will have made it burn slowly." He sounded regretful.

"Then you were up there, were you, at the time of the murder?"

"I wass here and I wass there."

"Oh, Sawnie, admit that you were up there," said Miss Walshe. "You left the gate early."

"The money had been taken. I put it where it belongs."

"You see, he is perfectly honest," said Miss Walshe. "Pray let him go. I will speak to him later about the chain." She evidently saw more of Sawnie than anybody.

"Madam, we can bring him in for malicious damage at least," said Inspector Allen. "Meantime, I must ask you to be quiet or you must leave the hall."

Hawke said nothing. There was no doubt that a court would regard Sawnie as of diminished responsibility. He smiled over at Miss Walshe.

"He truly is the genuine Insshe of Insshe," she said desperately. "He—"

Tom, who had come back after a silent breakfast, as being *persona grata* with the police, if not with his wife, leaned forward despite himself.

"Were you the observer, Sawnie, who told Miss Walshe about the drowning of the little boy in the river last year?" he asked. The Insshe of Insshe stared across with renewed disdain.

"Why should I not, when it iss what I saw?" he said reasonably.

Miss Walshe broke in gently. "Sawnie has been very good to me in various ways, chopping wood for my flower containers and such things," she said. "Do not blame him for the killing. I myself didn't have to plan at all. I knew Willard Norton-Insshe had – had injured his face that morning with the motor, and would be unlikely to appear in the procession, which of course meant he would be in charge of the souvenir table instead. It was an opportunity, when his back was turned, to approach through the marquee which was prepared for the clan society's Annual General Meeting, go out by the open flap – the table was set outside, as it was a fine day – and stab him while everyone was watching the procession and the pipers. I bent first and pulled the knife out of his sock. The whole operation was quite simple."

"So you want us to arrest you, Miss Walshe, for murder?"

"As I have told you already, it does not matter. It is preferable to the arrest of an innocent man."

Allen's mobile bleeped at this point and after listening, he bent closer to Hawke; the two officers conferred together without uttering the irrevocable words quite yet. An expression of incredulity spread over the DI's face. He beckoned Tom, who came over.

It was the pathologist's report. Forensic had finished with the late laird's body and the relevant tests. There was no new discovery about the manner of death, except that a main artery had been severed completely by the blow. There were no finger-prints on the knife, as might have been expected. However, there was one circumstance which might be of interest. Hawke leaned over to murmur to Tom.

"Evidently Norton-Insshe had had a vasectomy," he murmured. "Not too recently. Possibly about five or six years ago."

"Eh?" said Tom.

He had a mental picture of the dead man descending the stairs at Inshtochradh; could it have been only yesterday morning? He must have worn the condom to impress Dora, others to impress his wife: there could have been no real reason. Perhaps, however, it might be on a par with bringing Lady Charlotte's breakfast tray deliberately round by the front staircase in order to be seen. Either it paid to advertise, or else Norton-Insshe himself had been an exhibitionist and fantasiser, no doubt to compensate. At any rate, he was dead. Tom made no reply to the information other than raising one eyebrow.

"I think," said the DI, "that we should perhaps send for Lady Charlotte." She would have had time by now to get over the first shock.

He continued quietly putting questions to Miss Walshe while they waited. It was like, Tom thought, a game of solitaire; discarding suspects one by one until you arrived at – what? He listened to what the old lady was saying now. Hawke had pointed out to her that knives were seldom a woman's weapon.

"It has happened before," she said calmly. "Look at poor Lucretia. I dare say she had no option, given the state of things in early Rome. Now, sadly, rape is an everyday occurrence."

I did quack. Perhaps after all Lucretia had quacked for Tarquin, and that was the real trouble. He heard Miss Walshe continue, "Poison, you see, is extremely difficult to obtain these days, and Willard cooked all his food himself except for, perhaps, tea and a biscuit when he was up here at Great House."

"Did he often come to Great House?" That, Tom thought, would be what the DI was probably after; they sat, all of them, waiting like waxworks, except for the true laird who still stood, chain on his shoulders, motionless. No doubt Lady Charlotte would claim the chain when she came in, ending his hour of glory.

"Oh, yes, he visited the house here at least twice weekly, going over accounts, keeping an eye on the pictures and so on. He knew a lot about the value of art on the international market, though he was *not* what I would call appreciative of it for itself. He – I considered, as you ask, strangulation from behind, garotting the victim; sultans used to have it done to their unsatisfactory sons. Suleiman the Magnificent, I recall, did so once, or it may have been some other . . . My memory begins to fail me, Inspector, although I used to have what these days is termed total recall. You will suffer from old age yourself, you know, one day." She smiled behind her spectacles, having regained what seemed like full equanimity, for the time being.

"How old are you, Miss Walshe, if I may ask?"

"I am seventy-five years old. I was born in India, where my father, whom I do not remember, had been one of the last to serve in the Honourable East India Company when he was younger. At the time I was born he was exactly the age I am now, having married very late. My mother was much his junior. She died of cholera when I was six years old, and I was brought up by the Governor's wife."

"It's different out there now," said Inspector Allen heavily.

"A sad difference. There was very little wrong with the British

Empire, though one never hears a good word about it nowadays. We took care of them, those people. They are like children still. The whole business of handing over government was a great mistake, but nobody learns anything from history."

As if in answer, Lady Charlotte entered the room, the deerhound by her side. She seemed in some way taller and more confident. She was wearing the *arisaid* over a long white dress. She went straight to Sawnie, ignoring the other men who stood up politely on her entry.

"I am wearing it for you, Alasdair," she said in Gaelic. "I saw them bring you in."

Miss Walshe had gone on talking in an undertone to herself, as though silence was inadvisable. "They should give him back his black knife," she was saying. "He uses it all the time and keeps it sharp. He is very clever with his fingers. He used to whittle wood with it while he was Lord Insshe's shepherd here, in the old days when we still kept sheep. My pupil, Lady Charlotte—" she raised a thin hand "—has a little wooden figure he carved for her. It is upstairs."

Allen moved impatiently. "When are we to find out the truth of this matter?" he demanded. "A murder has been committed. So far, two persons have admitted to the murder. That is impossible, though the motive is the same. Both Miss Walshe and, er, Mr Cattanach allege that the late Mr Norton-Insshe drowned your son last summer in the river near here, while supposedly teaching him to swim. What is your reaction to that, Lady Charlotte?"

It was a brutal question. She drew a breath, but continued to fix her eyes on Sawnie, who stood silent, gazing at the floor.

"Is it true?" she said. Then in Gaelic, "*Chuala mi nathubairt thu. Thuir dhomh fresgairt!*"

"I have kept silence for your sake," he replied, in the same language. "I did not want you to know. Matters were bad enough for you with him, as it was."

Finnegan started to translate laboriously. "She's sayin' she has heard what he's supposed to have said, and to give her an answer. Then—"

"It doesn't matter," snapped Allen. He began to fire questions at Sawnie himself, while Lady Charlotte, grown white of face, nevertheless stood her ground by him; it was evident that the pervading odour of lice did not deter her. She had altered in some indefinable way, Tom thought; no longer a crane, but a more majestic bird, native to these parts; a great crested grebe, or a young heron, perhaps, standing alone by the water's edge, soon to catch fish for itself. At least, he thought, she hadn't known she was being molested every night by her son's murderer; that was one blessing.

She had begun to speak, in the high childish voice he remembered from Inshtochradh.

"Ronnie was a Down's syndrome case, as you will have heard. I loved him very much. His – my husband was ashamed of him; he liked everything to be what he used to call normal. He used to threaten to put Ronnie in an institution if I didn't do everything he said. So, I – I did." She blushed, the rose colour spreading over the fair skin of her neck and cheeks. The summer sun had otherwise hardly affected it.

"Willard wouldn't let me have any more children after that," she continued. "It – the Down's syndrone – doesn't happen twice in a family as a rule, but he couldn't understand that; there were, after all, things he didn't know. He used to say a second child might be like that as well.

"Ronnie was a lovable little boy. You remember him, Alasdair *gradhach*? He never did any harm in all his life. He was eight when he – he was drowned. He couldn't, of course, have managed the estate for himself later on. It's probable he would have died, as they do, in any case before thirty. My husband wouldn't have known that, and anyway—"

She spread out her hands, the large fine hands of an aristocrat, roughened with gardening. "I don't think I can tell you much more; I don't often speak as much. There was one thing." She talked now like someone in a hypnotist's chair, as if the relief of bringing it out outweighed the bitterness. "Once I – I thought I was pregnant a second time. Willard was furious; he'd always taken precautions. He–he beat me, and then – then I think tried to make me miscarry. I didn't, and he took me to a private clinic in Edinburgh saying I must have a check-up. They gave me an anaesthetic by injection. When I came out of it they said I'd had a curettage, but I knew that wasn't what it had been. By then, I was past caring."

Miss Walshe was crying silently, the tears by this time running past her spectacles and down her lined cheeks. "Oh, Charlotte, I didn't know," she said. "Oh, my dear, my dear."

"You seem very fond of your pupil, Miss Walshe," remarked Allen.

"She – she was entirely taught by me. She only briefly attended any school, the one in the clachan that isn't there any more. I – she—"

It was all getting too near the bone, Tom thought. He leaned forward again, and spoke to the standing cateran in the great gleaming chain with its rowan-berry emblems. The pair were, grotesquely, like a couple ready to launch into Highland dancing; but of that there would be none, now or afterwards.

"Why," he said, "didn't you use your own black knife, Sawnie, to do what you say you did? Why did you take the late laird's one out of his stocking, if that is what you did then?"

"It wass more suitable to do so. Himself's own knife wass used for few things, except for dressing himself like a farmyard *coileach*. I used my own, for eating and that."

"I gave him the chain myself," said Miss Walshe desperately. "I took it from the dead man's shoulders."

"I will not let a woman save my life," the Insshe of Insshe began. The DI broke in.

"Miss Walshe has done her best to do so. What is the truth? I want the truth. You cannot *both* have killed Norton-Insshe, though you both had reason."

"I killed the bastard," Sawnie said. "He himself had killed the heir to all the centuries. The blood in the child wass the oldest blood of all."

"Group O, universal donor," said Hawke. They had found the record cards at Inshtochradh.

Lady Charlotte stepped forward then and took the black knife from Rowbotham's bemused hand. She held it against her for moments.

"Do not trouble, I will not kill myself," she said. "Had I intended that it would have happened nine years ago, or else four. There is a piece of evidence I should like Alasdair to fetch for you if you will permit it. It is upstairs."

She turned to Sawnie as if to give him his black knife; a constable moved, but Charlotte's hand forbade him. She laid the hand then on Sawnie's shoulder, in the way of outlawed MacGregors in the dark long ago to an ally who needed aid. Again she spoke softly in Gaelic.

"*Beannachd.* There is a window open. Go with God."

He vanished instantly by the tower stairs, his tattered kilt flaunting like Columba's royal banner. Hawke jerked his head at Finnegan to follow.

"*Stad,*" said Lady Charlotte quietly to the deerhound, which set its great body at once in the way. This made for the second's delay that was needed; a long cry sounded then from above, the sound of a man flinging himself down from the high rock out of an open window, then silence.

"You bloody fool," yelled Hawke unfairly at the Irishman. He shouldered his way out of the room, and down to the now quiet field from which tents and all else had by this time been taken away except, within the last moments, for one thing: a dead man lying on the shaved grass, the great ornate clan chain twisted and gleaming about the shoulders and the broken neck. Am Insheach had died with honour.

"You were not going to lay a finger on the father of my son, to put him in prison," said the Lady of Insshe calmly; and laid the black knife squarely on the desk in the reception hall.

"We still can't be certain he did it," said the DI later. "However as he's dead, I suppose—"

Tom knew otherwise. A clansman had obeyed the command of his chief, his lady, instantly. Theirs not to reason why; so it had always been in the Highlands. *I dreamt a dead man won a fight, and I think that man was I.* They'd used that, once again, in the Second World War.

After things had been straightened out as far as could be done he went back to the Renault, and drove about by himself for a long time. He felt no need for food or drink, and knew nothing for certain except that he did not want, quite yet, to encounter Dora again.

Eighteen

He went back to Taigh Mór in the end, and told DI Hawke what Dora had found earlier in Miss Walshe's Bible; it was best to do so. It cleared up one aspect for them, at least. The DI was grateful.

"What you've told us fits together everything nicely, Brack," he said. "The whole story – and we've been in touch with the internet – begins with poor Lord Insshe's dynastic and disastrous marriage to an upper-crust bride who turned out to be not only a bitch, but a totally uninhibited whore; one of these degenerate sports which turn up every so often in the very best families."

"So-called," muttered Allen. "In plain fact they're the same as everybody else, but won't admit the resemblance in public."

"Po-faced as a rule, certainly. However, this lady's peccadilloes could not be hidden, as she had the bad taste to pursue them while Insshe was out in India on a delicate diplomatic mission in the days of the changeover. For the hostess to be known to behave as Sonia Insshe was by then behaving more or less openly was a disaster of international magnitude, and didn't impress the watching millions one bit."

"She ran off in the end, I gather," said Tom, having heard a little from the McIntosh couple when he'd dropped in briefly for a drink at the Rowan Tree, from which they were departing now there was no need for them to remain. Hawke nodded.

"And in the way of rewards in this world, ended up as the mistress of a senile millionaire who had controlling rights in a worldwide hotel chain. It was like old whatsit in America with his film star that shouldn't have been, and he spent millions setting her up as one and financing bad films, and building a stone palace for her somewhere out west. She looked the same to everyone else as any shopgirl behind a counter, but the old boy went crazy about her and stayed that way until, if I recall, he died. The same thing happened with Sonia's millionaire. He knew well enough she was unfaithful, but he still went on drooling. One of the people Sonia was unfaithful to him with was a male cook, name of Norton, origins not high-class. He appealed to her tastes, however."

"Good God," said Tom. "And meantime her lord at home had consoled himself, diplomatically, with a nice cool English débutante met, no doubt, at the annual garden party at Delhi; the protégée of the erstwhile Governor's lady, no less. Insshe must have had persuasion, or no doubt Mavis was sorry for him. A deserted diplomat is a lovesome thing."

Hawke nodded. "However it happened, and we'll never know everything now, they had Lady Charlotte, who at that rate isn't a lady at all, and brought her home, pretending Sonia had given birth out there instead of, by then, no doubt having had herself sterilised by way of general precaution. Certainly Norton would have had to have his vasectomy years earlier than it happened if Sonia hadn't done something of the kind to herself; condoms aren't foolproof. The old sugar daddy – it's a phrase out of fashion, I know, but by then so was he – died and, as might have been foreseen, left Sonia the hotel shares and everything else except for an allowance to be paid to his wife, who'd been in a mental home in Los Angeles for thirty-five years."

"Faithful type," said Allen.

"We aren't finished yet. Sonia and Norton ran the hotels themselves for a time, which is no doubt when Norton perfected his art – he was already a chef of talent, no question – then sold the chain at a profit, went helling together round the States for quite a bit, during which time Sonia grew as infatuated with Norton as the old sugar dad had been about her. That meant Norton had to work for his corn. During that time she almost certainly talked to him about Insshe and Great House and upper-crust life she'd left, filling him with notions about what he ought to be and couldn't, or it didn't look like it, because his own past had been trammelled somewhat, as they say. However he was quick to learn, and by the time Sonia died of a heart attack in the middle of you know what in Cincinnati, Ohio, Norton found, surprise, surprise, that she'd left all she had to him, except for the allowance poor Insshe had been paying her all those years to keep away and say nothing about not having given birth to Charlotte herself. He loved Charlotte, you see; she was an Insshe, you can tell from the portraits. That nose can be taken anywhere. Also, she's ambidextrous, an hereditary aspect of the clan. I expect you noticed how she handled Sawnie and the knife."

"So," put in Allen, "Lord Insshe had been paying blackmail money which impoverished the estate, for the sake of the good name of the house, as it were, for a couple of decades, let's say. Why didn't he divorce the bitch?"

"Probably because in those days, if you remember, divorce still wasn't the acceptable thing in the very best circles. A divorced man, for instance, couldn't become a Privy Councillor. However, Insshe by then was no doubt past all that, and only wanted to stay home in peace and watch his grandchildren grow up."

"What about Mavis?"

"She'd appeared, of course, after a short time, as little Charlotte's permanent governess. They weren't seen outside often enough together for many, if any at all, to guess that she was the child's mother, or if they did let the thought cross their minds up here, they kept quiet; they're loyal in these parts. She was the laird's daughter as well as the Lord's, and in the Highlands, it's blood that counts."

"Group AB," put in Allen wearily.

"I'm coming to that. When Charlotte was eighteen, along comes this brash but worldly rich man prepared to save the Insshe estates from crumbling – *if* he's allowed to marry Charlotte and become the next laird in a kilt and feathers."

"A farmyard *coileach*. A cockerel. Knowing all the time that Charlotte wasn't legitimate and he could put the screw on her, and my lord, at any time he liked. Pretty."

Hawke fingered his chin. "In fact, I don't think Lady C. knows yet that she isn't who she is supposed to be. It was, after all, part of Norton-Insshe's entire sham façade to keep appearances up to snuff in every way, probably including verisimilitude at home. He'd married the Lady of Insshe, and that continued to be that. The old lord died soon after the marriage; in fact, soon after learning Charlotte was pregnant. What he didn't know, of course, was that the baby was Sawnie's. As for Norton, his conceit would never have let him dream that his mousy little bride had dared to run crying, probably at once after the wedding night, to a louse-infested tinker she'd known in childhood and who saw her made comfortable, as they say. It's also possible that Norton-Insshe, as he'd become, found it refreshing after his experiences with old Sonia, to deflower a sexless, colourless little top-drawer British virgin, but of course we'll never know."

"How did Charlotte herself know the boy Ronald was not her husband's?" asked Tom. The whole story was sordid and sad.

"Well, there's a certain way of telling in this instance, though she probably knew anyway; women have a notion somehow about those things."

"Now we're getting filthy," observed Allen, for the first time grinning and showing widely-spaced teeth, his own. "How would Charlotte know for certain, before finding out about blood groups?"

"Well, whether she knew or not, and I'd say she did, let's come to the second pregnancy, which really would be Norton's doing. We can prove that, because for the only time in his life Sawnie went off for two years at the precise times of in and out, to work on an oil rig. The life didn't suit the dignity of a Highland laird, however, so he came back, no doubt with a little money, but not in time to have participated. By then, Charlotte had been made to have the abortion, and Norton-Insshe had decided, in case he let go too soon another time in spite of all the Dutch caps and condoms in the universe, to have his vasectomy. You see Charlotte's own death would mean that he had no further rights over Insshe; it's entailed in the female line as well as the male. Failing Ronald, or the aborted child, Charlotte alone was the heir."

"Imagine his feelings, when he discovered Ronald hadn't been his in the first place, and the second venture might have turned out all right," put in Allen, who had occasional flashes of ingenuity. "By then, he couldn't get himself any more. If Charlotte's life had been purgatory before, it'd be hell after."

"Soon, as one result, he killed the boy, having planned it for two years," Hawke said. "After that he continued to play the laird, marching round in the annual Games procession, presiding at the clan AGM, holding on to the presidential office despite sour faces and hints from old Colonel McIntosh, who was next in line. I can't say I seriously considered old Tosh as the murderer for the sake of wearing a mere clan chain, although you never can tell in these parts. He might have had other grudges as well."

"Perhaps the laird raped Mrs Mac at some point while they were staying? Not my personal taste, but tastes differ," said Allen. "They wouldn't admit, you know, to having stayed at Inshtochradh, but their signatures were in the book all right, three years back. No doubt Miss Walshe was conditioned to put the sheets in the washing machine pronto on the departure of lady guests."

"What was that about blood groups?" asked Tom, the blood by then pounding in his own head. There was no doubt they'd been thorough, the police. He'd feel safer in the south, though there was no logic in that; they knew where to find him if they decided, in the end, that they wanted him. The memory of dead Sawnie came, lying still and twisted below the high tower window here at Taigh Mór. The pathologists had taken him away on principle, with the grey look pathologists acquire, in some way having come to resemble the goods they investigate. However, suicide wasn't a notifiable crime north of the Border. He wondered what Lady Charlotte's position was as regards incitement to it. He'd keep quiet, however; Hawke had begun to enlighten him about blood groups.

"A donor van called about four years ago; we've checked. It must have been shortly after Lady C.'s abortion. She was well enough, however, and so was he, to show the flag and give blood, being grouped in both cases along with the folk from the clachan. The odd thing was that the only thing they had in common, that husband and wife, was that they turned out both to be AB. It's a rare group, and couldn't possibly have produced Ronald's own, which turned out to be Group O. Ronald, of course, was done not as a donor, but no doubt in case he ever had to be treated in hospital for whatever. How soon Norton-Insshe looked at the cards is nobody's business, but he was intelligent enough to put two and two together after talking to the technicians or maybe a GP. Sawnie's group, of course, will be O.

"He then realised, as you've said, Allen, that he'd thrown away his birthright for a mess of pottage, or rather an even nastier mess of sperm-free semen."

"Well, perhaps Norton-Insshe was hoping everything would grow back if he kept trying," Tom said, and told them what he'd heard below the open window at Inshtochradh. Too late, he realised that he'd involved Dora.

"I didn't know earlier that you were married, Brack," said the DI smoothly. "Congratulations."

"You knew damned well. You saw our signatures in the hotel register. I told you at the beginning that I'd killed Norton-Insshe myself. In fact, I was annoyed with him for not providing tea-making facilities in our bedroom."

"It isn't the time for joking, Brackenbury," said Allen sourly, "and we hope you'll keep most of this out of *The Perceiver*? It's a privilege, you know, to be allowed to work with the police."

"It widens my outlook," said Tom. It was best, he knew, to keep things light.

Later, he drove back a greatly aged Miss Walshe to her own house in the Renault, as she stated that she didn't think she was quite fit to drive herself in the Morris today; dear Charlotte hadn't wanted her, though, at Great House and it was best to come away. "She simply stood there at the door, clutching the little wooden figure Sawnie carved long ago. She said she wanted to be left alone, and she'd be in touch soon."

"What happened to the black knife?" He questioned if it was safe yet to leave Lady Charlotte quite alone in Taigh Mór with a *sgian dubh*. However, Miss Walsh smiled.

"Dear Charlotte is very brave, and completely without any

foolishness of that kind. I trained her carefully from the age of eighteen months, which is when children begin to remember things. She is quite safe with Sawnie's knife. You heard what she said in the hall; if she'd been going to kill herself, it would have happened earlier."

Tom remembered Lady Charlotte's resolute little mouth below the long nose. There was steel there, perhaps even a certain insensitivity. No wilting lily, no violet by a mossy stone, could have endured all she had. The upper crust was tough.

He murmured that Miss Walshe needn't worry about her Morris; he would return on foot and bring it back to the schoolhouse before nightfall. "After that we must be on our way," he said. She turned to him.

"Oh, please. Stay with me for a little while. I – I do not want to be left alone quite yet. You see—"

She began to tell him her story, partly as he already knew it; but there were personal things.

"Poor Charlotte," she kept saying. "Oh, poor, poor Charlotte. I know some of what she endured from that man, but *not* about the abortion. That was horrible. I expect, as she said, it was quite early; I hadn't noticed anything."

"Did you know already," he asked, "that Sawnie was the first child's father?" It was a direct question; but she was the kind of person who appreciated directness.

She did not answer for moments. Then, "Yes," she said. "I knew. They had been friends, you see, from the time Charlotte was a child. For a little while, to try to accustom her to other children, I let her attend the little primary school which is my house now. She didn't like it there and we took her away; she was always very shy, but she and Sawnie, who was there then – they were much the same age – made friends. As I say, he became a kind of protector, and later on, when he was Lord Insshe's shepherd, Charlotte used to go up and help him with herding the sheep ready for dipping, and sometimes even clipping the fleeces; and of course there were the births of lambs. Crows come, you know, at once if it isn't watched constantly, and peck the new-born lambs' eyes out, dreadfully cruel, but that's nature. Charlotte helped Alasdair with all of that. It was natural for her to run to him when the facts of marriage revolted her. They were happy together, those two. I never gave them away. After all I – I had been guilty of the same impropriety in my own youth, but you know nothing of that, Mr Brackenbury."

"I know," he admitted, but not telling Miss Walshe about Dora's discovery. Panic showed in her eyes behind the glasses, the first time he'd seen it.

"Please – please do ensure that Charlotte does not ever know that I am her mother. She was never told, you see. It would destroy the last thing she has: her pride in being the true, hereditary Lady of Insshe. I have kept the secret all my life, and so did her father."

And you submitted all that time to being treated as a governess, as a subordinate, he thought. He wondered how long the actual liaison had continued. As if she read his thoughts, she answered him.

"We remained only good friends, Lord Insshe and I, after the child was brought home from India and thought to be Sonia's. He had to pay Sonia, you know, a great deal of money regularly to keep her quiet. That was why the estate became encumbered. Sonia was a most wicked woman. I do not judge people as a general rule; we are told in the Scriptures not to do so. However, she made Lord Insshe's life unbearable, both before and after the time when she lived with him as his wife."

Brackenbury put his cards on the table. "Why didn't you ask him to divorce her and marry you, the mother of his child?" he asked. "He would have been pleased to, surely?" *My own dear heart.* Mavis Walshe smiled suddenly, her face lighting up.

"I wouldn't let him," she said. "Not only would it have affected his position and possibly even Charlotte's – divorce was frowned on still in those days, especially in the Diplomatic Service, although he soon left it – but, also, I would have lost my own nice little pension from the East India Company. You see, I am almost the last unmarried woman left alive who is the daughter of one of their officials, and they had this tradition – a very thoughtful one – of providing an income for such girls who didn't marry. Altogether, I considered it more advisable, for everyone's sake including my own, to leave things as they had by then become. For one thing, it would have given free rein to Sonia's tongue, and nobody wanted *that*."

"You cannot have been happy about Lady Charlotte's marriage in the event?" he said.

"I was not, but I said to myself that I would probably not have been happy about anyone's marrying so shy a girl, and Willard had a certain charm, you know, as well as a great deal of money. I did not, of course, know of the connection with Sonia until after the marriage, and neither did Lord Insshe. That discovery, I still think, however it was made, killed him. However, as Charlotte was expecting Ronald by then, and I knew whose child Ronald really was, I said nothing. It is always best to keep silence in such situations, especially when there is nothing at all one can do. Charlotte had been aware that by marrying Norton-Insshe – he took the name, of course, at the occasion – she was saving the Insshe estate. That meant a great deal to her. The rest, of course, was unpleasant, more so than could have been foreseen. After Ronald's death – how I remember that little boy, with the great hound forever beside him, up at Taigh Mór, happy, because he was always happy, there is no evil in those little people – and then—"

"Diarmaidh tried to save him, I believe?" He was deliberately exploiting her; nobody else would tell him such things now.

"Diarmaidh was devoted to Ronald, and to Ronald's mother."

He recalled that Norton-Insshe had claimed the dog's prior affection: that was typical. "Tell me, Miss Walshe, about the late laird's treatment of your daughter after the child's death. I know this is painful for you. I assure you that I will reveal nothing you say to the police or to the media. I am merely interested in the case for its own sake, especially as Sawnie is now officially assumed to have killed Norton-Insshe."

"I am certain that nothing of the kind—" she was beginning indignantly, then suddenly, as if a mask had dropped over her face, began her tale of how Norton-Insshe had virtually kept his wife a prisoner, forcing her to keep account for him in writing of how she spent every moment at Taigh Mór, keeping her afterwards at Inshtochradh as if in an ivory tower, taking her meals upstairs so that she met nobody. "He would never trust her again after he found out that he himself was not Ronald's father," she said. "I knew it was that matter of the blood groups; Willard found out in that way. He wasn't the kind of man who would have killed Charlotte, let alone divorced the Lady of Insshe. Either would have destroyed his position in society, the first of the kind he'd ever had. He took, instead, slow and careful revenge; Charlotte said nothing of it, but I guessed at least a part."

Tom said nothing. He couldn't expect this gentle and correct colonial lady to be aware that, as well as keeping Charlotte under supervision all day, Norton-Insshe exhausted her sexually each night. There had also grown, no doubt by degrees, the creepy, secret ambience of the Gothic façade that was Inshtochradh, the probable discouragement of long-term visitors there; the exhibitionism and worse when they came: for example, what Dora had had to endure. This same fantasising had also been present in the determined annual leading of the Games procession in full fig, the packets of unnecessary condoms, the wearing, for far longer than was officially allowable, of the clan society's chain, One more status symbol, perhaps; a kind of defiance, a denial by a man of obscure birth of what he'd quite pointlessly turned himself into: a sterile male, victim of his own illusions. And yet, Norton-Insshe hadn't been all bad; nobody was. He'd been, for instance, a gifted cook and good gardener; he'd kept exact and honest accounts for the estates, at least as far as anyone knew. A pity there had been quite so much money at his disposal; left to make his own way in the world, Willard Norton might have become a happy and successful market-gardener, head chef, or supermarket boss. Life didn't work out that way, however, and now he was dead.

"Independence is a pleasant thing, Mr Brackenbury," said Miss Walshe with clairvoyance, still no doubt thinking about the Honourable East India Company. "I see you have brought me home; how kind. There is plenty of room, you know, for as long as you and your wife care to stay. I shall go up to bed for a little, I think."

He saw her in, agreeing that she had certainly better rest, and asked Dora to make her a cup of tea. He then said he would walk round and bring home the Morris from Taigh Mór car park. "It's no trouble at all," he protested, adding that it was again a fine day and he liked walking. Miss Walshe, standing in her schoolhouse doorway, then said a memorable thing.

"It is true that I have cancer," she said quietly. "Such a pity that they would not take my word for what happened, and that poor Sawnie had to die."

She went inside, then shortly reappeared clutching a small bundle of hand-shredded paper. "I should like to put this in the dustbin," she said. "They collect rubbish from the shed tomorrow, weekly. One greatly misses open fires."

She went across to the bin, opened it, put whatever it was inside, and returned to the house. Tom didn't go in yet to speak again to Dora. She would take tea up to Miss Walshe presently, no doubt.

He walked instead back to Taigh Mór. The Morris was sitting modestly in the car park, and he was about to insert Miss Walshe's borrowed keys when he became aware of Allen, regarding him aggressively now the DI wasn't present to monitor things.

"You've got away with it nicely, haven't you, Brackenbury? If that old girl hadn't laundered the sheets from Inshtochradh, we might perhaps have found out a thing or two more."

"I don't understand you, except that you're offensive." It was best not to sound conciliatory; attack is the best form of defence. Tom waited.

"We examined the so-called laird's bedsheets, and they were marked with a certain semen type, granted sperm-free, we might have found also in your bed, as well as, naturally, your own. That's what I believe happened, Brackenbury, but I won't say more; the tinker chap is dead, and gets the blame, the case is wrapped up and you're a free man. Remember, though, that I'll be looking out for you in future. I thought I'd mention it privately, that's all. We know you were away on that milkman and beauty-queen case two nights ago, because it was in the papers after you'd faxed it to your editor. Norton-Insshe wouldn't have missed a chance like that if I know human nature."

"Perhaps you don't." Tom got into the Morris and drove off, glad his hands weren't shaking. The insolence of Allen had almost made him sock the brute's jaw like he'd done lately to the deceased laird. That would hardly have made for a happy ending, whatever happened next.

He drove the Morris back, stabled it, and went into the house. Dora was just making tea. "Miss Walshe asked for it not to be sent up for about an hour, so I waited," she said, her back turned over the kettle. She might have been addressing a stranger. He did not reply. Dora went on talking.

"I told her I would," she went on, "and when she thanked me for cleaning up the house, I told her cooking and housework was about all I'm good for. She looked at me and said, 'Nonsense, you're an intelligent woman'." It was pleasant to hear that. "It makes a change." She busied herself with the tea-things.

"Dora, we ought to pack and go. I want to get on the motorway before the heavy traffic."

"Do we have to go back quite so soon? Why? You booked for a day or two longer at the beginning. Miss Walshe needs looking after for a bit, she's shaky just now. I don't want to leave her."

"Lady Charlotte will look after her, no doubt. It isn't our business."

"I think we should stay all the same, at least till tomorrow, to be sure she's all right. Lady Charlotte won't do anything till then. Miss Walshe said she was upset, and having heard what's happened, I'm not surprised."

"No, we must go now," Tom said firmly. He didn't want to spend another night with Dora here. Did he want to do so anywhere? He still didn't know. He didn't know anything, for the time being, one way or the other.

"I'm going round to the newsagent's," he said. Pack our things, and I'll get the car brought round to the door." As he'd said, they could send flowers to Miss Walshe from London.

He took some moments to check the tyre pressure on the Renault. By the time he had brought round the car and got inside, he would have expected, knowing Dora, that she would have had their two suitcases ready. However, there was only his own. Dora herself was seated in the room on a high chair, her small hands clenched together.

"Take your case," she said. "Mine isn't coming, because I'm not going either. I'm staying with Miss Walshe for a bit till she's all right again, and then I'm going home to Brennan. I don't mean to your cottage. I mean my own house in the village. I'm leaving you, Tom Brackenbury. I thought it was as well to mention it, in case you didn't notice."

Her voice was colder than he'd ever heard it. It reminded him of steel; perhaps of a black knife sliding into flesh. He heard himself speak.

"I seem to remember, only a few days ago, your promising to love and honour me, for better or worse – and many other reasons besides."

"It was a mistake to marry you, I've always known that, but there were reasons you haven't heard. I can let you have them if you want."

"I'd rather hear your reasons for wanting to leave me. This marriage will be in the Guinness Book of Records for having lasted for less time than anyone else's this year. I suppose that's something."

He felt that he was in some kind of fourth dimension, a state of madness; this couldn't be happening, he would wake up at Brennan to find Dora bringing him in a tray of early morning tea, or polishing the furniture in household gloves. He'd wake up somewhere like the prince in the fairytale, or more probably the frog.

She spoke slowly and carefully, as if she'd thought it out while he was away. "Last night I said I was afraid," she told him.

"That was true, because I was afraid of you. You know why, and you know you were thinking of all that while you had sex with me. That's all I am to you, something to keep your house clean and to fuck in bed. Commander Oldham was no different. He didn't know anything about love and neither do you. I offered you love last night although I was so afraid, and all you did was the usual. You were careful not to empty yourself, you were so determined that I mustn't have a baby because you don't like babies. Well, I'm having one, and it isn't yours, and it certainly isn't what's-his-name's with the knife in his back, because there wouldn't have been time to find that out since yesterday."

"How did you know about the knife in Norton-Insshe's back, Dora?" Tom asked quietly. "It isn't yet released in print."

She turned her averted head and stared at him; he was aware of the clear blue of her eyes between their thick fringed lashes. "I saw him, of course," she said. "You didn't know I'd been down."

"Dora." He stood motionless, except for a muscle twitching at the side of his mouth. "I don't give a damn that you killed him. You had every reason, after all. I only want you to know that I was beginning to love you, that what I minded was that you hadn't confided in me, that you let me find fresh trodden grass under your sandal last night before I guessed. When people love each other they don't need that kind of discovery. Since I married you, I've found out more, far more, than a woman's extremely bedworthy body and the other things I knew you were: decent, cheerful, reliable, honest. I thought at least you *were* honest, Dora, but you haven't been so with me. I had to ask you just now how you knew about the knife. I didn't know till now that you were having another man's baby. I suppose it's Oldham's?"

"Yes. Wait! Tom, I – oh, I thought *you'd* done it, with the knife, I mean. That was why I was afraid last night. I told myself I was sleeping with a killer, and you hadn't said anything either. Both of us thought the other had done it. I suppose it's funny in a way. I walked down because I wanted to see the lady pipers, and I thought if I let you see me you'd be cross."

"Very cross." He strode over and picked her up from the chair. She had burst into tears. He set her on his knee, soothing and comforting her, kissing her, murmuring gently. "Dear little Dora. Darling Dora. It's been horrid, I know. There, now. There, now." He patted and stroked, holding her close. Presently, she grew calm, and Tom wiped her eyes. Tell me about Oldham. Did he rape you, as well?"

"No. I was sorry for him because he was blind. Besides, I wanted a baby. I wanted it more than anything in the world, and now I'm going to have it. Miss Reston saw us, and she must have gone and shut herself in the kiln. I felt awful when I heard, much later, as you know. I'd only done it at all because of the baby. I knew you wouldn't want one. When it was confirmed, I came down and married you. That wasn't honest. I knew that at the time."

"I will remain objective for as long as possible. What did Oldham say about the baby?" Oldham must be at least seventy by now, dirty old man.

"He wrote a cheque for five hundred pounds and told me to go and get myself seen to, as he didn't want 'little strangers' as hc called them," said Dora. "That was really why I came to London, to you, I mean."

"Thank you. Tell me some more about the baby presently, but first we will return to the matter of yesterday, and what you saw. Was Norton-Insshe's body wearing a chain on its shoulders or not?" He was asking things out of order, as they came to mind. Dora moved against him, her soft breasts brushing him.

"No, I don't think there was any chain. The parade had ended and I saw the dog streak over, then got round the back of the marquee – I'd walked down the side path, because you hadn't left me any money to get in with, so I had to go outside the rope and round the edge. I saw the parade in the distance, and heard the pipes while I was still walking on. I wanted to see if there were any souvenirs for sale on the table outside the big tent."

"You couldn't have bought them without any money."

"No, but I wanted to have a look, because I'd meant to get some from Miss Walshe at the shop and then we'd left in a hurry. Anyway he was lying there, with the knife in his back, and after the dog got there everyone began to turn round and look, because for one thing it started to howl. I thought I'd better make myself scarce, as I was certain you'd done it. Oh, Tom, perhaps the police think so as well?"

"The police are by no means perspicacious enough. Dora, before telling me about any more of anything at all, perhaps it's time to take Miss Walshe her tea. Then we can talk about everything by ourselves. I expect she wants to sleep." She slid off his knee and went to prepare the tea-tray. The kettle boiled soon and she made tea and took it up.

Brackenbury sat there frowning. Oldham. Mary. Everything. He—

"Oh, Tom, Tom!" Dora was calling softly from the landing on the stairs. "Tom, she's dead. She left a note. I think you'd better come up."

He took the stairs two at once, and went into the upstairs bedroom at the end of the passage.

Mavis Walshe lay peacefully, her face already smooth and unlined. There was an empty bottle of drugs on a sidetable. The note lay beside her on the table, also open: '*I killed Norton-Insshe; please assure the police. I do not want Alasdair's memory smirched. He was innocent. Please tell the inspector this and add that I regret causing further disarrangement, but as I told them I had not, in any case, long to live. MW". The signature was firm.*

"I don't believe her," said Dora, looking down at the dead face.

"Neither do I. Also, if she'd saved up enough painkilling drugs to take an overdose as has obviously happened, she must have been in increasing pain for some time. A brave woman."

Tom had already taken down the great Bible. It opened naturally at the page Dora had found. Between the pages was nothing but the envelope. Mavis Walshe had destroyed all evidence of her daughter's real identity, unaware that the police knew in any case. The fragments of evidence, he was aware, lay in the dustbin still, not yet having been collected. He would let them go. Hawke would say nothing. The case was tied up, with Sawnie labelled as the killer. Tom's conscience nagged at him on behalf of the dead Highlander. It would be, no doubt, in tomorrow's papers; talked about for a time, and then forgotten. He himself wouldn't forget.

Dora had come over, and he put his arm round her. "I'd better telephone the doctor and the police."

There was still the envelope to show, if they should look. He closed the Bible and replaced it on its shelf. Her farewell note would be read; that was perhaps enough. *Miss Mavis Walshe, Government House, Delhi.* It showed nothing now, except that an era had come and gone. No doubt they'd all met up somewhere already; Mavis, Ronnie, Sawnie, James, Lord Insshe. *In my Father's house are many mansions . . .*

He went to the telephone.

When he came back Dora said, "Tom, who do you think really did it? Do you know?"

"Yes, I know. Apart from me, it could only have been one other person, leaving aside several hundreds present who disliked the late laird thoroughly."

"Who?"

"Lady Charlotte."

"I thought you said she couldn't have, because of the parade?"

"Wait till after the police have been, and the doctor. I'll tell you then."

Nineteen

"Now tell me about Oldham," said Brackenbury. They were driving down the A9. "I knew him less well than Mary did. I came across him, as you know, at the time of the Partridge murder." He recalled the long stone house in a valley, the white fenced field in front containing its grazing racehorses; the Commander was a rich man. He'd been in the Fleet Air Arm when he'd lost his sight in an enemy encounter in the Far East, a few days before Hiroshima; the story he'd spread about a road accident had been invention. He must have been quite young then, also brilliant; promotion had come early. Mary had been devoted to him. It had been, though, a classic case of the invalid's response: *you're fond of me, you say? There must be something wrong with you. In any case I don't need a nurse.* Tom was surprised at his own lack of resentment at having been, as it were, pre-empted. He listened to Dora's tale as impersonally as if he was conducting a newspaper interview. Many of those by now had left him incapable of surprise.

"I knew Miss Reston had loved him for years," Dora was saying. "That's what I told him when he came after me the first time. He laughed; we were in the garden at your cottage, I'd been picking nasturtiums, and he said, 'There's no such thing as love, m'dear, only sex'. I knew Miss Reston let him, but he said, 'You can't have much of that yourself with Brack since your husband snuffed it; Brack's hardly ever here'. I told him we didn't at all, that the whole thing was respectable. 'Well, you must need it', he said, and went on to say that Mary was getting abject, like a trained pointer bitch, and my voice sounded prettier, a pleasant change, and could he feel me to find out what I looked like, because he couldn't see me, of course.

"I knew he was blind, as I let him run his hands all over me; I'd expected it to be only my face. He said then, 'You're a nice little armful, good flight deck', and asked if I wouldn't make a blind man happy. If he hadn't said it that way I mightn't have agreed. As it was I let him into the house and let him do it only that once, as I told him, because I wasn't to be made use of. He laughed again – you know, that short hard laugh he has – and said he'd like to make use of me, as I called it, often, and he'd pay. After he'd gone I found he'd left a twenty-pound note. I was angry at first, and was going to post it back to him. Then I started thinking how useful money is, and it was then I had the idea about the baby."

"He'd be too careful, Dora. He hadn't given a baby to Mary Reston." Mary wouldn't have wanted one, however; always covered in clay, it had never left the places under her broad square fingernails: he would always remember.

"Well, I thought it might happen in time, if I could get him to hold on a bit," said Dora. "He came back, of course. It happened two or three times after that, and I think Miss Reston guessed, because he would only stay to tea with her first by then, instead of staying on. He would come on after that and 'do' me, as he called it. He always left twenty pounds, and I used to put it into a building society account in Penarch, saving up for the baby. I still wasn't pregnant, though."

"Then, I take it, old Mrs Dobbin died and Basil asked you to come down and keep his house?"

"Yes. I didn't want to take it full-time because I had the job of looking after the cottage for you, and never knew when you might be there. However, I said I'd go down two or three days a week, and leave meals ready. That was when Miss Reston came and put her hands round my throat, and he rang her up to say he'd cane her bottom. I was sorry for her, but he hadn't asked her, after all, and I wanted the baby.

"When I went there I'd do the housework, then he used to like to take all my clothes off. I was beginning to lose hope by that time, but thought he might as well go on with it. One day we were lying on his sofa and I hadn't a stitch on, and suddenly I looked across at the window. There was Miss Reston, staring in. I don't know how long she'd been there. She must have walked down, because I hadn't heard her car. Her face was like one of those pumpkin masks, you know, twisted and ugly."

"What happened then?"

"Well, she went away from the window. I screamed, which I don't often. The Commander jerked inside me and came, and he got up swearing. Then I told him Miss Reston had been there and had been watching us. The Commander fastened himself up and went to the door with his white stick, calling, 'Mary. Mary', but she'd gone. I think he was quite fond of her, you know. I can't think why he didn't marry her."

"Because he was blind. She made him feel inferior. You didn't." Tom's throat was dry and he no longer wanted to listen. "Go on, Dora dear."

"Well, I got dressed quickly, and things went on as usual, but she must have gone straight away and shut herself in her gas kiln. We didn't know for weeks; everyone thought she'd gone away somewhere, perhaps to stay with friends. Then they found her, as you know. You can imagine how I felt, because by then I knew I was pregnant."

"How did he take it? The pregnancy, I mean." Nobody knew, or would ever know, what Basil Oldham had felt about the death of Mary.

"Well, it was my fault for telling him, just after he'd had the news that they'd found her. I'd waited, you see, till I was quite sure. He was furious, then went straight to his desk and wrote out the cheque I told you about, gave it to me and said – I told you that as well – 'You go at once and get yourself seen to, my girl. We don't want little strangers'. That was when I packed and came to you, because I *did* want the little stranger and still do."

"Will Brennan welcome back a single mother, if you're still thinking of leaving? You know they'll tear you to bits, especially if they know it's his? They'll say you took advantage of a blind man hoping for his money, and that isn't all."

"They wouldn't have known whose it was. I wasn't thinking of leaving now, unless you don't want me with the baby. You always said children make you tired. Single mothers get an allowance and probably they'd reduce the council house rent as well."

"And you would live on there as the local Scarlet Woman?" Where is the cheque now?"

"It's in my handbag. I haven't had time to put it in."

"You will give it to me. I will then return it to sender."

"It's mine. I don't care what they say in Brennan, I'm going to call the baby Jerry and look after him myself."

"You are evidently quite determined that it will be a boy?"

"If it isn't I'll put it back where it came from, on the Commander's doorstep. That'll shake him and his milk bottle."

"You are becoming not only wanton, but vulgar, Mrs Brackenbury."

"I was always vulgar inside myself. Didn't I tell you I wasn't good enough for you? I wasn't the Commander's class either, and we both knew it. It would have been like Lady Charlotte."

"Didn't Lady Charlotte see enough of Sawnie to give him a message herself?" Dora asked presently.

"Probably not after her marriage. You must remember that Norton-Insshe kept a strict eye on her movements after he found out there had been a lover who was Ronnie's father, although he'd have been incredulous if he'd guessed who it was. As things were, he probably thought it was someone she'd met earlier shooting or at the cull."

"What's the cull?"

"The time they go out each year, all of them, to cull too many stags in a herd of deer, otherwise the two leading males, the old and the young, may fight to the death in season."

"Just like people."

"Well, perhaps not quite; but the feeling's the same, no doubt. The thing is that Lady Charlotte was accustomed to blood and the swift use of the *sgian dubh*, because the stalker's *coup de grâce*, as we call it, the final blow, is delivered straight into the carotid artery in the side of the stag's neck. Also, she'd have seen deer *gralloched*, that's gutted as soon as dead, to hang for venison. That was one thing about Norton-Insshe the locals despised him for: he couldn't bear the sight of blood; one of the men questioned told Hawke, and for that and other reasons he used to rent out the shooting, and the cull itself, to commercial parties who came up from the south. They gave him a good price for venison and braces of pheasant. He didn't, of course, let his wife go out on the hills any more, which, knowing what we know now, was perhaps as well."

"He liked herbs," said Dora. "He showed me neat rows of them all, in the walled garden."

"So that's how the rose got into the tooth-tumbler. Skeletons are rattling out of cupboards, Mrs B. This is the Penarch by-road, coming up."

"You're taking me back to Brennan whether you want me to leave you or not?"

"We are certainly going to Brennan, Dora. Unless you have strong objections, we will stay at the Lamb and Flag and make public our marriage."

"You want to, still?"

"I want to, still. Let me continue, however, about Lady Charlotte. I suggest that the message in Gaelic ran something like this: '*When you find my husband dead at the tent, you may take the clan chain*'. Sawnie would never question that from the clan chief, although—"

"The chain had certainly been taken by the time I saw him. I remember now there wasn't one."

"Yes, it couldn't have been there by the time you saw Norton-Insshe, because we know he was dead by then or the dog couldn't have streaked over. You see, the whole point is that a dog – and Lady Charlotte knew her deerhound and the way Diarmaidh's mind worked – a dog would break away from its mistress in that way for nothing but the moment of death. It wouldn't worry about internal bleeding. It was in its own blood to watch a stag finished off after being brought down by dogs, but at that time Diarmaidh was on the lead. Charlotte stabbed quickly as she was emerging from the empty marquee ready to lead the procession. Any cry Norton-Insshe made would have been drowned by the pipes. He would have thought nothing of it as she approached, as he knew who it was. He might even assume it was some domestic matter when she bent to take the knife from his stocking."

"The dog knew him, though. He used to take it out. We saw them at Inshtochradh."

"That doesn't mean anything except that he was fantasising as usual when he told me the dog was devoted to him rather than to its mistress. Norton-Insshe didn't inspire devotion in anyone but Charlotte's supposed mother Sonia. Birds of a feather. No, the dog was Lady Charlotte's and knew it, and although it had never roamed the hills with her, being a gift made by the clan society when her son was born, it was devoted, not to Norton-Insshe, but to her, and to Master Ronnie.

"The little boy grew up for eight years with the great dog beside him all day, up at Taigh Mór. They couldn't send Ronald to school or let him play with other children. Children can be cruel. He had his mother, his unknown grandmother Mavis, and Diarmaidh to guard him and love him. When a dog loves, it's for life and after death."

"Why wasn't the dog with Lady Charlotte that first day in the Pullman? She'd left him behind."

"No doubt he was expected to be part of the scenery when visitors came to Inshtochradh, so she was instructed to leave him behind. Norton-Insshe was, as you say, mad in his way, a perfectionist; nothing was forgotten."

"So when Diarmaidh streaked over and howled, he wasn't really howling for Norton-Insshe at all? What I can't understand is how Lady Charlotte managed to kill the man when she was busy leading the procession."

"Diarmaidh was howling because he smelt lice. Sawnie had just been there to whip the chain, and Sawnie had been there likewise, watching, when Ronnie was drowned. You remember we heard how Diarmaidh tried to save Ronnie and dived in, but Norton-Insshe must have beaten him off, thinking nobody was about, then went on holding the little boy's head under till he was dead. Diarmaidh would never forget that, or the scent of Sawnie nearby behind the trees. He would associate one thing with the other. He was howling for the death, not of Norton-Insshe – that might even have been a howl of triumph – but for the memory of Master Ronnie, last year. He hadn't exactly been encouraged to howl at the time."

"But how could Norton-Insshe have been killed by Lady Charlotte when she was busy leading the procession and everyone was watching her? The dog was with her, and went round with her two or three times, with the pipes playing. I saw it as I came down. Norton-Insshe died when she couldn't have been there."

"Yes, that was the big moment, the parade. While it was going on her husband was no doubt still bleeding slightly, not yet dead as she'd assumed, unless she knew – and she may well have known, but kept her knowledge to herself, having seen the deer die often – that a severed artery closes up instantly at both cut ends so the bleeding isn't severe. On the other hand, if you merely puncture or partly sever a vessel, the blood gushes out. When I saw Norton-Insshe he was hardly bleeding at all. He would die by inches, of a blocked heart after the blood couldn't get through its normal circuit; or else Sawnie gave the black knife an extra shove or twist with his own body when he wrenched off the chain. Norton-Insshe would have died sooner or later, and Charlotte knew it, and all she had to do was simply keep going round and round with the pipes blasting *Belphegor* and nobody looking at anything else. I don't say she told the deerhound to let everyone know; he would do that from instinct, acknowledging a death.

"Norton-Insshe could have been lying there dying, with his breaths rasping, and they wouldn't be heard for the pipes; and nobody would look that way because of the procession. Charlotte certainly had her revenge for all he'd done to her and to Ronnie."

"It all sounds a bit far-fetched to me," said Dora.

"You still think *I* did it? Here we are in Brennan, darling. I'll drive you first to your house, then pick you up, then we'll go to the Lamb and Flag."

"Where are you going?" she asked suspiciously.

"To return the Commander's cheque after you have kindly given it to me."

"I thought you said I was free to express my personality. Supposing I want to keep it?"

"Dora, give me that cheque at once. You will also tell me how much you have put into the building society account from time to time from your immoral gains, and I will refund him totally."

Dora fished out the cheque from her handbag and sat wordlessly back. It would be nice to see her own little house again, but she wouldn't now leave Tom. It didn't matter whether or not he had killed Norton-Insshe; if so, it had been done for her sake. She wouldn't say another word about it when he came back from the Commander's.

Twenty

It seemed a long time till Tom came back. Dora lifted and laid a few things here and there in her little house; she didn't somehow feel like doing much. When she heard the click of the gate she turned, and saw him as though she was seeing his long rangy figure for the first time, through the window, coming up the short paved path; his craggy face smiling, one lock of hair, that indiscriminate straight hair nobody else had, falling over his forehead. She opened the door, and he bent from his tall height and kissed her.

"Was it all right?" she asked. Tom laughed, and kept his arm round her openly until they'd shut the door. Now everybody in Brennan would know, but it didn't matter. Curtains always twitched in a village. She expected they'd thought anyway long ago that Tom and she, at the cottage . . .

"Of course it was all right. If our hearts were ever weighed in an Egyptian pair of scales in the underworld by antique gods, yours would balance, Dora, and mine would go down like lead."

"Did he take back the money without any fuss?"

"He says you're a nice piece and I'm lucky, and he took back the money and says he'll put it on a horse. That's his chief excitement now poor Mary Reston's dead; he misses her very much."

"Did he mention the baby?" She'd tried to reconcile the fact that it was still present and correct in her, that it hadn't been lost with the goings-on of the past few days. It was certainly tough. Last time, with heaving Mrs Partridge's deep freeze, and the time before—

"*I* did. He's going to leave it something in his will, he says. I am to ensure that you have the best possible attention in London; he would have paid for that, but I wouldn't let him. Anyway, you are coming back with me to the Lamb and Flag; I will tell everybody that we are married, we will book a room overnight and I promise, Dora, I will make love to you properly, very gently, as the mother of my child."

"I thought you didn't like children?" Dora was blushing. She'd wanted for some time now to tell Tom how much she really appreciated what he was doing for her. Perhaps tonight would do.

"Well, only sometimes. They have been allowed to become socially impossible. After it is born, which is not, or shouldn't be, for some time yet, I will assist you in training whichever it is to behave itself, speak civilly to its elders, and be seen but not too often heard. If it fails in any of these respects, I shall smack its bottom and it can take me to court. If you interfere, I will do the same with yours."

"There's one more thing I still don't understand about that business at Insshe. Why didn't Sawnie try to stop the little boy's murder, or at least tell someone? Why did he simply go away?"

"For several reasons, my dear Watson. Firstly it was bred in the bone with him to be cautious of the law. His ancestors had hidden successfully in the heather long enough to become tinkers in the second and third generations, avoiding judgment. Joe Jolly is another such. He and his lurcher will poach game, certainly and regularly, but they'll never be caught. These folk do nothing obvious, nothing quickly, except to steal, and Sawnie was honest. If a Highlander has a grudge, though, it smoulders like a fire in the heather till it's time to act. Sawnie's second reason would be that although Charlotte loathed the marriage and he knew it, he knew also that she endured it for the sake of the money Norton-Insshe put into the estate. Sawnie wasn't bright enough to work out that Charlotte would get it anyway on the man's death, as will almost certainly happen. Sawnie merely waited for his revenge, for Charlotte's sake and Insshe's, till it should be time. He would no doubt have killed the false laird if she'd ordered him to, but all she told him was to take the clan chain after Norton-Insshe was dead. She knew that would implicate Sawnie, but Sawnie merely did as he was told, knowing it was his right, as he thought – the subtleties of the difference between a clan president and a hereditary chief wouldn't be clear to him – to wear the chain, with its gold medallions of the rowan clan device."

"She isn't a very nice woman at that rate. What else?"

"Why, that he loved her. We heard him say at Taigh Mór, 'I have kept silence for your sake'. He kept it, and she killed him. There were reasons for that."

"It's all very sad," said Dora. "Nevertheless, I don't see why Lady Charlotte couldn't have made sure that he got the chain afterwards in some other way, if he wanted it so much?"

"He certainly wanted to *think* he was the clan president, and she knew it," Tom said. "It's not so certain whose actual property the chain now is, but in any case there were reasons why she had to have him killed, as well as her understandably loathed husband."

"Had Sawnie killed? You mean she arranged for it to happen? But she was fond of him. They'd been lovers, and he was her son's father."

"There is another thing he was, apart from the fact that he might, not being entirely stable, have become a danger in one of perhaps three ways. Firstly, with Norton-Insshe gone, he might have pestered her person, lice and all. I don't think he would have blackmailed her over her probable written message, although he would keep it, and it was almost certainly kept hidden under his *bothan*, with dry bracken or else heather on top. I'd like to bet that Lady C., has been up there already as soon as the police were out of the way, hunting for the piece of paper and probably finding it to destroy. She is an efficient woman. She ran Taigh Mór like clockwork, including that precisely lettered monstrosity of lobelias and the clan motto."

"I thought that was Norton-Insshe himself?"

"No. Norton-Insshe left Taigh Mór to his wife entirely except to vet finances; after all, he paid. It meant less to him than secret Inshtochradh, where he could be king of the castle without any argument. Anyway, Sawnie was a danger to her in that way, also probably for two more reasons.

"Firstly, he might soon have realised, or been caused to realise, that he didn't have to obey Charlotte as the head of the clan, because he was the clan head himself. The attainder on Jacobites, which Sawnie's ancestor was, was revoked some time after 1770 or so; that's from memory, I'll look it up. The Highlanders who had escaped abroad came back years later to their regained acres, often finding their houses burned to the ground and having to rebuild. The ones who'd taken to the heather instead will often have died, leaving sons who were used to that life and no other and, like the gypsies now, would never be happy under a roof. Sawnie's line of descent was one of those, and it's probable that all his ancestors, knowing who they were, married one another irreproachably to continue the line. After all, they took the name of Cattanach in a kind of irony, knowing the old tradition of the battle with the Clan Kay, which was their own. At that rate they would be less likely to be identified, and by the time the 1770 amnesty came along they'd got used to it.

"That in effect made Sawnie, and not the descendants of the hated fourteenth laird – in other words Lady Charlotte after her father – the true heir of Insshe. Sawnie himself wasn't bright enough to have put two and two together in time to save himself from jumping out of the window to his death below Taigh Mór, but otherwise he might, as I say, have been brought to a realisation. There are clan societies and a good deal of interested and objective research these days, and somebody sooner or later might have traced the real Insshe of Insshe. All Sawnie could do in the way of general protest meantime was to mine the statue on the hill and blow it up, the routine method of expression of those who have an inherited grievance without always remembering what it is. Certainly, if anyone had told him the Insshe acres were really his, there's no saying what he could have been persuaded to do. He might quite seriously have offered to marry Lady C. now she was widowed, which would have been unsuitable, to say the least; or someone might have got Sawnie to assert his rights, especially as he had some money in the bank, or more probably, under the bracken, after his spell on the oil rig – which, by the way, is probably how he got hold of enough depth-charges to blow up the fourteenth laird."

"If Lady Charlotte had known she was illegitimate, like you said, the best thing would surely have been for her to marry Sawnie and then they could have been lord and lady, and lived happily ever after?"

"Yes, *but she didn't know*, that's the irony. Insshe, we know, was her pride, and to find out she hadn't any right to it would either have killed Lady Charlotte, or else made Lady Charlotte kill. We'll never know which. She might, for instance, even have opened the Bible you found at Mavis Walshe's house, seen the letter – you said it wasn't fully replaced in its envelope – and guessed, as you did, that she herself was the baby in question. In any case, marriage with poor Sawnie, unless he was deloused and fumigated, was hardly a feasible proposition for a lady like her."

"She sounds a bitch," said Dora. "In a way, I'm sorry for McNorton now. He didn't like blood, and he was good at growing things, and he had himself doctored when he didn't have to, and all the rest. It must have been horrible, dying like that with the pipers blowing away, and no one able to hear or notice, or even care."

"Yes. Everyone thought of Lady Charlotte as the downtrodden little daughter and then wife, but in fact she was a most determined character, well able to make her own decisions and carry them out when the time came. She wanted the money for Insshe, so she married a vulgarian in spite of the woman she thought was her governess trying to stop it. However, Charlotte certainly didn't enjoy marriage. She made use of poor Sawnie to comfort her, and things perhaps went further than either of them had expected. Thereafter, Charlotte became increasingly the Lady of Insshe, presented with a deerhound at her son's birth and all the rest. I doubt if she intended to kill Norton-Insshe until after he made her have the abortion, and perhaps not then. We simply don't know; we do know that she didn't realise Ronnie had been murdered. She may have been simply sickened of Norton-Insshe's nocturnal attentions.

"Anyway, we can say Charlotte had made up her mind that things were not going on in that way, especially as he kept her prisoner and couldn't or wouldn't give her more children. Sawnie would have done the killing for her, but she couldn't rely on the timing, and the bicentenary seemed the perfect occasion after I'd punched Norton-Insshe's nose so he couldn't appear in the procession."

"She must have thought very quickly then of how it was to be done."

"Oh, she'd known for long enough it would be done with his own *sgian dubh* – the small black knife – as soon as his back was turned and there were no witnesses and no proof. As the laird sat there in full fig, and she, the Lady of Insshe, came out of the great empty marquee looking insignificant in her plain grey coat and skirt, with the pipes blasting away already, she simply bent and slid out the knife and stabbed him, but that time under the rib-cage, hard enough to sever an artery, which would take some minutes to produce its effect on the heart. Then she began her march round, having already sent word to Sawnie to come and take the *slabhraidh*. She'd got the Gaelic message through via Mavis, but Mavis, of course, was her devoted slave. Sawnie left the gate early and came for his rightful chain."

"All of it's awful," said Dora. "Are we going to the Lamb and Flag? It's getting dark."

They went to the familiar local, remembered well by Tom from the days when he'd first come there intending to paint Bigod Peak. Old friends at the bar congratulated them; everyone wanted to stand them drinks, and by the time they'd had fish and chips, it was getting on for eleven. They went to their room. Dora leaned out of the window for moments, and breathed the fresh country air.

"I'll get used to living in London, I suppose," she said. "There are parks, aren't there?"

"Yes, but as I told you I will try and find us a place in the Cotswolds with a garden, leave you there during the week and come down at weekends; provided, that is, you don't go on making blind men happy during the week."

"Of course I won't. I only need you to make me happy."

Later, while Dora slept, he thought over the whole matter. Something nagged at him; he couldn't put a finger on it. He gave up trying in the end and turned over on his side, falling asleep at last.

Much further north, Colonel McIntosh had stopped listening to his wife's metallic chatter and had finally, and with relief, seen her up to bed while he indulged in a final dram. He was glad everything was over and that he would, without doubt, be elected the next clan president; Lady Charlotte was herself, of course, too shy. It had been a simple matter to stab the so-called laird, suddenly seeing the latter's unprotected back on the sales chair beyond the marquee, waiting to sell those tacky souvenirs at his table. He himself had felt nothing at all while he moved swiftly through the great tent and out, did the job – no different from stickin' wild pig in Nepal, in fact simpler as the target was sittin' still and unaware – and had the forbearance not to take away the great chain of office, merely saunterin' out to watch the procession. Having left the chain on the dead man's shoulders had taken discipline, but at that rate nobody would suspect him, as there seemed no motive. He'd always kept a cool head in the army. In any case the *slaibraidh* would come to him in proper course when everythin' was over.

The fact that long ago, the one occasion he and Cis had stayed at Inshtochradh, he himself had come in late to find his wife lyin' on the sofa drunk on whisky, and in a state that showed the feller had been with her, mattered nothin' now; Cis had been skittish elsewhere in her day. He'd dragged her up and had taken her away, and said nothin'; doubtless she didn't even remember.

No, it was the *slaibraidh* that mattered; the clan chain.

The pipes had been wailing already and soon drowned any sounds Norton-Insshe might have made. He himself hadn't waited for anything, assuming the law would set its machinery in motion, as had happened. Lady Charlotte had just made her way out in front as he finished the job on her husband, and wouldn't be back till she and the dog had been round and round the field, with everyone watchin'. He'd remembered to wrap his handkerchief round his fingers before slidin' the *sgian dubh* out from the man's still living calf.

It hadn't been planned, any of it. He had done it without reflection and felt no remorse. The feller was better dead. Now there would be shootin' again and the cull, and he himself would preside at the Annual General Meeting, whenever and wherever it was held, to express regrets.

The prospect amused McIntosh. A shot of Highland blood, his own mother having been an Insshe, was better than whisky. There was no doubt it made for the occasional flash of irrational behaviour in which no Sassenach would indulge, but the English were a chilly race.

Also – again, the Insshe inheritance – he himself was ambidextrous, and if the police had been more perceptive they might have spotted it. At one time he'd been worried when that feller Hawke had asked him to stay within call, to wit an extra night at the Rowan Tree; but it had come to nothin'. Amazin', even in the namin' of these new concrete slabs of hotels, how one could never get away for long from the clan.